Amelia Kyazze is a [...] photographer. Before becom[...] two decades working fo[...] refugee organisations, writ[...] the Balkans, Africa, and Asia.

She lives with her Ugandan-British husband and two children in Lewisham, southeast London. When not writing or taking photographs, she mentors other writers, facilitates creative writing workshops, and enjoys running, jazz music and London history.

www.abkyazze.co.uk

instagram.com/abk_writing

Also by Amelia Kyazze

Writing as A.B. Kyazze

Into the Mouth of the Lion

Ahead of the Shadows

THE CAFÉ ON MANOR LANE

AMELIA KYAZZE

One More Chapter
a division of HarperCollins*Publishers*
1 London Bridge Street
London SE1 9GF
www.harpercollins.co.uk
HarperCollins*Publishers*
Macken House, 39/40 Mayor Street Upper,
Dublin 1, D01 C9W8, Ireland
This paperback edition 2024

1

First published in ebook by HarperCollins*Publishers* 2024
Copyright © Amelia Kyazze 2024
Amelia Kyazze asserts the moral right to
be identified as the author of this work

A catalogue record of this book
is available from the British Library

ISBN: 978-0-00-860590-2

This novel is entirely a work of fiction.
The names, characters and incidents portrayed in it are
the work of the author's imagination. Any resemblance to
actual persons, living or dead, events or localities is
entirely coincidental.

Printed and bound in the UK using 100% Renewable Electricity
by CPI Group (UK) Ltd
All rights reserved. No part of this publication may be
reproduced, stored in a retrieval system, or transmitted,
in any form or by any means, electronic, mechanical,
photocopying, recording or otherwise, without the prior
permission of the publishers.

For Yvette, who will always be my favourite girl.

And for Colette, who inspired themes in this book and so many other aspects of my life.

May her memory be a blessing.

Prologue

August 1977

Amara tested the weight of the rotten peach in her hand. It smelled of fermentation and decay. The juice dripped between her knuckles and threatened to run down to her wrist. She decided against squeezing it yet, better to save it for when they got near the racists. She placed it back in the bag with the other rotten fruit that the lady gave her when she arrived at Clifton Rise in preparation for the protests.

She scanned the crowd for anyone she knew, although the group was thousands of people. There was a kind of party atmosphere. As the National Front were streets away, this felt like a friendly convention of open-minded people. Amara had never seen a group like this. Black like her, white hippies with dreadlocks, brown faces with freckles, students with festival T-shirts, Sikhs with turbans, local councillors and people from the Irish club. Catholic nuns were standing side by side with tall men nearly double their size. There was no category that contained them all.

She was there because of a conversation under a streetlamp a couple of weeks before. He had found her in her usual spot, reading in the doorway of Lewisham Library.

'Come join us, let us show the National Front what Lewisham is really like,' he had said. His dark copper skin was smooth, his teeth white but chipped at the front. Like her, he had just finished uni. 'They like to say, "If they're black, send them back." Well, this is our turf. We're going to send *them* back to where they came from.'

He was so involved, he volunteered for anti-racist causes by handing out flyers after dark. 'This is the big one,' he said. 'If we embarrass them here, they'll be humiliated.'

She looked at the flyer in her hand. 'The *Socialist Worker*?' she asked. 'I dunno…'

'No, it's not what the media says. They are just working people, fighting the racists and fascists in their own way. We're coming together to expose the lies of the Front, and the police covering for them. We have the strength in numbers of Black people here in Lewisham. You're one of us.'

She listened to the speeches, wondering how they were going to stop the fascists from marching down Lewisham High Street. All the time she was aware of the fruit in her carrier bag, getting more mushy as the time passed. Under the veneer of an 'anti-mugging march', the National Front were confident that they would have the numbers of people coming from across London to intimidate the locals. They might even bus people in from the Home Counties. But they hadn't reckoned on the spirit of Lewisham, that's what the last speaker said. He was a tall Trinidadian man wearing a formal white shirt and black tie. He spoke eloquently about community spirit and said they were going to break through the NF lines. 'They say they will destroy race relations here,' the man concluded. 'And to that, I say, "You can't destroy us. We are Lewisham, we are London, and you shall not pass!"' The crowd cheered wildly, people whistling with pinched fingers.

Amara felt hints of her asthma coming back in rattling breaths and wished she had brought her inhaler. So stupid to leave it at home! What if she had a full-blown attack? But it was summer, and she hardly ever had an asthma attack in the summer. Still, sometimes unfamiliar situations brought back her old nemesis. She looked around and wondered if she could escape down a side street if she needed to. Then she saw an old lady, standing out on a balcony holding a sign. In large capital letters it said LORD KNOWS I CAN'T MARCH BUT YOU CAN BE MY FEET. The lady was defiant, looking down at the crowd. After seeing that, Amara didn't try to leave. She had her feet on the ground, would use them the best she could.

'This is the voice of London!' the Trinidadian man

shouted, and the people cheered wildly. There were thousands of them.

'We're going to New Cross!' said someone behind her. The crowd started to funnel into the side streets, moving towards the racists. On one side of her was a tall white man, dressed in simple clothes with a grey beard and long hair in a ponytail. He introduced himself as a Quaker but said little else. To her other side was a woman about Amara's height, with cornrows under a beautiful orange patterned headscarf. She spoke French with a tall man next to her, who had round glasses like an owl and a well-combed afro. While they were standing around, the woman would occasionally lean on his shoulder and they'd share a kiss. They also had plastic bags of fruit on their arms, probably collected from Clifton Rise as well.

The backstreets emerged not far from the station. She could see what the organisers had said to expect: there was a line of police protecting the racists. It was hard to make out their number, but it seemed smaller than Lewisham's turnout. Still, to have the force of the law protecting you, that meant something.

The protestors linked arms, and Amara was swept to the left by an orchestrated wave she didn't understand. She stumbled and nearly fell. The plastic of the handle of the carrier bag of peaches rubbed sharp against her skin. She wondered when and where she should use them. She prayed that her asthma wouldn't come back. She didn't have the power to fight more than one nemesis that day.

The linked chain of protestors moved past a young man

high up, perched on a traffic pole with a megaphone. He was shouting out encouragement, and as Amara got close she could see it was the man from the library that night. She wanted to stop, to show him that he had inspired her, but there was no way out of the formation of the line of protestors. She realised with fear that she was moving closer to the police, and behind them, to confront the National Front.

She had never seen a fascist in real life up close, just on the news. They were small and angry, this tight group of white men protected by the police. She could make out some women but there were more men, many with some kind of combat clothes, and small moustaches.

'They're Honour Guards,' the owl-glasses man said, indicating a group of taller, younger men who stood stiffly together. Amara nodded as if she knew what that meant.

All at once, the linked chain pulled her forward towards the Quaker's side and someone with a megaphone shouted 'Now!' Amara was pushed towards a police officer and the crowd pressed her against his uniform. He was an older white man, with blotchy skin under a day-old beard. He smelled of cigarettes and sweat.

The shouts were so loud nothing coherent could be heard. The line moved back again slightly. People started to throw things, and Amara remembered her peaches. She managed to reach into her bag and sank her hand into the top piece. She threw it as hard as she could towards the racists. As it left her hand a cold rush of juice ran down to her elbow. It arced over the policemen and she didn't see where it landed. She reached for another one.

'Oh no you don't,' the policeman said, and grabbed her wrist. He had bloodshot eyes and broken capillaries across his nose. She pulled back, her thin wrist slipping from his grip. Another protestor, a young black student wearing a Malcolm X T-shirt, moved just in front of her, with a rock in his hand.

'You bastard, don't you DARE!' the policeman roared, and beat the kid on the head, neck and shoulders with his baton. Amara heard screaming but she couldn't tell if it was from the student or someone else. She wanted to stop and help but the chain of protestors pulled her hard in the other direction.

'FORWARD!' someone shouted into a megaphone, and the snake of linked arms was again pulled towards the police and the fascists. She could see their faces, shouting and indignant.

Where did they think the black people could go back to? She was born here, for God's sake! She felt rising indignation and fear in equal measure.

A flare screamed up to the sky. More things were being thrown: clumps of dirt, rotten tomatoes, other fruit, chips of bricks. She lost her footing and her knee slammed down into the ground, but the Quaker man lifted her back up. The French woman smiled at her, encouraging her to go on. It was clear that the anti-racists had the numbers, but the fascists had the police. Who would win?

The chain pulled her again towards the front, and the

police and the racists. This time she moved close to a policeman who seemed much younger, maybe a new recruit. He did not meet her eyes as he scanned the crowd. A line of sweat dripped down from under his hat, slipping in front of his ear, but he made no move to wipe it away. It could have been his first protest. She wondered what he was prepared to do, what the orders were.

Shouts came from all directions. The French woman and her owl-eyed boyfriend were shouting and swearing in French and English. The fascists were singing songs that sounded like football chants, with the words garbled. Amara saw fear on some faces, determination on others. Placards with NF slogans on them stuck up in the air, saying TAKE BACK OUR COUNTRY, IN GOD'S NAME and COLOUREDS GO HOME.

Part I

Chapter One

December 2010

Gina turned her back on all the customers and sank her fingers into the sugar bowl. They probably wouldn't care. All the gossiping ladies, the new mums bouncing babies on their knees, and the freelance writer guy in the corner (double-shot of espresso, twice each visit), they were too absorbed in their own lives to take any notice of her.

She didn't stand out. She had curves but her clothes were shapeless as a smock, an ex-art student with no paint to show for her art. Her hair was cut short with a bit of gel for minimal fuss.

She knew she wasn't allowed to put her fingers into the bowl. Lizl, the manager, with her health and safety checklist, would have been alarmed had she not left early that afternoon. But at this time of day, no one was looking. Gina couldn't help herself.

The sugar wasn't granular – that was the best feeling of all. Here it was in uneven blocks. Not cubes, no – this wasn't that kind of place. They resisted conformity, these different shapes that were not round nor square. They had odd angles and ridges that were strangely satisfying when she rolled them between her thumb and forefinger. Some were brown, some were white. None were mixed.

She thought back to her sugar sculptures. Such a mess. Why was she attracted to disasters? That's what Javier always said. And then when she didn't answer, she hoped it might sink in that he, too, might be another one of those disasters. She was an artist, you couldn't expect overnight success. She just happened to choose a very tricky medium. She sculpted with grains of sugar. Not blocks, like these. She preferred to work with the granules, like sand slipping between her fingers, to make art that was ephemeral. That's what she said in her artist's statement. There's a long tradition of that, say, from Buddhist monks doing their sand mandalas. Take that, Javier, with your criticism. She'd said that, about the sand mandalas. And he'd said something like *But you've never been Buddhist a day in your life*. Which totally missed the point, as usual.

Anyway, the sugar sculptures had real potential. No one else was doing them. True, they took a painstaking amount of attention to get right. And they were so fragile. But that was their beauty. She did them for her final uni show. She had tried many different methods to find the right sugar-to-water ratio, also the perfect amount of golden syrup. It held the pieces together, with a sepia-like glow. But you couldn't have too much syrup. The figures would look jaundiced, and that was no good. Timeless, that was the effect she was looking for. Something that anyone could relate to, recognise even. But tragic, too.

She had thought that Romeo and Juliet would be a good choice. But when the time came to display her art, and she lifted the plastic cake-carrier lid to display her precious, fragile beings and gently lay them on the display table, horror ensued. Some wind or disturbance made them quiver. Then, a thoughtless bump came in the form of Martin Lee, the bloke who spent all year working on the same eco-vehicle forged from recycled exhaust pipes welded together. Just one knock made Romeo's head fall off and roll to the edge of the platform.

Gina looked at the figures: Juliet prone on the tomb-slate (it was the death scene). Romeo there on his knees, ready to take the poison, but with no head. She had to admit they barely resembled their namesakes. Romeo looked more like a praying mantis after sex.

She had three thoughts in quick succession:

Fucking Martin. Such an idiot.

For fuck's sake, why didn't I take a picture?

The head looks like a skull. Should have done Hamlet instead.

Javier had been there to witness her humiliation. He was always there, perched on her shoulder to watch the moments when her potential triumph curdled into failure.

• • •

She was interrupted from her memories by Joanne, a pensioner who often came in late in the afternoon, clutching the free evening papers. She requested the ginger tea, as usual, and then made resentful noises when it came time to pay (Teapigs organic, £1.95 per cup). She usually lingered but no longer asked for a hot-water top-up, once she learned that Gina had to charge 60p for it. People still got the water, in order to squeeze out some flavour from an increasingly ineffective teabag (while adding lumps of sugar to make up for it). It was already too pricey, considering that you can get generic tea for 80p for a box of 80 around the corner at Sainsbury's, but Gina didn't make the rules. As a personality, she was more of a rule follower. That's what Javier said. In his Spanish accent he made it sound like he would rather storm the barricades of Madrid than be like her. Or maybe that was Paris, the barricades. Anyway, she was never that good about European history. He said that a lot too.

Spotify was playing an 80s list, and some of the mums were openly singing along to A-ha. Motherhood must push you to the brink, and you lose some inhibitions, Gina thought. Like assuming that other people wouldn't mind hearing your rendition of 'Take on Me' – caffeine-heightened, slightly off-key. But who was she to say? She was a bit indifferent to A-ha, really. Being born at the end of the decade, most of the 80s references passed her by.

The A-ha mum didn't see that her baby had thoroughly destroyed the croissant she had so lovingly placed in front of him. Plump fingers just shredded it to bits. Complete carnage radiated out in a perfect circle from his fists, also in rays extending in all directions from his highchair. The mum paid no notice. Maybe she was too tired. Must be exhausting, to have a kid like that. Destroying everything he got his hands on. She always looked down trodden, that woman. Ordered lattes with a double shot, but it seemed like those barely did the trick of keeping her eyelids open. One day she was probably going to just lay her head down on the table and sleep, croissant crumbs embedded in her fringe.

No one would really mind. Archie's was a lenient sort of place. Lord knows they were understanding when Gina left the kettle on to boil dry (cracked it). Or when those mince pies caught fire (smoke detector wailed). They went for the cake-delivery service after that. All the cakes, even the little pies just needed the microwave. Everything was served at room temperature from then on. Gina tried not to take it personally. It was a good job, really. Close to home, and not demanding. Lizl was a nice manager, and in the slow times – not immediately post-school-drop-off time, of course, but the slow, after-4pm shift, when just a few hangers-on lingered – she had space. She could daydream as she wiped the tables and pulled down the blinds, encouraging the last people to drink up and make their way home so she could close.

If she needed to, she could emerge from her thoughts anytime, like coming to the surface in a pool, if people needed a top-up or a new customer came in (the bells on the door were helpful). But really, as A-ha changed to early

Madonna's 'Borderline' and no one really saw her or minded, she could just stay behind the counter and feel the different shapes in the sugar bowl and think about what she wanted to sculpt next.

She was working on a theme. Her 'Elves and Fairies' theme, as Javier disdainfully said, but it was more than that. Actually, none of the figures had been fairies. She tried to do Boudicca, who everyone knew wasn't a fairy, but an actual queen in history. It was the Queen, poised just before the suicide. But that proved a little complicated. The Suffragettes, that was the next attempt. But it was tricky to show the scene with the jailors and the force-feeding. The sugar granules didn't do things like vomit very well. Gina didn't want to just do the ladies in traditional clothes with the placards. That had already been done so many times.

So she was currently projectless, fishing around in her mind for the next idea with potential. She took up a brown (demerara) sugar lump and looked at it more closely. It wasn't round, but it was trying to be. She tried to see if there were caverns inside. It was basically solid, although with ridges that could potentially serve as eyebrows, on a skull for a mouse. Or something less pointy-faced.

A skull. Yes, Shakespeare was always a good pool of ideas. People would recognise that. She could do *Hamlet*. Or maybe a more modern literary twist. *Rosencrantz and Guildenstern*? But would people know what she was doing? Tom Stoppard was loved by many, but he was no Shakespeare. She rolled the sugar-skull back and forth between her thumb and fingertip. *Macbeth*, maybe.

Chapter Two

December 1952

Bella pulled her sleeve over her fist and rubbed a circle through the fog on the window of the bus to see if they were nearing London Bridge. The condensation and the smog outside made the view opaque and vaguely frightening, like having gauze over your eyes. She could make out some of the landmarks but not many. She hoped she wouldn't miss her stop.

A black cab swerved in front of the bus, making it pull up short. In the front seat, Bella's hand hit the glass to stop her momentum. She shook it lightly to get rid of the tingles.

The *Vogue* magazine had fallen off her lap and she stretched down to pick it up. Shame, it was wet on the corner but it was all right. She took off her glasses and breathed on each lens to clean them. Her wool coat hem wasn't the best fabric, but it was what she had to hand. The lenses were thick, getting heavier each time she needed a new pair. She hated having to wear them, but she had little choice. Ever since she was young her eyesight didn't match up – each eye was different, and neither was right. Her reflection in the glass had eyes that looked bigger than other people's, and they didn't look quite in the same direction. She'd grown used to it, but when she caught other people's glances, she was reminded of what an odd one she was.

On one of the side streets, there was a queue outside a butcher's. One man pushed another so hard that his hat came off; he responded with a heavy thump to the first man's chest. This knocked him back and into the ladies standing behind. The bus moved past before she could see how the scene fully played out.

Scarcity brought out a peculiar side of strangers, she found. Sometimes they could respond with violence, other times with generosity. At the boarding house where she stayed with the other nurses, there was rarely sugar on the table for tea, one of the last remnants of rationing. Yet if someone had a new suitor, that was the first thing to sweeten up the relationship, and often the girls did share.

She was glad to be up high and moving in the opposite direction from the queuing below. Scenes of public confrontation made her feel unsettled. If she was on foot and saw a commotion starting, she would cross the street and move away as fast as she could. It was a habit, one of many protective lessons from Paris before the war. Like all the other Jews, they tried not to call attention to themselves in tense times. If anything felt like a crowd was heating up, they were the first to disappear. It was the safest way to be, after France fell to Hitler: learn as much English as you can, make a plan, and disappear. That's what her parents taught her, and she executed it faithfully. It was a pity they didn't manage to do the same.

But what do you do? Bella was not made to be crushed by sorrow; it wasn't her nature. Another habit she gained from her mother was to make quick decisions to set a course of action. Once she had determined the answer, it was very hard for her to change her mind. Perhaps her path was unusual, a young unmarried Frenchwoman with no family in the country. To be the youngest person to graduate from the nursing programme just after the war, doing the exams after just two years, not three – that was nothing to be scoffed at. Five years on, she could be proud of what she had achieved, and she was ranked second to the Sister. Nursing was her way out; it was her calling and her future when her past rapidly fell away.

When she saw that the bus had crossed the bridge, she pulled the bell and hopped off near the market. It was just a short walk to the hospital. Mud splashed on her boots as she landed, and she screwed up her face in a frown. Now she would have to stand in front of the doctors with their haughty attitudes and English accents, with boots wet and smelling of horse. What a disaster. Yet Bella would never be ashamed of herself; if anything, her emotional armour raised itself higher. That was how she had to be, to survive alone in this city.

• • •

It wasn't Bella's duty day, but when her ward Sister had asked if she would step in to give a talk to newly qualified doctors, she was happy to oblige. She welcomed the idea of giving the lecture; nurses were seldom allowed to give any kind of direction. She liked the feeling of turning the hierarchy on its head.

She was worried about being late and started to run. One hand held the flaps of her coat together against the rain and wind, as she hadn't had time yet to replace the lost button at the top. The other clutched her bag so it didn't swing away. Sometimes she felt like a paper doll version of herself. She could see it now, like the ones they used to play with back in France as a young girl: two-dimensional, coat in a triangle shape like a child's drawing, skin the colour of the paper beneath. Eyes too big – they would suit a comic drawing or a satire.

As she crossed the gate into Guy's Hospital, she smoothed back her black curls and licked her lips to make them less pale. She'd forgotten her red lipstick at home. Upstairs on the second floor, lights in the interior hallway flickered yellow and the place smelled of cigarettes. Not wanting to seem out of breath, she forced herself to slow down to a walk and to try to breathe normally.

At the door to the lecture hall there were three doctors before her, smoking. One said 'Greetings', and the others nodded their approval.

As she peered inside, she could see others were smoking in their seats. She had heard some say they thought it was good for the health, soothed the nerves. But even though doctors said it was true, something in her couldn't believe it. If the London smog was bad for your health, how could it be good for you to put smoke directly into your body? No, it defied sense. But that's how people could be, putting faith ahead of logic. They did that all the time.

A Black man sat in the front row. She had never seen a doctor like him, but there was no mistake. He wore a good suit and had a notebook out, ready for the lecture. He was tall, with the length of his legs folded up neatly so others could pass. His face was striking, with strong cheekbones and a smooth surface with no stubble. She wanted to know more about him, yet did not want to be caught staring.

He looked up at her for a moment, and his expression was unreadable. The eyes were dark brown encircled by pure white, and he seemed to have no wrinkles or marks at all. Then in another moment he smiled, and the lines crinkled up the sides, but his lips did not part. A formal smile, one with respect. But no enthusiasm, she judged. Of course not. She was just a funny little woman with heavy glasses and a strange accent, as he was about to find out.

The other doctors filed into the room and took their seats. No one sat on either side of the Black doctor, but a few spoke to him or nodded. His pen was poised in his hand, and he seemed to be anticipating what she was going to say. Her normally robust self-confidence shivered slightly as the head doctor gestured for her to take to the podium. She could already feel their eyes running over her red dress, not a fashionable one, and wrinkled from the bus ride. But there was no time for doubt. She jumped right in.

• • •

Adebayo was struck – like those old baobab trees on the plains that were split by lightning but kept growing. Alive, yet completely transformed from how he was before. For a moment he questioned what had actually happened.

He tried to concentrate on her words. She was presenting about the procedures for giving an injection and taking blood from a child patient without inducing panic. Nurses were much better at this, as everyone knew. It was the touch of a woman, most likely. But also other things – better technique, attentiveness to vital signs, coming down to their level and using psychology so as not to let arrogance interfere; this was the topic of her lecture.

She spoke English with an accent – was it French? It was nearly perfect, but he could sense small differences. Her expression didn't flicker in those moments, so he wondered if she knew where the slight mistakes were, or if that didn't matter to her.

But it was more than her words that held him captivated, it was her conviction. In all his doctor's training, he could not remember a time when a nurse, let alone a young woman, had spoken to doctors that way.

A Jewish star rested on a gold chain around her neck. He knew the symbol from the newsreels during the war, but he had not seen anyone wear it so openly in London, defiant of history. Her red dress, tied back at the waist, made her stand out dramatically against the drab lecture hall walls.

He watched her lips as she spoke. She seemed like she

didn't care if her words caused offence, as long as she was technically accurate and morally right. He could not take his attention away from her for a moment. The presentation wasn't long, and received soft applause at the end. Others may have been doing it to be polite, but Aday meant it.

Would she stay to take questions afterwards? He needed to speak to her.

His hands were moist as he waited his turn. Other doctors had interrupted the presentation with their questions, but that wasn't any way to treat a woman with respect. Besides, he was used to waiting until they had finished their say, otherwise some of them might grow aggressive, and that wasn't how he wanted the atmosphere to be today, in front of her.

He moved slowly, so as not to startle her; he knew he could have that effect on people. He waited until she stopped speaking to the last English doctor, and then she turned to him. Her eyes were magnified by the depth of the lenses. It was her only flaw, a sign of her humanness. He told her that her lesson was extremely good.

'You think so?' She leaned away from him then, as if she thought he was mocking her.

'I do. It makes the procedure less damaging, and also helps the medicine to be absorbed, as the vein will not be constricted with panic.'

'That's what I keep saying to people, but they don't listen.'

'I would listen, if you said so.'

She smiled then, as if judging his motives. He felt that

perhaps he had been too forward.

'In any case, it was an elegant presentation. Miss...' He left a space for her to say her name, but she just let his words hang in the air. He looked at the notes in his hand where he had written *Nurse Monteaux*. 'Miss Monteaux, am I pronouncing that correctly?'

She nodded.

'Thank you very much for the lecture.' He walked away without saying more. She was a puzzle, this nurse. Many people in England, he found, were like that, but this was the first woman he wanted to figure out.

This woman would demand effort. She had a guard around her. You could sense it by the way she held her narrow shoulders, or the way she played with her necklace when others were speaking. She would not be simple, this woman. She wouldn't accept the plainness of life; no, she wasn't ordinary. From what he had seen, this beautiful woman was brave. She would have the courage and strength to stand up for what she believed.

He had to find a way to see her again. He didn't know how, but he was certain.

He tried to keep an eye on her without being noticed. She did not look at him again. She was distracted by another doctor coming back with an irritatingly uneducated question. He took a moment to glance at her hand – no wedding band. But he knew nothing about Jewish customs. He didn't even know if they wore wedding bands. Were they allowed to marry a person of another faith, of another race? He knew nothing, that first time they met.

Chapter Three

Gina set the alarm at Archie's and then pulled and bolted the door. It was an old door and squeaked in protest, like it always did in the rain. She looked back once again to confirm that she had pulled down the blinds. Did she turn all the lights off? She squinted back to look through the gap to see if there was any tell-tale glow in the kitchen hutch. No, it looked grey in the shadows. She could be sure that her concentration hadn't lapsed this time.

Joanne, the pensioner, was about twenty metres away. Gina had given her the end-of-the-day croissants, no charge, as always. She didn't even say thank you, but that was normal too. Joanne held them in their brown waxy bag, and just ate them right there, on the street in the rain. That bag must be disintegrating in her fingers. Gina looked down and pretended not to see. Nanna would never have let her do that, in the rain.

Hell, she wasn't even allowed to eat and drink coffee at

the same time. It was '*impolit!*' Nanna declared. But when asked, she could never really explain why it was so.

'It simply isn't done!' Nanna said, her French accent always making the words sound more emotional than other people's expressions. When pressed further, she just said, 'It's the French, we don't eat standing up. We don't do the eating and the walking. It's just not what eating is *made* for.'

Nanna said that kind of thing a lot. She thought things were made for what they were set to do. And people, they were made a certain way, and only for certain things. You couldn't change that, either. Take Nanna – she was made for romantic storylines in her audio books. She liked drama, but nothing too gory or tragic. And nothing about the World Wars. Unlike other grandparents, she did not like that period of history. Give her any other period of history – The Black Plague, Salem Witch Trials, anything, and she relished it. But not the European wars, God no.

A motorcycle slid up next to Gina and revved its engine. She knew without looking that it was Javier. He wouldn't take his helmet off, not in the rain. It made him look like an android, not a flesh-and-blood human. And she hated being on the bike in this weather. It always felt like punishment – like accelerating through an endless cold shower.

He cocked his head to urge her to get on the back of the bike, but she shook her head. He revved the engine again and motioned a bit more forcefully. She gestured for him to go without her. He put both feet down and turned off the engine, flipping up the visor so she could see his eyes and an angry square mouth.

'What the fuck, Gina?' he spat. 'You making me wait, in this shit?' His Spanish accent made her want to laugh when he said that word – it always sounded like 'sheet' – but laughter was the last thing that would work for this situation. Javier was not made to be laughed at. He was made to be worshipped, or so he thought.

Gina didn't know what she was made for. But she knew she was not going to be clinging to the back of a wet leather jacket in this weather.

'I don't need a ride,' she said. 'I'm cool.'

'But I left my notes at your house last night,' he said. 'I need them before my meeting with the prof tomorrow.'

'So go ahead without me,' she said. 'You know I hate being on the bike in the rain.'

'I can't go there by myself; the old lady's there.'

'Nanna's always there. She doesn't go out.'

'The old cow hates me.'

'Well, she certainly wouldn't like you calling her that.'

'You know what I mean. Give me your keys, maybe I'll sneak in while she's listening to her radio nonsense.'

'Nothing's wrong with her hearing; she'd sense you.'

'Yep! She's like a bat. Blind, and with fangs too.'

'Fuck off,' she said. He knew he would get a rise out of her if he went on about her grandmother.

'Forget the notes, they're just shit anyways.' He put the helmet on again and bashed his foot against the kickstand. He pulled away, not looking back at her. She watched his leather-clad back and round helmet recede until he turned a corner to get to the South Circular.

She used to love the bike, in the summer months. When they first got together, it was part of what made him exciting: the handsome older man with the foreign accent, offering a chance to zoom past traffic and avoid taking the tube. He was so affectionate with her, caressing her cheek before gently putting the helmet on her head to keep her safe. He was enthusiastic, intellectual, and drew people to him. He liked the big ideas of history and made sweeping statements that made you sit up and listen.

Javier had an intensity about him. He had a way of noticing her early on and pulling her out of a crowd. When she was in her second year of uni, there was nothing she would look forward to more than having that intense energy flow her way. He would tell her how beautiful she was; she was special, like no one else. They spent all their free time together, and it never seemed quite enough. Her friends objected to Javier insisting she cancel plans with others, but she didn't mind. He needed her to himself, he said. Didn't like to share the attention.

But somewhere along the line that intensity shifted, and she'd noticed that while confined in the tight circle of two, the focus was mainly on him. She was in the shadows, and when she looked around, her old friends were no longer there. They had moved on, moved out and not stayed in touch. Three years later, she had Javier, and she had the responsibilities of looking after Nanna. She didn't have anybody else.

She knew she should be more sympathetic to his troubles; his PhD was not going well. The funding ran out after the fourth year, and he now had to teach first-year students in order to afford to stay in London. He was not made to be a teacher. He did not have the patience for it. But there was something else about him too that made you stop feeling sorry for him. Something had just gone bitter. Like a teabag left in too long. And everything around him became stained and bitter too.

It was Friday, and December had such early sunsets that Nanna's sacred hour had already arrived. Gina saw the Shabbat candles as soon as she opened the front door; the thin candlesticks were in the kitchen window, down the narrow hallway, facing the back garden. Gina wondered what the neighbours thought about the old blind Jew living there for so many years. She wondered if any of them knew anyone like Nanna. She defied convention. Unlike many other Jews her age, she had no synagogue and was not living in a tight orthodox community in North London. There was nothing orthodox about Nanna, never had been.

At eighty-one, and with her advancing blindness, she was more or less confined to the house. Still, she had people in her life. She had Gina, and also Oleg, their lodger. And Oleg's girlfriend, whatever her name was. Oleg had been living with them for years, ever since he came from Russia to study engineering. He kept to himself but was nice enough. He reliably paid the rent, stuck to his portion of the fridge and cabinets, did the washing-up promptly. If he had a drunken night out with too much vodka, they never knew.

Gina secretly hoped he did every once in a while, just to ensure that someone in the house was having a good time.

Oleg was respectful of Nanna. He wasn't a big talker, but he asked how she was feeling, helped her change a fuse, that sort of thing. He also probably helped her light the Shabbat candles tonight, as otherwise Nanna would have waited for Gina to arrive before being able to do the weekly ritual. With her eyesight failing, she was worried about dropping a lit match and it catching on something. That was another reason why she did it over the sink. So, if anything happened, the tap was right there, danger averted.

The timing was tricky, as the candles were supposed to be lit at sundown, but the sunset changed so wildly throughout the year. Now, in the dead of winter, it was before four o'clock. Gina's shift ended at five, so she was grateful when Oleg stepped in.

His girlfriend was new, and very quiet. At first, Nanna was convinced she was mute. But no, she was just shy. Eastern European, and maybe feeling cautious with her boyfriend living in another woman's home, even if that woman was tiny and frail and didn't even weigh 95 pounds. Nanna could still seem intimidating, Gina had to admit. She was addicted to volatile French debates coming over the radio at any hour of the day. The French were always ready for a good debate. And Nanna would shout along right with them, not caring if anyone was in the room. She would slip into her native tongue with such ease, and launch into a rousing tirade on whatever was the latest controversy.

Gina was used to it. After taking GCSE French (grade C, not great) she could follow her grandmother's train of argument but she was no good at writing or spelling. There was no interruption once Nanna got into her debates with her radio chat hosts.

Poor girl, the girlfriend. When she first came into the house and was introduced she answered at such a low volume that even Nanna – whose hearing was increasing in strength, like a superpower almost – missed it. She and Gina tried afterwards to compare their impressions. The name was something like Catherina, or maybe Karolina, or Martina…? And despite being introduced another time, they again just failed to get it. And after twice, well … you couldn't ask again, now could you?

There was no sign of Oleg or his girlfriend now, though. Gina shut the door behind her and bent down to pick up the cat and rub him behind the ears. He was the latest of Nanna's cats, a long distinguished line of rescued animals, firmly part of the household until they died and then were buried without ceremony in the garden.

The house wasn't well lit and had a low warm orange glow. The ceiling light – 1970s-saucer style – hovered over Nanna's recliner like a UFO posed to strike. Otherwise it was just the parallel flickers of the kitchen candles.

Coming home was Gina's sanctuary, and her refuge. Although Nanna loved a debate about the outside world, politics, movies or books, she never used the same interrogating tone with her granddaughter. For Gina, she reserved a kindness that seemed special – not even the cats had earned that. Perhaps it was because Gina knew that her grandmother was ordinary and extraordinary at the same time. Gina didn't know who to pray to, but when she did worry, she prayed to the universe that nothing would push Nanna over to the other side, not just yet. She needed her, like a talisman.

Javier was a bit of a problem. He didn't have that kind of relationship with his grandparents. They – rest in peace – were buried in a small town in Spain and were old friends of Nanna's. Or maybe those were his great-grandparents? Gina couldn't remember. Anyways, it was how they met, the family had sent him over to London for a summer to improve his English. This was before he got a place at UCL for his PhD in History (studying the roots of fascism in Western democracies, a topic that kept him cheerful).

Perhaps it was a cultural thing, or maybe it was a Javier thing, but he looked at family the wrong way. He seemed to see them as a barrier to his progress, tying him back to a past he was desperate to discard. He was always telling Gina she had to cut the tie, strike out on her own (with him, supporting him).

He didn't get it. Really, family was an embrace. That's how she saw it, anyway: Nanna was what held her in place. Gina didn't really have other family to speak of. A birthday card arrived every year, often late, from her mother in Jamaica. A phone call every now and then, with news about the tourist industry. Gina didn't have expectations of anything different. Jamaica was Amara's home now. For her health, that's what she said. Even though she owned a line of hotels, she said there was not a lot of money to fly back to England.

Gina's father was never mentioned. She just had Nanna, but that was enough.

'You don't like him,' Gina said, matter-of-factly. That was one of the good things about living with Nanna. You knew she loved you, and you could speak up about things without it being a confrontation.

'Of course I like him, *cherie*. If you like him, I like him.'

'No, you don't. You never have.'

'Well,' Nanna turned to face her. Even though the woman was nearly blind, it felt like she was the only one who actually saw Gina. She bothered to take the time to sense what was really on Gina's mind. 'I don't like how he speaks to you sometimes. He was not, as we say, made to be very polite.'

'I know, I know. I've said things to him, told him to be nicer to you.'

'Oh, it is not me, my darling. I have one foot in the grave...'

'Don't say that! You're fit as a fiddle!'

'Oh please, my child. I am past eighty. Don't tell me half-truths. I am so grateful for you and for every day I have left, and of course the cat is here...' She absent-mindedly stroked him, until he changed his mind and sprang from her lap. 'But you know, losing your sight, it is a bit of a mixed blessing. You hear things that you never heard before. I was too busy, too stimulated by my eyes, to hear it before. Things like how he pauses before he says thank you, as if he has to remind himself, or he has a tiny battle inside himself each time, whether to thank you or not. Or how he sucks the air in through his teeth, before he asks about me. And who am I? I am just an old woman. But if he really cared about you…' She left the words dangling in the air, and Gina knew exactly what she meant.

Two sets of footsteps came up the stairs from the basement flat. One set was very heavy and booted, the other light and high-heeled. Gina and Nanna stopped talking and turned to Oleg and Juliana or whatever her name was as they made their way towards the door.

'Going out?' Nanna asked.

Oleg grunted agreement.

'Thanks for helping Nanna with the candles,' Gina said.

'Not a problem.' Oleg wrapped a woollen scarf twice around his neck. It covered his chin and the lower half of his mouth, preventing any further discussion.

The girlfriend raised her eyebrows and gave a shy smile, without saying anything. Oleg opened the door and held it for her as she stepped through. Her legs in tights looked unprotected against the cold, but she wore a puffy pink winter coat and propped up the hood over perfectly lacquered blond hair. Oleg held out his elbow like an old-fashioned gentleman, to help her over the threshold in her heels.

As the door shut, Gina held onto that impression of them: their silhouettes from the back, with a grey fog of rain outside making a smooth background. They could have been Matisse cut-outs. Their shapes were so different: one round, grey and padded, the other thin but protected by pink puff, made taller by the shoes.

'Like a bear with a stork,' Nanna said after the door shut. Gina hit her lightly on the arm, as her laughter started to rise. She hoped Oleg hadn't overheard, that they had walked away and not paused to open an umbrella. Nanna continued, trying to be quieter though still laughing. 'You know what I mean? He's so heavy and round, and she, well... Or maybe she's more like a flamingo.'

Sensing Gina's admonishment, she sobered up a little. 'I don't mean they look like that, I see just a blur of colour and shapes mainly. It's just that they felt like that. A flamingo going out in this cold...' She continued to chuckle at the images in her head. 'Oh, I don't mean to be unkind, darling. It's just my imagination amusing me.'

Chapter Four

December 1952

For lunchtime on his surgery days, Aday always walked to the café. The smog was so intense he wouldn't have believed it if he hadn't been trying to navigate through. The grey was omnipresent and pressed in on all sides. His hands were visible, but as he looked down at his shoes the shapes blurred away from him, indistinct with the deadly fog.

London had experienced nothing like this in the last hundred years, or so he had been told by his colleagues. As a newly trained doctor, he had recently seen many cases of lung irritation, pneumonia or worse. There wasn't much he could do. He prescribed inhalations and bath salts for those with aching chests. He recommended that they leave the city and go to the seaside, even though it was winter. Hospital admissions were arranged for the worst affected, although in many cases that did little good. The weather in this country was horrendous. He couldn't wait to finish this year of rotations and get back on the boat home. It had been nearly six years, and that was enough.

He walked cautiously, pausing as he approached the kerb. He couldn't see across. Midway a tram was moving at a fraction of its normal speed. A man walked with a torch in front of it, flinging the light back and forth to try to increase the visibility. Why anyone would travel today was beyond him – unless they were going to help people, as he tried to do. In any case, no one but a fool would move fast, but if he kept his senses about him, he could make it.

He needed lunch. If he didn't get regular meals he risked a drop in blood sugar, and the last thing a patient needed would be the doctor collapsing during a surgery visit. So many of them were nervous around him already. He was six foot six and the only African among them. He often wondered which intimidated people more.

There had been a small number of other foreigners studying with them in medical school, but not many. Most of the Kings College classes were a wide sea of pale winter-white faces. His skin was not remarkable where he was from, and he had never felt "coloured" until he arrived in London. Before then, it didn't even occur to him. He was just Adebayo, one of the younger brothers of the King. He was special owing to his family's status, but not unique because of his skin or face.

At university, he had hoped that his intellect, and his drive to serve and to heal, would be what would distinguish him from the others. But his expectations of the English were too high. Along with the other subjects from the colonies and abroad, he would always be viewed as an outsider.

At medical school, he had earned the best qualifications in the class. But he found that people like him were only tacitly allowed to remain, as long as they kept quiet. He quickly understood the order of things. He didn't speak out or cause trouble. His performance in the final exams spoke for his skills and attention to science, but he did not draw attention to himself.

There were spells of outbursts and spitefulness against him. One professor accused him of cheating, not believing that someone from Africa could have his level of comprehension. Luckily, other professors vouched for him. There were worse moments: hateful words spat at him from the windows of a tram, or from the mouths of drunken ex-servicemen in the street. He learned to steer well clear of mobs, particularly if there was anger in the air.

Confrontation was not for him. He did not feel his role on this earth was as an agitator, someone to upset the order of things. No, he was a healer. He had his work and it was enough.

He had become used to it, over the years. The stares and the open mouths when people first saw him. The children who wanted to touch his skin or his hair and then ran back when he turned to greet them in the Queen's English. He didn't mind the children. They were innocents. Still learning, they were forming their intelligence. He could see that he could startle people, through no intention of his own; to be a good doctor he had to recognise that and adjust.

He understood his patients, too. They had their worries about their illnesses, and he could see that a doctor's role was to put things right, as much as was possible. He kept his voice low and soothing with them, especially if they were meeting him for the first time. Some wouldn't open the door for the home visits, not believing his qualifications. Many had never seen an African doctor before. He carried his medical licence in a protective cover in his briefcase, for those moments of doubt. That usually worked if someone in the household or a neighbour could read. But sometimes nothing worked, and he was sent away. That was a true defeat, when fear won out over science.

It tired him sometimes, the constant reading of people's past and present mental states. It added layers of complexity to the presentations; there was always some mystery to sort out in each case. To manage his emotions, he turned to routine; he walked the same route to the hospital every week, and ate at Archibald's, the café on Manor Lane, most days. It was easier to interact with just a few good people, and to keep a professional distance from the rest. He didn't share more of himself than was needed. People who knew him called him Doctor, and he didn't ask for anything else.

. . .

He settled into his seat at the café. For a change today he decided to sit at one of the barstools facing the street. Rain fell in diagonal lines, hitting the glass and the pavement in a way that defied expectations.

It had been several days, but he still could not stop thinking about that nurse. She was the first woman who had caught his interest, and held it. He had to see her again. Of all the women he had met in the years since he had arrived in England, she was the only one who sneaked into his dreams, breaking up his sleep. She probably had barely noticed him, forgotten about him already. But if he wasn't mistaken, when she looked at him with those green eyes huge through her thick lenses, he thought there was a comprehension there. He couldn't actually remember the shade of green, or whether they were speckled or uniform. He needed to see her again to find out, or else he might go mad.

The door of the café opened with a ring of the bells attached at the top. In walked a small, old, white man, drenched from the rain. His back was slightly curved over with illness or despair, Aday wouldn't be able to tell which without an examination. He watched as the man stuttered through some English phrases to order some soup and a coffee, and sat down on another barstool at the window. Spanish, Aday judged, or perhaps Portuguese. Probably a labourer out of work, due to the smog? Or, worse, a man who had lost the last of his money and couldn't afford to go anywhere else.

The man looked so despairing, staring through the wide

pane of glass being hit by rain at a haphazard pace. A tear broke free from his eye and ran down his face. When his coffee arrived he cupped one hand around the mug, while the other hand pulled tight at his collar, trying to get warm again.

Aday had to say something. 'It's good,' he said.

'Good?' the foreign man repeated.

'For the smog,' he continued. 'The rain shows that the weather is in transition, and the smog will lift. What doesn't blow away will be washed down the sewers.'

The man may have had a little trouble following.

'Whatever your problems, my friend,' Aday continued, 'they could similarly be washed away.'

The foreign man smiled then, and wiped at both cheeks with his free hand. The waitress brought out soup with bread for him, and Aday's sandwich. The bread was thick and dented slightly with a couple of dirty fingerprints, but that was the way it had been during these dirty days of smog.

'Fernando,' the man said, touching his chest just above his heart. 'From España.'

'I'm Aday,' the doctor said, 'pleased to meet you.' He reached for his sandwich. He only had a short time before he had to get back to his surgery.

Fernando studied him for a moment, and then moved to take out his wallet. He took out a black and white photo of a girl aged about sixteen, Aday guessed. She was standing in Spanish dress, her back against a pier with amusements behind. The photograph was frayed at the edges and cracked at one corner where a fold had scratched the emulsion. It was clear it was a valuable item, perhaps the man's most treasured possession.

'Christiana Ruiz Martínez. I look for Christiana. She is older now. From my village.' He turned the photograph back towards himself so he could look again. 'Beautiful, no? *Maravillosa.*'

'Yes, I would say so.'

'I try to find her, after so many years. Her husband died; my wife left. We had love once, so long ago. But I walk for days – no, weeks – in this smog, trying to find her. And my breath, it hurts. My heart, too, is hurting. It won't last, not a chance.'

'You need to find her?'

Fernando seemed to be in pain as his breathing sped up. 'Yes. You know her?'

'I do not know her, my friend,' he said. Fernando's face fell with a silent crash. 'Do you think she is nearby?'

'Si, señor, she is in Lewisham. I was told so. But I did not know Lewisham was so big, bigger than many villages together! I have no luck, no one to tell me how to find her…' His voice trailed off as he looked down at his soup, having not yet tasted it. He would probably be disappointed; the cream of potato was not the best choice here, Aday knew from experience.

'There might be one thing that could help,' Aday said, as he stood up to have a quiet word with Gertie. She agreed and he went behind the till. He found what he was looking for and brought it back, accidentally slamming the large white book on the countertop and making the spoon handle bang against the bowl.

Fernando looked at him without comprehension.

'The directory,' Aday said. 'She might be in it.'

Fernando looked down at the book, so thick it took both his hands to open it up. The long lists of numbers and names might not make sense to him, Aday realised.

'You've never seen a phone book before?' he asked, trying not to sound like a grandfather would to a child. 'It's a list of everyone in London, if they have a telephone. Do you think she'd have a phone?'

Fernando nodded.

'What was the family name again?'

'Ruiz Martínez.'

'Hmmmm ... complicated name...' He flipped through the pages as he had many times before. 'I don't see anything under Ruiz. What about the other one? Martínez?' More flipping of the pages. 'Here it is. There are seven C. Martínez's listed.'

Fernando had to squint to affirm that yes, indeed, there were seven. 'Which one is her?' he asked excitedly. 'One of them has to be my Christiana?'

'So you can give them a call, each one, and see if that's your woman. Or you can try to find her at home.' He pointed out the addresses alongside the numbers.

Fernando looked up at him as if he had no words for gratitude in English or Spanish that would suffice. Then he stood up quickly, fumbling in his pockets.

'Don't worry, old friend,' Aday said. 'I'll cover you for lunch.'

'*Gracias, señor*, I'll never forget this!' Fernando grabbed his hat, felt for his handkerchief around his neck, and ran out the door.

'Wait! Where are you going?' Gertie shouted after the old man as he dashed into the smog. 'You can't take the directory!'

Aday chuckled as the doorbells chimed as if mocking her. He sat down again on the stool and pulled the plate towards him, the same lunch he had every weekday.

'Don't worry,' he said. 'He'll bring it back. Have faith.'

Chapter Five

Gina heard the bells ping again. A young man walked in who moved like a marionette unsure of the master of the strings. He had that student-type beard, the kind where they didn't think they needed to clip it into shape. A red woolly hat was a bit too tight on his head, accompanied by a thin blue scarf that looked like it had been knitted by a well-meaning but talentless relation. He pulled off the hat when he reached the counter, leaving exposed a sloppy mass of brown straight hair, some sticking up with static. He smiled at her, revealing crooked teeth.

He studied the handwritten prices on the chalkboard behind her. 'That's a bewildering number of herbal teas,' he said.

'Yeah, we get that a lot.' she said. 'But some people have their favourite and are disappointed if we don't stock it.'

He nodded, too vigorously. 'Yes, I can see that.' He seemed stalled, not knowing what to do.

She felt sorry for him. 'Or a coffee? We can do coffee.'

'Yes, that'd be great.' Then he paused, looking at the separate list of coffee varieties.

'Just a normal coffee?' she suggested. 'It's called an Americano. With milk?'

'No, no milk. Black is fine.' He looked relieved and reached to swing his backpack around to his side, threatening the ketchup and brown sauce bottles on the end of the counter.

'You pay when you leave,' she informed him. 'Like an old-fashioned diner.' She hoped he would also remember the tip jar, next to the till. He had nice eyes. Grey-blue, they were a bit big for his face. He seemed a little sad at the edges, even though he was smiling.

There was one unoccupied table, close to the back door. She pointed it out to him and said she would bring the coffee over. Archie's was a forgiving place for eccentrics and students and everyone else. She hoped he wouldn't forget to pay. Sometimes people did.

He kept looking at her as he moved to the table, walking backwards a few steps, in danger of bumping into the freelancer's table. The writer looked up and glared at him, worried about coffee spilling on his laptop. The new guy didn't seem to notice. Whatever was going on in his head, he wasn't concentrating on his surroundings. He sat down with a screech of the chair legs on the floor.

. . .

The café was busy, but small enough that Gina could keep an eye on the coming and goings of customers. Joanne was there, as always, reading the free papers and making her herbal tea last. One of the usual young mums (the main A-ha fan) came in later today, bringing her mother. The grandmother looked sure of herself as she bounced the chubby baby on her lap. The boy pressed up and down on his wobbly legs, testing them out and springing around haphazardly. The grandmother must have been getting a good arm workout, keeping up with his moves and making sure he didn't fall. She seemed happy, as her cappuccino drifted to room temperature, letting her daughter have a moment to finish hers.

The student guy stayed all afternoon. He finished his coffee and ordered another, letting it cool as he became absorbed in his work. In an A3 sized sketchbook he worked (HB pencil) on intricate drawings of a futuristic-looking building. Maybe he was an architect. She looked over his shoulder when she went to collect the second coffee cup, but he waved her away.

'Still working on it,' he said. It wasn't clear if he was talking about the cold coffee or the drawing.

Five o'clock came. The gossiping mums and the writer made their way to the door towards wherever they called home. Gina pulled the shades down and turned the music up a notch to signal that it was closing time. Even after the others left, the new guy stayed. She went to quickly scrub the WC and then came back for the final washdown of the tables. She did every one but his. Eventually she had to say something. Even the free papers lady had left, after eyeing the last of the unsold croissants.

He was a tall guy, hunched down low over the drawing pad. He was making very small lines, all stacked up to make in the end a very big image.

'We're closing.' She stood behind his chair as she said it. It didn't seem like he heard her. 'Excuse me, mate? I need to close, sorry.'

He sat up with a jerk. For a moment he looked around as if he didn't know where he was or how he'd got there. He saw the darkness beyond the window. 'Oh, sorry. I didn't realise it was so late.'

'No problem, it's just that it's time to go.'

'Of course, of course.' He rushed to fold the cover back over his drawing, she hoped he wouldn't damage it by moving too fast on her account.

'It's okay, I have a couple of things to do first. But I need to close the till. Do you mind?'

He looked at her with big eyes, as if he couldn't fathom her meaning. 'Mind?' he said.

'Paying. For the two Americanos?'

'Of course, of course.' He seemed like a guy who repeated himself. Did he say everything double?

'It's £4.50, unless you want the last almond croissant to take away.'

'Yes, yes. That's fine. Great, croissant, great. June would like that.'

'I just have one, is that okay? It's £1.25'

'Fine, fine. Thanks so much.'

He left in a rush. No tip.

She let the door close with the bells, and only then did she see that his woolly hat had fallen on the floor under his chair. When she went outside to try to give it to him, he was gone.

He came in again, about a week later and seemed unusually happy. With most of the customers, even if they were regulars, their eyes went to the menu or the cakes on display when they spoke, rather than to her. But he walked up to the counter, looked right at her and said hello, with such a cheerful expression on his face. It was like he was an old friend meeting up after a long time, not a customer. She doubted herself for a moment – did she know him from somewhere?

He didn't say anything more for a bit, so Gina said, 'Can I help you?'

He suddenly seemed flustered. 'Oh yes, what did I have last time? A regular coffee? And that almond thing, that was lovely. Really lovely.'

'Almond croissant. No problem, I'll bring it over.'

'Sure.' He seemed a bit deflated that the conversation ended. She turned to make the Americano. 'Black, no sugar?' he added.

She nodded. Maybe he was an odd one. Better not to get

involved. Just deliver the coffee and the pastry without dropping it, that was her job. It hadn't been a good day so far. Javier had wanted her to stay at his place last night, but she wasn't keen to leave Nanna on her own.

'You've got that lodger guy there,' Javier had said.

'It's not his job to look after Nanna, you know that.'

'Why not? He lives there, doesn't he?'

'How do I know if he's around? He's not family. He pays to be there, not the other way around.'

'Well, maybe you should give him a discount. Or on the other hand, get him to pay more when his pretty girlfriend stays over. If he doesn't want to pay, then he has to do the dirty work. Cleaning the floors, scrubbing the toilets, all the glamorous jobs.'

She hated it when he started to talk like that. Like he had no kindness for people, for Nanna especially. Nanna, who should have earned that from the whole world a long time ago, for everything she had been through.

'If you think you're getting lucky tonight you're an idiot,' she said, and got up to get her coat. He grabbed the belt loop of her jeans and pulled her back down to the sofa.

'Don't go. I was just joking.'

'It's not funny. I love my nan, and you just talk rubbish about people.'

'It's funny, in a way. Come on... You know I have a different sense of humour to you.'

She moved to get up again, but he held her back.

'Let me go,' she said.

He said nothing, just held onto the belt loop with a naughty-boy look on his face.

'Let me go, for God's sake!' There was no way in hell she was going to stay here. But he just did the Javier thing, stubborn as hell.

She jumped up, hearing her jeans rip as she fell back to the couch. He was laughing at her now. A loop of denim was in shreds in his hand. There was a hole at the top of her jeans. She didn't give a care. No way was she staying there another moment longer.

But coming home wasn't a victory lap. She had missed the last train south and the night bus only went to New Cross, so she had to walk the rest of the way. She thought about Javier, and tried not to think about him. He had been into the romantic gestures when they first got together – showing up at her studio unannounced, with flowers for no reason. He seemed dedicated, unlike many other guys at uni, who were commitment-shy. He insisted on their exclusivity from the time of their first date. At the time, she had thought it flattering, and unusual. His decisiveness was a relief, after years of trying to guess what other people were thinking.

She wished she had someone to talk to. All her friends had disappeared the summer after uni, and other than Javier and Nanna and the customers, she couldn't think of anyone else she had spoken to all day. Who could she tell her troubles to? Not Nanna, she wouldn't want to worry her. She was twenty-two now, shouldn't be bringing her romantic problems to an eighty-one-year-old.

In any case, Nanna was long asleep by the time she got home. She had left the hall light on, as she always did when Gina was out.

She wondered if Nanna had remembered her new blood pressure medicine. The prescription was supposed to help with the oedema in her feet. They were so swollen lately, and Gina had to work hard to get her to see the doctor. In the end, Nanna agreed that the doctor could come to them. But that meant Gina telling Lizl at the last minute about the change of shifts, and Lizl was a bit short with her today. Maybe she was losing patience with Gina's situation. Or maybe there was something else she forgot. In any case, it didn't feel good to be Gina, not at the moment.

She remembered that the architect guy had left his hat last time, and gave it to him. That made him smile.

After everyone else had left, he was the final customer again. She took his payment and started counting the money in the till, the last step before closing.

He sort of spat out the question: 'Do you like art?'

'Sorry?'

'Art. Sketches, you know.'

'I was an art student, if that's what you mean.'

'Great, great.' He smiled very widely. Again, she noticed his teeth first, but then also his eyes. They were kind eyes.

'Why do you ask?'

'There's an exhibition. In Old Street, at the Royal Drawing School.' He handed her a postcard with a dark charcoal sketch covering the front. It was a landscape, but it wasn't clear where from. It was eerie and dark with vines and swirls. Might not even be a place in this world.

'The private view is in a few weeks,' he said. 'It would be great for you to come. Really great.'

'Is it your work, then?' She scanned the back of the card, but there was no list of artists, just an address for the school and social media links.

'No, not mine. I'm not artistic.' She looked at him puzzled and pointed to his sketch pad.

'No, I mean, I'm just a practical guy. Structural engineering background. If people need drawings for a loft conversion or an elaborate garden shed, I'm your man. This,' he gestured to the pad, 'is just to keep my mind off things. Just doodling, playing with futuristic ideas.' His eyes came back to the card. 'The show is for June, my girlfriend.' He beamed when he said her name. 'She's the artist.'

She still didn't understand why he was giving it to her; she didn't even know his name. 'That's great, but…'

'You might be busy, but it would be great if you could stop by. You see, June, she … kind of struggles with … keeping in touch with people. It would be good to have a nice friendly face there. It could really cheer her up.'

He looked so eager, she couldn't think of a reason to say no. 'Ok, I'll see if I can stop by.' She hadn't been out in Old Street for ages, not since the last of the Goldsmiths friends moved away; it could be fun.

He put out his hand for an old-fashioned handshake. It

was so awkward, she had to laugh. But better than a hug from someone you didn't know, she supposed. Then he put on his odd hat, zipped up his bag, and practically ran out of the café. At the door he stopped and said, 'My name's Tom, by the way.'

'Goodbye, Tom by-the-way.' He smiled at that, and it made her smile too.

'Friends? Guys and girls can't be friends.'

A few days later, Javier was back on his regular refrain, about the inherent differences between men and women, or guys and girls, as he said. Sometimes he said 'chicks,' but today he remembered that she didn't like it.

'He seems like a nice guy, and anyway, he was talking about his girlfriend.'

'I bet he was using it to hit on you. Oldest story in the book. Make up a girlfriend to seem hard to get.'

'Is that right? Is that what they write in the handbook for shifty blokes out to pull a girl by deception?'

He looked at her suspiciously. 'I don't know what you mean, deception. Did you tell him about me? You should have told him about me.'

The postcard for the show at the Royal Drawing School was pinned to her corkboard. They were sharing a drink from an old bottle of wine in her room. She had a little sink, but they didn't bother to do more than rinse the glasses before refilling them with the wine. It wasn't good quality wine to begin with, and now it tasted a little vinegary.

'Anyway, I like the sound of it,' she said. 'Since graduating, I haven't seen any art shows. It would be good to get out and see something new.'

'Well, I'm not going,' he said. 'I've seen more disastrous creations than I hope to see in all my life.' He finished his glass and poured another.

Sometimes she really didn't know what she'd seen in him. Didn't he use to rave about art and act like a connoisseur? 'I thought you liked art,' she said quietly.

'Oh, you know what I mean,' he said. 'It can be so fake, all this student-y stuff. Trying to make a statement and pretend it hasn't all been done before.'

She looked at him, wondering if he would read her mind and stop talking.

He eventually glanced up, and changed his expression from one of annoyance to that young boy's look he used when he tried to get on her good side. 'Not *your* work, my darling. I'm not talking about you.'

She ran her tongue over the front of her teeth. They felt rough and needed a clean.

'Look,' she said. 'I need to talk to Nanna about something. Can I see you later?'

He looked hurt, taking an extra few seconds to get up from where he was lounging on her bed. 'What, now? You're kicking me out?' He exaggerated the last word, as if he was a cartoon character, not a man.

'Um, yeah. I need to catch you later. You know, in the week. After your teaching.' She put the cork back in the bottle and put it on her bedside table. She pulled him up to standing and started to straighten out the duvet on the bed. Everything was such a mess right now. She just wanted to make something come out a bit better than before. Was that too much to ask of the universe? To let her improve something?

He moved with deliberate slowness as he put on his leather jacket and tied up his Converse. His helmet lay next to his feet, round like a cue ball.

She wanted to brush her teeth, but didn't feel like doing that in front of him. Maybe she should shower too.

'Well, my darling,' he said, when he couldn't find an excuse to stay longer. 'Parting is a sorrow.'

'"Parting is such sweet sorrow" is the quote,' she said as she led him down the stairs to the front door. In the living room Nanna was sitting in her recliner with her feet up, listening to French radio. She raised one hand in greeting to Javier, without expectation. He said nothing and pulled the door hard behind him. As Gina heard the motorcycle start up, she hoped that he hadn't drunk too much wine to drive.

'*Cherie*,' Nanna said. 'Come give me a kiss.'

She came close, leaned down and kissed Nanna once on each cheek. As she pulled back, Nanna's eyes were watery but smiling.

'Have you been crying?' Gina asked. 'Something's upset you?'

Nanna held one of Gina's hands in hers. 'No, my dear.' Her voice crackled a bit, like she hadn't spoken in some time. 'It's just a radio programme, about orphans. You know how I am about hearing anything about children being hurt or neglected. I can't take it.'

'Then you mustn't listen to that one,' Gina chided her. 'I'll change the station.'

'No, *cherie*, it's fine. It's finished. Well, it hasn't finished, it's a serial, you see. Comes back tomorrow, at the same time. But I'd like to finish it.' She looked up at Gina, as if searching for permission. 'Then I can hear how it turns out. And I think it will turn out well. I live in hope, in any case.' She put her hands down in her lap, pulling gently at the throw over her legs. 'I'm made to be hopeful, you know that.'

Gina looked at the aged hands together, resting on the knitted blanket. They were swollen with arthritis and laced with raised veins. You could trust those hands. They were truthful, battered hands and she loved them so. She brushed her cheek against Nanna's hair and said, 'Oh Nan,' but couldn't say any more. She wanted to say something about being annoyed at Javier, or the disappointment when she dropped the pot of herbal tea at work and it smashed, but she also had an overwhelming feeling that she wanted to brush her teeth. She didn't want to smell like the cheap red wine going sour. Nanna deserved better than that. Hell, everyone deserved better than that. She'd pour the rest of the bottle down the drain.

As she moved to the stairs, she said, 'I made a new friend today.'

'You did? That's nice. What's her name?'

'It's a guy. His name is Tom.'

'Hmm? What does Javier think about that?'

'Doesn't matter. He's just a friend. Anyways, he's invited me to an art show. In Old Street. I think I'll go.'

'That's nice, dear.' Nanna's attention seemed to drift, and she said no more.

Chapter Six

January 1953

Aday told himself he was looking for her because of her lecture; she said it was imperative for doctors to understand the new research to ensure that the procedures did not have a damaging effect on children. As a new doctor he could take that message up and push it through the system, if he just could learn a bit more about her.

He had her family name – Monteaux. Nurse Monteaux. He didn't know her given name, but the surname was a place to start. Most likely, she lived with other nurses in one of the boarding houses connected to her hospital. But which hospital did she serve? He looked again at the notes he took at her lecture, but to no avail. He had been so focused on watching her that he took very few. He admonished himself for the lack of professionalism.

He confided in a colleague, who suggested that the

Matron's office would have records of all the serving nurses. He started with Lewisham Hospital, where he worked. The Matron's office faced the parking lot, wedged under the stairs. He had never been there before; indeed, not many men had. Nursing was the domain of women, and the intrusion might not be welcome.

Walking in, he startled the receptionist, which was a pity. No, he wasn't a porter, he assured her, and not a delivery driver either. He stood there in his doctor's whites and showed his identification with a gentle smile.

The woman facing him wore glasses halfway down her nose, and had a wary expression. 'Never seen a coloured doctor before,' she said. To whom, it wasn't clear, as she was otherwise alone in the room with a typewriter and piles of files. But there was no luck to be had, not at Lewisham. He tried again back at Guy's Hospital, wondering perchance if that was why she had given the presentation there, but to no avail. Charing Cross Hospital was no good; neither was Queen Charlotte's Hospital. It was only at St Mary's, near Notting Hill, that he made progress.

'Yes, we have an Isabella Monteaux here, working in the children's ward,' the secretary in the Matron's office said to him with some satisfaction. She was young and had ginger curls that fell into her face as she spoke, whereupon she pushed them back behind her ears again.

'Well done, my good woman! Great detective work!' His voice may have been too loud, but he could barely contain himself.

'And she was asking after you, you might like to know,' she added, a broad smile on her face.

On another day Aday would have protected his feelings from surfacing, but today it was not possible. She had asked after him as well! How extraordinary. It was meant to be, a meeting of the minds. He just knew it.

Was she mad to agree to meet this doctor when she had seen him only once? Bella only had a letter from him delivered through the hospital. Written very formally, the letter thanked her for the presentation and asked if she might be willing to meet him to discuss further her ideas about how to improve the welfare of children.

When she first held the note in one hand, the other came to her mouth to smother her smile. She knew from the heat on her cheeks that she was not doing very well at hiding her emotions. She quickly folded the paper into her pocket and walked away from the Matron's office. It was best not to reveal too much to strangers when you were alone in this city. That was one of the rules she lived by.

She wrote back in as formal a language as he had used, accepting his invitation to meet the following week for a cup of tea at a café near Lewisham Hospital. She posted the letter from a post office near Paddington, where few people knew her.

Ten days later she had to navigate her way from Notting Hill down to southeast London, where she had never been before. Two buses and an hour later, she was flustered. She did not like to be late, but in truth she was. The rain had flattened her curls and the colour of her coat was muted, closer to a muddy brown than the enthusiastic orange it had been when she started out. She bit her lip and straightened her back. It had been a long time since she was this nervous about speaking to someone, particularly a man.

The windows of the café on Manor Lane were masked with condensation from within. She had to push hard on the door, as it was surprisingly heavy. Inside was warm and smelled of tomato soup and fresh bread. The ceiling was a dark iron sculpted surface that flowed and curved and looked like a work of art. She was distracted by it longer than she should have been, and then her eyes came down to look at the customers.

There were many ordinary people in groups of two or alone. And then there was him. He was at a corner table with a red checked tablecloth like all the rest, but the similarities ended there. He wore a dark blue suit, like the one he was wearing the day they met. His hat and coat were hanging on a hook behind the table, as if he was in his own office. He stood up when she came in, pushing the table slightly to get his legs out. The salt and pepper rattled a bit in protest but did not topple. He looked directly at her and smiled widely.

'Nurse Monteaux, so wonderful to see you here.' He relieved her of the heavy door, closing it behind her. A layer of warmth settled where the cold air had been. 'May I call you Isabella? Please, come sit down.' He gestured to the table as if he owned the place.

'Gertie?' he called out to the waitress. 'Could we have some tea please?' He helped Bella out of her wet coat and asked if she would like it hung up to dry. Momentarily at a loss for words, she nodded and he took it over near the radiator. With care, he pulled out the shoulders and sleeves into their proper shape, and laid it over the tops of empty chairs to dry out.

When she found her voice she said, 'Doctor Falade, am I pronouncing that right?'

'Indeed. How was your journey? I am sorry about the weather.'

'Not your fault, of course.' She paused and pulled some papers out of her bag. 'I wanted to show you some more evidence about the children's blood transfusions and testing. Look here.' She pointed to graphs printed on thin paper. They were the results of a trial of treatments for children's blood disorders. He was surprised she had access to research; nurses were normally not involved in work of this kind.

She saw his confusion and explained. 'My ward sister is spearheading a new procedure, but we had to gather more evidence to convince matron to change the protocols.' She continued to explain the research cycle with better clarity than many of his lecturers at university.

'This is excellent,' he said. 'May I keep a copy of that?' She gave it away freely. 'I will see if I can talk to the matron and the sisters at Lewisham to do the same. Ah, here's the tea.' The waitress brought a pot of tea and two currant buns.

'They seem to know you here,' Bella said.

'Yes, I eat lunch here most days. I love the food, and it suits my routine between the hospital and the surgery. Also, I find that, as a stranger to this city'—he paused and looked at her directly—'it helps to have people who know who you are, and who welcome you back. Sometimes strangers can act oddly, and it takes too much effort to change their views. Do you know what I mean?'

She nodded, looking down at her saucer, which had a small spill of tea painting its way along the curve. She did know.

'Let me tell you a story about a man I met here, not so long ago.' And he proceeded to tell her the story about Fernando and the directory. She put her chin in her hands and forgot about the currant bun, wanting to hear all the details. It was extraordinary, this man finding the name of his loved one again after all those years! She didn't want it to end.

'What happened to him?' she asked.

'I haven't the faintest idea. Gertie is still upset about the directory going missing.' He chuckled to himself. 'But a new edition is due out again next month, and then maybe she'll forgive me for trying to help a stranger in need.'

The conversation dwindled, and they each paused to drink more tea. Hers was cold by now. She had forgotten to be nervous, but now it came back to her. Her hand went up to her curls to see if they had any life left in them. They were still slightly damp, and who knew what a mess they were in. She took off her glasses for a moment to wipe the lenses, and then laid them down on the table beside her. He was transformed into a watercolour: the brown in his face, the white of his shirt, the blue of his suit, and a background of the café in a relaxing blend of rainy day colours.

'Why do you take off your glasses? Can you see without them?'

'Not very well. I have needed glasses since I was very young.'

'Then why remove them?' he insisted.

She could hardly tell him it was because she was convinced she looked better without them. Those ladies from *Vogue*, they never had glasses that made their eyes look a different shape. 'Sometimes I just want a change' was all she said.

Chapter Seven

The café windows were fogged over on the rainy afternoon, but it was a busy place. The mum-and-baby group was there again, so Gina put the 80s music a little louder for their benefit. She noticed that the babies were getting more sure of themselves on their little legs. The mum who had brought in the grandmother last time was back to being on her own with her kid, the croissant-crusher. She let him test out standing on the floor, but kept hold with one strong hand so he didn't wander off. He wobbled and slipped, landing on the cushy nappy with a small 'whump'. The baby looked at the room with surprised eyes, like he was deciding whether to cry or not. His gaze for some reason rested on Gina's face, behind the counter, and he held her with that look. For a baby, he certainly seemed to have quite a personality building in him.

'You're okay, Buddy,' the mum said, scooping him up on to her lap. The baby still stared at Gina. It was a bit disconcerting. The mum followed his gaze and smiled as she rubbed his hair away from his face.

'He likes your earrings,' she called out in Gina's direction.

'Sorry?' Gina wasn't sure if she was talking to her, but it seemed like she was.

The mum got up and approached the counter, baby on hip and holding an empty coffee cup. 'Your earrings. They're so sparkly. Babies like that. But I could never wear them, not while he's in this grabby phase. Did you make them?'

Gina touched the earrings she got from Camden Market years back. 'No, not these... I make other things. Sculptures.'

'Really! That's so cool!' The mum's tired face brightened as she put the cup on the counter. 'I used to do art, before I had Buddy. Could I have another caffeine hit, before I have to wrestle him into the buggy with the rain cover? He fights me every time.'

'Sure thing. I'll bring it to your table.'

'You should bring your sculptures in sometime. I'm sure the customers would love to see them.'

Gina didn't know what to say. The woman had never spoken more than a coffee and croissant order before.

She saw Gina's hesitation and laughed. 'I can see the idea might terrify you. But seriously, I wish I had done more with my art before I had this guy.' She bounced the baby again on her hip, perhaps hoping he wouldn't totally understand the sentiment. 'Things were quite different.' The baby still stared at Gina, as if he wanted to deny any part in this drama. 'I should have seized the moment more often,' the mum continued. 'I know that now.'

'Sure, I'll think about it. Thanks, um ... what's your name?'

'It's Alison, and this is Buddy.'

'Buddy and I know each other,' Gina said, and the baby didn't seem to object. She reached out to try to shake his hand, but he held his little fists back. He hadn't made his mind up about her, not yet. Babies are funny like that. They won't pretend to be something they're not. You gotta respect them for the determination.

'How do girls make friends?'

Tom's question seemed earnest; he didn't realise that it was a bit awkward. It was like he needed directions in a foreign country, and couldn't speak the language.

Gina didn't answer him straightaway. 'That depends,' she stalled.

'Some people do it naturally,' he said, looking into his coffee cup sadly. She gathered that wasn't the case for him and June. She had taken up the habit of sitting down at his table, after the other customers had gone home. It felt easy, and no one was there to disagree.

'I don't know about naturally,' she said. 'You just click with some people, or you don't.'

'Do you click with people?' He looked up.

She shook her head. 'Actually, I shouldn't talk. I think

I've been losing friends since uni. There's hardly anyone left, except Javier.'

'Why? You're so approachable.' He said it like it was the best trait ever.

'I don't know about that.' She thought of her loose group of art friends who were all gone now A number of them had made plans to move in together in a shared house in Manchester. An artists' collective, self-governing and such. She stayed behind in London, because of Nanna. They were probably all vegan by now. Or broke. Or both. Or maybe they made a success of things, and would be heading towards the Turner Prize before you knew it. Who knew? They weren't in touch.

'People drift.' She shrugged her shoulders.

'But then you meet new people, no?'

'That can be the tricky part, I guess. In London.'

'In London,' he echoed, looking out the café windows. There was a comfortable silence between them.

'I didn't grow up here,' he volunteered after a moment. 'I'm from Bristol, originally. I always thought I'd go back there, but June...' He swished his cold coffee remains around in a jerky circle. 'She said, "No way."'

'Why?'

'It's the art scene,' he said. 'Nothing compares to London. Unless you go abroad, I guess. New York, or Berlin.'

'Yes, well ... London seems to attract interesting kinds of people, and we never leave. Or the opposite. My mum, she literally says she can't breathe in London. She'd die if she lived here, gets asthma attacks with the rubbish air. She only came back to have me, give me to my nanna, and then go off again.'

She had said too much. Why did she bring up Mum? She had probably embarrassed him. He didn't say anything.

She stood up like she was clearing the table, sweeping croissant crumbs into her open palm. She squeezed her fist tight and felt the pieces with their mixture of sharp edges and crumbly bits.

'That's, um...' He seemed to be searching his mind for the right thing to say, then gave up. 'That's difficult. I'm sorry to hear that.'

'No, it's okay.' She made her voice sound cheerful. 'My nanna, she's the light of any room she's in. You should meet her. She remembers everyone she's ever met. A better memory than mine, I tell you.'

'Does she do the crosswords? My grandfather used to do the *Times* crossword every day, and he lived until eighty-one.'

'She's eighty-two next month.'

She put her hand in the sugar bowl and told Tom about her sugar sculptures. They had a laugh about the headless Romeo. With Tom, it didn't seem that bad. A disaster for the mark, yes, but ... he seemed entertained by it. Not in a mean way, but in a laugh-with-you, laugh-at-yourself sort of way.

'Why don't you bring June here sometime?' she asked.

'I'd like that, I really would.' He seemed hopeful for a

moment, but then the mood dropped again. 'But she works late, and she'd miss your opening hours.'

'Shame. Maybe on the weekend?'

'That's when she's in the studio, but that's an idea. She shares a space with some other artists from the drawing school. Would you like to see it sometime?'

'I'd love to,' she said, and she meant it. 'Any sugar sculptors on site?'

'I don't think so. You may be one of a kind.'

At home, she took out her tools. They were bundled together, as always, wrapped like a carver's tools in the faded green felt roll with the gold ribbon. She couldn't remember where she got the roll from; must have been a present from Nanna, or something she bought herself when she started her art degree so long ago.

She'd missed the feel of the tools in her hands. She unrolled them, each one in its own loop. They were simple yet beautiful, with smooth wooden handles. She'd forgotten how nice they were to hold. One had a square edge that made very satisfying cuts. Another was cylindrical and you could use it to make tunnels or embellishments.

When was the last time she'd used them? She couldn't remember. There always was something holding her back. She was too busy, with Javier, or with the café. She lacked a purpose: with no show or assignment, there was little justification to take them out and get stuck in again. After she scraped through her degree (barely mustering a pass), there never quite seemed a good reason to do it. But why did she need a reason?

She opened the cabinets and looked for the sugar. Demerara was in the corner, pushed aside for Nanna's Splenda. Behind, there was some other white sugar, out of date. She banged the bag on the countertop. Solid as a rock. Maybe if she slow-boiled it and then let the water evaporate, she could get something malleable, but it seemed like a lot of trouble. If she had the carving tools from uni, she could go at the block as-is, but her working style was usually more subtle than that. Brute force wasn't her thing.

She looked in the larder, hoping for something gooey like molasses or golden syrup to mix with the demerara. In luck! Tate & Lyle didn't fail her. A bottle, sticky on the outside, about one-third full. A bit out of date, but who would notice? – it was not for eating, anyway. It was last used to make some flapjacks when watching a movie at home. When was that? Before they had disconnected Sky Cinema when Bella's eyesight grew too weak and she found trying to watch the films too tiring. Probably about two years ago.

She took out some bowls of different sizes. In one large bowl she put hot water, hot as she could stand it. She took an extra plastic bag and stood the cement-sugar brick in it, to see if the heat would do the trick – soften the brick without getting it wet. She needed the sugar to respond to touch.

She poured some golden syrup in another bowl and microwaved it for twenty seconds. Then she poured a good amount of the demerara sugar right into it. She mixed it with a teaspoon, and it moved nicely. Textured with the grains, but in motion, like a river. Or a snakeskin or something. She pulled out the spoon. She knew she shouldn't but she felt like giving it a lick and so she did. It tasted a little stale, like it was dusty.

She pressed her right hand into the mixture. It was warm and comforting, like the scrubs you use at the end of a long soak in the bath. She rubbed it between her thumb and forefinger, making circles under the gooey surface. What should she make? Her mind was blank, but her hands wanted to keep moving.

She felt the block of sugar standing in the hot water and was satisfied that it was starting to soften and relax, but it was still quite solid. She took out a knife, gently carved out a crescent-moon shape about the size of her fist and placed it on a plate.

She took out her tools, one by one, and drew patterns in the bowl with the syrup. She carved a zig-zag design, copying the pattern all around. She drizzled the gooey mixture over the crescent moon. Little bubbles came to the surface as the liquid trickled down. She loved how you could never predict how gravity would affect your inventions; the density of the sugar was different every time.

At uni she had access to some great tools. There was this metal table that vibrated, to get all the air bubbles out of the silicon moulds. And a kiln, for casting the fimo models before pouring the sugar mixture in. It was easier to do the art when you had the right facilities. The creative energy came faster when the possibilities were supported and you could go in any direction. Away from all of that, she had to learn to be more of a self-starter, and she wasn't usually a self-starter sort of person. Maybe she could make a mould with aluminium foil? Or get some silicon herself? She'd have to look into it.

Some of her friends thought she was going to go into cake decorating after graduating. When they heard about her work at the café, they thought it was a natural progression. But she had no appetite for glazed flowers and wedding figures on top of a cake. No, her art meant more than that. She just needed to figure out what, exactly, she was meant to do.

In the end, nothing she made today was going to stand up and be displayed or praised. It was just her getting back into it. Fun, experimental, and ephemeral. Like the sand mandalas.

She decided to make those flapjacks after all (she found some oats in the back of the larder, somehow having avoided being nibbled by mice that the lazy cat failed to scare off). With the oven on and the smells from the cooking filling the kitchen, it was homey. After all that, she didn't mind tossing the crescent moon and the other pieces in the rubbish and rinsing the rest of the ingredients down the drain.

It was a start. Of what, she didn't know yet, but a start.

• • •

'She says it's like a haze that covers everything,' Tom said. He sometimes blurted out a phrase as if you had already been talking about it, although you hadn't.

'A haze?' Gina was with him at the end of the shift, running grains of sugar between her thumb and forefinger. Not the whole sugar bowl, mind you. Just the sugar cubes that were already crumbling apart – she helped them disintegrate a bit more. No paying customers were left, except Tom, and he didn't feel like a customer anymore.

'And then she can't be around people, can't be around me. Has no appetite, food tastes grey. She says that. How can a taste have a colour?'

He looked genuinely distressed, talking about June's moods. He was trying to find any compass points to navigate by, but he was lost.

Gina understood, in a way, but it was hard to describe it to someone else. And what did she know? Everyone might perceive it differently. It was like colours. We all said the colour is yellow, because that was the name we learned from picture books. But what if what you saw when you looked through your eyes was what I would call green? Was that why people had such dramatically different reactions to colours? But her mind was wandering. She wanted to help him, she really did.

'I can imagine,' she said. 'Just remember, no good-tasting food is grey. It must be a thing in nature, that brighter colours give you energy or vitamins. I think I read that somewhere once. Bright colours in our minds are associated with foods that give you energy. So if you are down and feeling low energy, you associate that with less colour, or the muting of colour.' She couldn't tell if she was making any sense. 'Anyway, it's hard to explain feelings from one person to another. It's good that she tries.'

'Yes, yes...' He ran his fingers through his beard, and Gina wondered if she should suggest that he see a barber. Didn't he have any guy-friends who could give him advice about that sort of thing? Or June should say something. He himself didn't seem to care that much about aesthetics. He wore the same odd wool hat each day, and often had food caught in his beard if he wasn't careful.

'It's good,' she repeated, 'that she tries to talk about her feelings. Some people just don't. They run away, or roll over and just try to sleep the winter away. My mum is like that.'

According to Nanna, Mum was just not a winter person. She was simply not made for the season. Got the winter blues, every time. It was connected to her asthma, of course. It wasn't a good combo, being depressed, sick and stuck in an old drafty house in what is possibly the greyest part of the country. No wonder she buggered off to the tropics. If Gina had had a chance and some sense of adventure, she probably would've done the same.

'But that's why you need to meet June,' he said. 'You'd get her, you see. I can tell. It's something about the artist in you. You're not very similar, but I think you'd get each other. I've told her all about you.'

At this, Gina glanced up. What was there to say? A waitress is a dingy café in a rainy corner of Lewisham, who can't get up the energy to fix her relationship with her moody boyfriend? Living with an old nan who is nearly blind and argues back with French radio? There wasn't much to be proud about, that was to be sure.

But the way Tom looked at her, he was like a friendly dog. A loyal, lovable dog, who didn't hide his needs. Dogs were like that. They were open about their affection, and what they needed. If they needed food, they would push the bowl towards you with their nose. If you left them alone too long, they would whine or shred the doorframe in rebellion. But if they wanted a rub, they had no shame about putting their head in your lap, their ears next to your fingers, and thumping their tail on the floor to show their pleasure. No, you could do a lot worse than that. It was honest, it was.

'The show – it's Saturday. You're coming, aren't you?' he said.

'I'll be there. Not sure if she'll have time for someone new, as all her friends will be around her and celebrating.'

'No, she's not like that, you'll see. It'll be great. Just great.'

Chapter Eight

February 1953

They weren't prejudiced, his colleagues at the hospital said, referring to high-minded people like themselves. They knew he was a good doctor. But you needed to understand the local people. They wouldn't come to a Black doctor even if they were sick.

As a practitioner, you had to have distance from the words and reactions of others. You could observe that their experiences in the war or in the colonies damaged their minds to the point where they could not see a stranger as anything but his colour. Lost the sense of the man.

But he had faith. He had done the training and earned his degree. He knew that he was meant to be a doctor, and that people would come to see that in him. Most of his patients were more or less accepting of him. For any doubters, his medical certificates were prominently displayed in frames on the wall. He had patients in the past walk up to them and peer more closely at the documents, inspecting the seal from Kings College. But he said nothing. People needed space with their own thoughts if they were going to change their minds without shame.

The ones who were cogent, not fighting off the demons of alcohol or madness of some sort, came to see him for what he was, a man using his knowledge to help them. The English stood in awe of knowledge. If they trusted that you had gained it legitimately, they stood back and let themselves be bathed in it.

He also had increasing numbers of patients from the colonies, or second-generation people, born in London and from workers in the shipyards in Deptford. They found him somehow, coming from as far away as Peckham, Greenwich, and even Notting Hill, sometimes. If they hadn't heard before, they were often the most surprised to see him; but once their challenging questions were answered – *Didn't you have to be English to get a medical licence? How did he succeed when so many other trained doctors were refused?* – they were his most loyal patients. Friends? Well, a doctor was never really able to befriend the people he served. There had to be some professional distance, or else you risked being emotionally involved. But he did have a loyal list of patients who came back when they needed care. Hopefully he had instilled in them some sense that coming to the doctor sooner, before something turned into an emergency, was less risky and less costly in the long run.

Through word of mouth, his patient list continued to grow. The place was short of doctors; south London didn't have nearly as many as west London or the Home Counties. For the three days a week when his surgery was open, he was quite busy. The other days he was at the hospital.

The names of the patients were often very similar. Lots of people were named James, John, William, as well as Mary and Sandra. But the next patient seemed different. The name was Spanish or Italian, if he wasn't mistaken.

The knock at the door was tentative, and Aday called out what he hoped was a reassuring 'Come in!'

The door did not move. Perhaps the patient was hard of hearing? He got up from his chair and put his large hand on the doorknob, just as it was pushed from the other side.

The old man was small, and Aday found himself looking down onto the top of his pale head, his thinning straight white hair splayed in a circle. The man tipped up his face and stared at Aday's with an expression of surprise and shock.

He was used to this, and stepped aside to allow the man to enter the room at ease. But the man did not move.

'Would you like to come in?' Aday said, keeping his voice calm and unthreatening.

'You! It's you!' the man said. His face was slowly moving into a smile, but still he did not advance.

Aday didn't want to keep the man in the corridor. Perhaps he had lost control of his senses? 'Please come in,' he said, holding open the door more widely.

'You don't understand, you are the one! You helped me,

saved my life!' The old man spoke with a strong accent. His face was flushed and he seemed anxious. Still smiling, he followed the instructions and walked into the room.

He was trembling now. Was it fever? He did not take his eyes off the doctor's face, and so failed to look where he was going and bumped into the chair. Aday let go of the door and put an arm on the man's elbow, helping him settle into his seat.

Sitting at the desk across from the old man, he tried to smile his gentlest smile. 'What seems to be troubling you, Mr…' He looked down at the notes.

'Almeira. Fernando Almeira.' The man was beaming at him. 'You saved my life,' he said again.

'Is that so?' Aday looked up from the notes, which held no past history. This must be the first time the man had come to the surgery. He saw a lot of faces at the hospital – was the man a recent admission?

'You don't remember?' The old man took off his coat and seemed agitated. Once he was freed from the sleeves, he spoke with his hands in big gestures, circles opening out. 'The phone directory? The smog?'

Aday sat back and smiled. Yes, the man from Spain. The day before the smog lifted. Such an eerie time, about seven weeks ago. 'The lover! Now I remember you!' He got up again to shake the man's hand properly. It warmed him from the inside to see the man again, smiling in front of him. 'That was months ago. Did you find her, in the end? Is that why you are still in London?'

The man held onto the handshake with both hands,

laughing and trying to speak at the same time, but he started to cough. Aday took his hand back and reached to give the man a handkerchief. He observed that the man shuddered with coughing spasms. Rapid breathing, blood vessels dilating. When the cough subsided, he sat down again.

'Mr Almeira, my dear man. That's quite a cough you have there.'

'You're a doctor? I've never met a…'

'A Black doctor? Yes, there are a few, but in this country we are a rare species.' He said it with a smile, although the number of times he had to repeat that phrase wore him down.

'Well, you were brilliant, absolutely brilliant,' the man said, a phrase he must have learned from the British. 'You saved me.'

'You found her, then?'

'Found her, married her…' He fumbled in his pocket for a moment. He pulled out his wallet and two pieces of paper. One was the tiny photograph that he had shown Aday before. The second was also small, but much newer. It was a photo of the man, in a nice suit, next to the woman from the childhood photograph. He could tell it was her: the eyes, cheekbones and high forehead were the same. Even though people of that age rarely smiled in photographs, the old man grinned widely. The woman, more subtly, smiled with happy eyes, the wrinkles coming out from the corners like rays. She wasn't wearing white, but he guessed it was a wedding photograph: a second chance.

'That's wonderful,' Aday said, but it wasn't the time to reminisce. He was a doctor, first and foremost. He took out his stethoscope. 'But I assume you are here about your cough? Would you loosen your buttons and let me listen to your heart and lungs?'

'Oh my heart, it isn't strong, doctor. It hasn't been for years. But it is still going, and Christiana made it whole again, thanks to you.'

'You would have found her, I just helped the process along.' Fernando's heart didn't have any alarming sounds, but there was a rattle in his breathing. Aday pushed gently at his shoulder to listen to the lungs from the back. Bronchitis, he was sure of it. Hopefully it wouldn't descend deeper into the lobes of the lungs. A man of Fernando's age might not survive pneumonia.

'You need these pills,' Aday said, as he wrote the prescription. Fernando's face faltered, and it occurred to him that the man might not be able to pay for the medicines. 'It costs a shilling. You do need to start them, right away.'

'I don't know how to get medicines in this country.' The man seemed lost again, like the time they first met.

Aday looked at his watch. There were no more patients today. 'Mr. Almeira, may I call you Fernando? Please, if you would do up your buttons and your coat.' He paused to quickly write his notes. As he stood up and pulled on his own overcoat, he realised he towered over the man. 'I will show you how to fill the script. And I want to hear all about your Christiana.'

· · ·

When Aday brought Fernando back to the café the next day, Gertie couldn't believe it.

'The directory!' she exclaimed, holding the heavy volume with both hands. 'So you found her?' she asked. She put the book down on the counter and placed an elbow on top to rest her chin in her hand. 'She was in Lewisham, after all?'

Fernando's English wasn't very good, but it had improved, Aday noticed. Using wide gestures, the man made a great story out of the tale to find his lost sweetheart. Having heard it before, Aday leaned back and watched the performance. The man's small frame shook with excitement as he told about knocking on his love's door, and her shock at seeing him. Aday chuckled to watch the eyebrows – long and reaching out, like the old man himself – dancing with excitement.

'Isn't that just lovely,' Gertie said to the other customers who were listening in. 'Love lasting that long. Like out of a fairy tale.'

The bell rang as another customer came in the door, and she had to hurry back to work. A few moments later, she brought the men two cups of warm coffee, and she placed them down in front of them like gifts.

'And I owe it all to you, my friend!' Fernando was in good spirits.

'It was just your Spanish luck, hitting gold that day.' Aday smiled into his coffee cup.

'Nonsense. If you hadn't taught me the modern ways, this directory listing... I would have been lost. And you know what?' He thumped on his chest. 'This would have ended. My heart, I know it would have.'

'Heartbreak is a myth, Fernando. It isn't actually connected to your physical heart.'

'That's what you doctors say, you scientists, but we know better. We lovers, we know when the heart loses faith, that's the day it will stop.'

'Well, let's pray that you never lose faith,' Aday said. 'I would hate to see that happen.'

Fernando liked to talk about himself, and even without a wider audience, he carried on about his new life with Christiana. He had moved into her large house, phoning their sons and grandchildren overseas on her fancy telephone to share the news. But his tone calmed down as he reached for his lukewarm coffee.

'And you, my good doctor,' Fernando asked. 'Are you married?'

Aday paused, wondering how much to tell. Everything with Bella was so new, so unique that he kept it to himself. He hadn't even written to his family about her, even though he knew in his heart that he was going to ask her to marry him. He decided that it was safe to tell Fernando. The old Latin lover might like the story, and there was nowhere else he needed to be that afternoon. He told Fernando about the day they met, the beautiful tiny woman with the huge eyes lecturing the roomful of arrogant men. How he felt at home with her, able to tell jokes and noticing every small detail.

He stored up stories to share with her; as he spoke to his friend he imagined how he would tell her about finding the old man again, and how she would be delighted that both Fernando and the directory were found.

'You are in love, doctor. That is clear.'

Aday didn't need to answer. He noticed how Gertie was listening in but pretending not to. 'Well, that depends on the lady, doesn't it?'

'No, no, no ... you know when it is love,' Fernando insisted. 'Your heart tells you.'

'I need to see how she feels,' Aday argued.

'Do you need to ask her father?'

'She has no family. They all died in the war.'

'So she is alone in this city? No one to protect her?'

'I'll protect her. And who knows? Maybe she will protect me. You should meet her sometime. She is very strong-willed.'

'You must come for dinner! The two of you. And meet my Christiana.'

Aday tried to object. Bella lived on the other side of London, and her boarding house had a curfew.

Fernando would have none of it. 'You're coming. Not tonight, that is fine. But for a Sunday lunch. I insist. We will meet this Bella of yours, and we shall see if she is as special as you say. Christiana loves family, and none of them are here. Her son, he is in Madrid with the grandchildren. My sons, they have families, but...' he gestured out the plate-glass windows. 'They are in America, and that is the other side of the world.'

Aday relented, on condition that he check with Bella. It might be good for her to meet Christiana, and maybe make a new friend. Perhaps meeting the Spanish lovers would help lift her spirits, and get her thinking about a possible wedding of her own someday.

Chapter Nine

Gina was nervous about going there alone. It had been awhile since she had been out in Old Street, and a Saturday night was always going to be a bit crazy. But she wasn't going out clubbing; it was an art show, for goodness sake. She didn't know why she felt tense. She had been to dozens of these kinds of shows when she was at uni. Loads of experimental things, performance art where you worried about being splashed with paint or fake blood or whatever. This was going to be a lot more tame. The Royal Drawing School didn't sound very experimental. About as establishment as you could get, really. Not like Goldsmiths. Goldsmiths was always trying to keep up its reputation as being cutting edge, nurturing radical art. But inside it was a bit more muddled. Or maybe that was just her.

Past the Wagamama and the Vietnamese resto so small

that it offered only takeaway, she saw the school. Wall-to-wall windows opened up a view of perfectly polished wood steps – and a beautiful wheelchair ramp at a slant that seemed like a work of art in itself.

The heat inside was intense. The noise too: the roar of happy people drinking the free booze and taking pride in art. Gina felt overheated immediately and tried to whip off her outside layers but got tangled in her scarf and nearly strangled herself before she even got through the door. There didn't seem to be anywhere to put coats, so she would have to hold her things on her arm all night. As she slowly walked up the ramp, with the display of drawings coming into view, again she asked herself what she was doing there.

The place was covered floor-to-ceiling with drawings. She had forgotten that the word 'drawing' could mean so many different things. Bright pastels competed with gloomy charcoals, whichever way the artist's mood wanted to go. Some drawings were so fiercely covered with charcoal there was no trace of the shade of the paper, just differentiation between black and grey. Others were lighter – less marking, less effort. Some were large, framed behind glass, a hefty sale price displayed underneath. Others looked so slight you thought they could be jokes. There was a series of small notebook pages, roughly torn, with just pencil sketches. Something that might have taken just a minute, but displayed like that, with drawing pins in a square of 5 x 5 pages, it looked significant. Maybe it was talking about the rip-offs in the art world or something. That piece also had an ambitious price tag.

The place was set up with temporary dividers, so that there was more wall space for hanging. There wasn't much room to manoeuvre as it was tightly packed with people clinging to coats and scarves and trying not to drop their wine glasses.

You could tell the graduates. The rosy-red cheeks of the ones who had finally accomplished what they wanted, set it up on the wall, and then raised a glass with their tutors. They had done it, won the awards, made the sales. Then there were the art dealers; you could see them too. Circling like vultures around the lucky stars, the ones they thought were the next big Young British Artists, ready to take on and shock the art world.

She wasn't one of the happy graduates, and she was terrible at making small talk. She certainly wasn't there to buy anything. This was a bad idea. She straightened up and pushed gently through the crowd to the wine table, where she helped herself to a glass of red. Could she gulp it down and get out of there without anyone knowing? She wasn't anybody important. Just a nobody off the street.

'Gina!' She heard Tom's voice, over-loud and clear despite the cacophony of the crowd. It made her smile. She turned around to see him, a head taller than most, same blue jumper that he always wore, waving to her from across the line of people seeking refills of wine. At least he had ditched the woolly hat.

He was acting like she was his best friend or something,

looking so happy to see her. She gently pushed through the crowd, nearly knocking some empty wine glasses off the table with her coat. Next to Tom was June, no doubt about it. She was tall, like him. Probably at least 5'9". Her straight black hair was cut short, with a bleached white shock to one side. She wore a lot of black eyeliner, like one of those high school goths who never really came out of that phase. Her clothes were black too, with tight leather trousers over thin legs, and a long black tunic on top.

'This is Gina, I've told you about her.' Tom seemed so pleased to see her, it was almost embarrassing. 'Gina, this,' he exhaled, 'is Juniper.'

June looked at her with a half-smile. Gina couldn't tell if she was embarrassed or if it was something else. Maybe she was shy. Gina remembered something that Nanna always said, that shy people can get judged before they even utter a word.

'Congratulations on your show,' Gina said. 'You must feel so proud.'

June shook her head and started to say something to object, but then stopped herself. Gina looked around to see that all the other students had friends, parents, teachers and art dealers around them, but Tom and June were alone.

'Which ones are yours?' Gina asked, searching the labels nearby for the names.

'Those,' Tom said, pointing to four large pieces in dark frames behind glass.

Gina walked up for a closer look. All of them were very dark, with extensive use of charcoal, pencil, ink and other materials. In some you could see that the paint and the ink had been used as a kind of adhesive, to pull together bits of collage. Newsprint, shiny magazine paper crumpled, fabric, and was that bark? Painted black with opaque acrylic, things began to lose their original identity.

The first three were hard to make out. The labels didn't help: *Untitled 1, 2 and 3* didn't give much away. But they were beautiful, in a way. Gina liked the first one, where a motion like a swirl caught up the different pieces in varying black and greys. The motion wasn't explained, but perhaps it didn't need to be. Another piece, *Frost*, didn't seem to fit the title. It too was all blacks, with a bit more grey. Silver crept into the shadows, making the vertical lines look like birch trees.

'Black is my colour,' June said, without expanding.

'I like it.' Gina didn't have to lie. 'Very powerful.'

'Just black and white, like my mind.' At that, June grinned.

'But there is subtle colour too,' Gina said. 'There, the use of that rust shade is hidden but definitely changes the piece. Gold too – that scratch there.' She walked closer to see better. 'No, you definitely snuck some colour in there too. I like the effect.'

June turned to Tom. 'You were right,' she said. 'You said she had an artist's mind.'

Gina looked back from the drawing. 'He said that?' She was embarrassed. 'Oh, no... I've not accomplished anything. Nearly flunked out of Goldsmiths.'

'Goldsmiths is for snobs anyways,' June said, taking

Gina's elbow. 'This place too. Full of phoneys. Wanna get out of here?'

'But it's your big show! Don't you want to stay to...' Gina stopped talking when she saw the look on Tom and June's faces. Like they had just been handed the keys to the flat of their dreams, and this wasn't it. She downed the rest of her wine in one, wrapped her ridiculously long scarf around her neck again, and made towards the door.

They found a place still serving food, despite it being past nine o'clock. The American Diner was a bit cringy, with its red and blue striped wallpaper and framed prints of baseball moments. But it was around the corner, and cheap, so it had to do. It did have some comfy booths going for it, though.

The three of them sat together sipping milk shakes (also an Americanism) and waiting for their burgers and fries (ditto). June and Tom sat shoulder to shoulder. Gina, sitting across from them, suddenly felt like this was some kind of interview. What did they want with her, anyway?

'This place.' Tom cleared his throat. 'The shakes are good, but it's not like Archie's, is it?'

Gina smiled. 'There's nothing's like Archie's,' she said. 'Unless you count all the other start-up semi-vegetarian-healthy cafés popping up in Zone 3 and then folding.'

Tom looked alarmed. 'You think it's going to close?'

'Nothing's been said about it. It's just that, you know, these small places can come and go... That place, it's been a café for decades. My grandfather used to go there in the 1950s. It was a simple café for lunchtime sandwiches and soup and such. But it closed and then I think it's been a Turkish place, a Chinese takeaway, and now, it's been turned back into a café. So...'

'That's quite a lot of history, for a little place.'

'Oh, I like it.' Gina reached for the sugar bowl, hoped her new friends wouldn't mind. Why did a place serving milkshakes and burgers have a sugar bowl? Americans didn't make any sense. She hoped they would start talking and she could come away from being the centre of attention. 'I like a bit of history. And a bit of change. People need change.'

The two stayed quiet. They made a funny couple, she thought. The goth artist with the geeky architect who didn't seem to give a toss what he looked like. What did they see in each other?

'So ... is this it then, for drawing? Or do you have more to do?'

'No, I've handed in my portfolio. Today was just for a bit of a party, and also for the art dealers.'

'Anyone show any interest?'

'Dunno. We can go back later and see if there are any red stickers.'

'Hope for you that there are lots of them. It would pay for more charcoal, that's for sure.'

'I might give it a rest for a while.' June looked into her milkshake, now half empty. She had chosen blueberry, but it was quite an artificial colour blue. Or maybe that was the fluorescent lighting, giving everything a green cast. This place really was the opposite of relaxing.

'You got your magnolia studio,' Tom said.

'Yeah, but...' June's voice faded into nothing.

Gina's milkshake was finished. To be honest, it was a bit too yellow to be convincing as vanilla, but it had those little brown specks in there to make you think it was genuine. Probably as fake as anything. 'What's that?' she asked.

'Nothing special,' June said.

'No, it's really cool.' Tom put his arm around June and gave her a supportive squeeze. 'The studio is the cooperative place I told you about. All sorts of different artists, no one judging you or giving you a pass or fail. I think it's great.' He was nodding, a bit too much. It was clear that he wanted it to be great, something to look forward to.

'It's just that,' June said quietly, 'I'm not usually so good in the winter. Sometimes I struggle even to get out of bed.'

There was clearly history, and The American Diner wasn't the place to get into that. They were all relieved when the waiter came over with three burgers, precariously balanced with too many crinkle chips. Probably straight from Asda's freezer section into the deep-fryer here, but who cared. Gina put a hearty dollop of ketchup on the side and took a big bite, to avoid having to answer any more questions.

· · ·

Gina didn't know why she was in such a foul temper the next time she worked at Archie's. She was worried about Nanna, that was one reason. Nanna's feet were really swollen, despite the change in heart medicine. Or maybe because of it? You could never be sure. Gina had called to get an appointment with the doctor, but Nanna wouldn't be moved, so they had to wait until the doctor could come to them. And the only time he was available was when Gina was supposed to be opening the café. She had been late and customers had been waiting.

Archie's was busy today, and there wasn't any time to slack. She wished sometimes that Lizl would stretch to another employee, but then again Gina didn't relish anyone being a witness to her foibles. Whether the upside-down cake had actually been a right-side-up cake when it came in that morning, that was her little secret with herself. And Lord, if there was someone new, Gina would have to train them, and that would probably be a recipe for disaster. Mistakes multiplied, that was the last thing the place needed.

And then there was Javier. He was in one of his moods, and this time it took forever to lift. He had heard about the night out at the Drawing School, and it had made him go a bit mental.

'You didn't invite me,' he had said. Not a question, an accusation.

'It wasn't my invite to give,' she said. 'I told you. Tom and June invited me, for her show.'

'Tom and June, Tom and June, that's all you ever do is

talk about Tom and June. Like Mickey Mouse and Minnie. A stupid entertainment show.'

'What is wrong with you?'

'You never think, do you? About me? About the sacrifices I make to stay in this country, for you?'

'What are you talking about? You don't stay for me, you stay to finish your PhD...' She regretted it as soon as she said it. She was not allowed to say those three letters in front of him, so touchy was he about the fact that it hadn't yet been, as he said, 'finally wrapped up'. It had been on the verge of being wrapped up for years now. He was not made to be a man who failed to finish.

'I stay for you, but you are so self-centred you don't see it,' he went on. 'You don't appreciate me. I need space to think, space to do my writing, and you ... you don't care at all.'

She hated him saying that. Of course she cared. It was just hard to keep on caring at every moment on demand. 'You know I care about your work,' she said, taking a soothing tone she hoped would do the trick. 'And I think about you all the time.'

'You do?' He perked up immediately.

'Yes, I think about you, and I've told them all about you.' It was a little white lie.

'You did? What did you say?'

'You know, things. About you, and about us.'

'I hope you didn't tell them...' He smirked and inclined his head to show he was thinking about bedroom stuff.

'Course not! You don't talk about that with people you've just met.'

'No? Well ... maybe I'd like to meet these two, this Tom and June perfect couple.'

She backtracked. 'No, they're not perfect. Actually... I don't think they are your type of people. You know, they are arty, and...' She couldn't get her thoughts straight.

'Yes, I think that would be magnificent.' He got to his feet with a theatrical flourish. 'You should arrange something, like a double date. Yes?'

A double date. Ridiculous idea. June would sink into a depression and Tom would just splutter out good-natured nonsense. Because he was a good person, and pointed out good sides of people. And Javier, she was coming to realise, didn't seem like such a good person anymore. Had he been before? She'd thought so, when they first started dating; he was a man who held doors open for her, and listened intently to her words. Made her feel like she was a unique beauty in a pool of mediocre faces. But over time, she realised that his intensity demanded a lot of energy from others. You had to go with his ideas and plans, or else it switched to a negative thing. If you objected, or talked about someone else, like a new friend you met – then that energy was immediately turned on you, like a hailstorm pounding on you. And you either took cover or you stood your ground. But it was hard to stand up to that hailstorm, when it came all the time. And Gina was more of a take-cover sort of person.

As the morning crowd settled down – lattes made, herbal refills done – Gina realised that she hadn't had breakfast herself. She had been so focused on Nanna's appointment, and then had run out the door. She had some coffee (double espresso) and unfortunately her stomach had that feeling when the acid was probably starting to dissolve the lining. The stomach suddenly let out a noise that was a cross between a groan and a squeak, like a dog anxious to get out. The writer guy, sitting at the closest table, looked up with a sour expression on his face (not fond of dogs). But he looked at the door, not at her.

She turned her back on the customers and cut off the end of the banana bread. No one would mind, really. You never sold the end. She needed sustenance in order to serve them better, that's what she told herself. She shoved it in her mouth, and it was so good. The balance of banana, cinnamon, walnut and – secret ingredient alert: almond essence – was just perfect. She ate another big chunk.

Then the bells on the door chimed, and oh dear, she needed to turn around and face the new customer. But the banana bread. She shoved into her mouth the last two big chunks of the piece and could feel her cheeks distorting all out of shape.

Chewing as fast as she could, still with her back to the customer, she reached around for a glass of water or something. Nothing was within reach. She heard the customer clearing his throat. It was a man, expecting to be served.

She chewed faster, starting to panic when the bread turned into a heavy paste. She didn't think she could swallow it down, not in one go. She thought about herself, choking on the floor, the only staff member there. The 80s music would probably mask her suffering; maybe no one but the author guy would notice.

Or she could pretend she couldn't speak English. If it wasn't a regular customer, they might not notice. She chewed faster, wondering how the mouth worked. Do you have to swallow food altogether, or can you just let a little down at a time?

'Um, hello? Gina?' She heard a familiar voice, and had to turn around. It was Tom, smiling uncertainly at her.

She gestured to her cheeks. Maybe she could claim that she'd had a dentist appointment, and so they were all swollen. But that was no good – she'd have to keep the chunks there for all her shift to keep up the act. And they would start to dissolve anyway.

'You okay?' He looked concerned, and paused before making his choice. She hoped her gesture translated something like 'All cool here,' while still trying to chew and thinking about how to swallow this massive amount of banana bread that she had so unwisely gorged on.

She pointed to the menu, hoping to distract him. He still looked concerned, but he did move his gaze to the list of teas and cakes. 'The banana bread any good?' She nodded vigorously. 'Okay, that and an Americano. You know how I like it.' He looked at her again, concerned. 'You sure you're okay?'

She nodded, but the glob in her mouth had reached a critical mass. She began to cough and choke and then the throat did what it is trained to do. It expelled all the contents of her mouth out over the counter, slopping over the menus and splashing down the other side.

As she coughed, she looked in horror at the banana and walnut chunks and thought – I should die now. Or be fired. Or both. In that order.

Tom came quickly around the back of the counter and held her shoulders while hitting her firmly on the back. 'You okay? You okay?'

She waved him off as the coughing subsided. She grabbed a cloth and started wiping everything as fast as she could. The writer guy stared in horror, but somehow Alison and the other gossiping mums didn't notice a thing. They were in their own Whitney Houston-induced haze, the high notes blocking them from sensing anything unpleasant.

When Gina caught her breath, she could barely look at him. 'I'm so so sorry,' she said. 'I hadn't eaten, I was worried about Nanna…'

He was smiling, seemed to think it was all funny. 'Don't worry, don't worry … it's all forgotten already.' He turned and found a free table, and took out his sketchpad. She really liked him for that, pretending it wasn't the worst thing he'd ever seen. She washed her hands and then went to make his Americano. How did he get to be the way he is? Anyone else would have been disgusted by a mile.

Giving him the mug of coffee, she had to ask, 'Why do you repeat yourself so much? You say things twice, in quick succession. Why is that?'

'Dunno... For emphasis, I guess. Now it's become kind of a verbal tick I have, sorry.'

'Don't be sorry.' She went back to cleaning the counter again. Double disinfectant, and no need to tell Lizl about what happened. 'Not a problem.'

Chapter Ten

July 1953

It was a small ceremony at the end of June. Her mind was made up long ago, after that first date at the café. Even before. When she held his letter in her hands like a secret she didn't want to share with anyone.

None of his family came. To be fair, Aday didn't send the letter in time. He tried to write earlier, but it was more important to get married than to ask for the King's blessing beforehand. Bella was in a hurry, once she set her mind to it. He said that he didn't mind that it changed his plans; he said no more about going back to Nigeria at the end of the year, setting up a practice there. His work was in London now, in any case: his patients were coming back to him again and again. And thinking about their life together was the best antidote she'd found for her melancholy, which raised its head every once in a while.

The only moments of doubt and darkness came when she thought about her family not being there. She had tried not to think about them in the years since she had escaped to England. Her parents had been English teachers; they should have been there with her when she first arrived, translating and navigating for her. But they didn't get out. She was alone, after everyone else was rounded up for the Vélodrome d'Hiver that July day. She had been hiding in the washroom behind the bath. She'd bitten down on her fist to keep from shouting with fear. She drew blood then, and still had small dents of scars to show for it.

But she didn't like to think about that time, or the months after when she was passed from stranger to stranger, moving first out of Paris, then to a port city and then across the Channel. She was never told who was helping her, or why strangers protected her. If it had been arranged ahead of time by her parents, their secrets were taken to the mass grave.

Bella escaped to England by lying under the false bottom of a fishing boat, smelling of fish, boots and sea-soaked wood. She heard planes overhead and prayed that her small vessel would be too insignificant to notice. She lay in a few centimetres of water, trembling, with her woollen clothes scratching, worried that the boat would sink. Counting down from a thousand, the way her mother had taught her to, was the only thing she could do to try to calm her mind. When she reached the number one, she started again.

She wanted to marry Aday because he was the only soul

to whom she had told these stories. He had listened to her in silence, holding her hand still and firm. She hadn't known how much there was to say until she started. She wanted to tell him everything: about her parents, about hiding behind the bath and the feeling of being under the boards of the fishing boat. Just once, she said her truth, and then she would never speak of it again. In the later weeks of their courtship, they emerged, a couple forged together by the painful truths, locked away for safety. They had each other, and that was enough.

At the wedding they had two witnesses: Fernando and Christiana took the roles that normally belonged to family.

Bella and Aday knew no other couple like themselves. There was no prohibition – it was just that no one else they knew had married across race lines. For Bella, that was as good a reason as any to try. She never felt the need to be like everyone else. In fact, after all she had seen, she was driven to do the opposite.

Besides, she was not rebelling against convention for convention's sake. She was marrying him because she had never felt so passionate about anyone else in her life. This must be love, she thought, especially when she had been convinced that she would never feel deeply happy ever again.

He wore a new suit to the wedding, paid for by an advance on his salary, and he looked so handsome she thought she might burst. Bella's long hair was up in a twist, with many small white flowers held in place in a circle. Her wedding dress wasn't fancy – they had no money for expensive cloth – but it was white lace and came to just below the knee. Christiana had come with her to find a seamstress who saved money by re-working old wedding dresses. Bella didn't mind; she rather liked it that another bride had worn the fabric before in a different incarnation: the hem lower, perhaps, or the pleats at the waist looser.

The ceremony was at Lewisham Town Hall, though she wouldn't have minded if it had been in a basement or a cave. She was with him, and they made their vows for life. She knew no rabbi, and in any case there were not enough Jews for a proper prayer service, no chance for a *Ketubah*, the contract for a long and fruitful marriage.

Bella had grown up with her parents' Ketubah on the hallway wall in their flat in Paris, and she remembered it well: it was an unevenly cut square piece of parchment, embossed in greens, blues and gold, with Hebrew lettering dancing around the shapes. She never had the chance to ask her parents what the literal translation was. After the occupation started, it was hidden away with the prayer books and then lost with everything else.

But she knew what it meant. From a very young age it left the impression on her that marriage was a contract that had joy in it, and that it was sacred. It promised both people that the two of them would love each other for eternity, body and soul, in good faith. Even without the parchment and the scripture, that was what marriage meant.

. . .

Aday was happy to hold their small celebration at the café on Manor Lane, inviting a few of his friends from the hospital and some nurses who worked with Bella. Gertie had reserved the café just for them, pushing tables together and covering them with white tablecloths instead of the red checked ones. Christiana had made a proper wedding cake with three tiers. Fernando brought a bottle of Spanish red wine, and a few of Aday's doctor friends pooled their money for a bottle of champagne.

Aday didn't usually drink alcohol. He had seen all too often how spirits weakened the constitutions of his patients, and the mess it made of their minds and their health. But for one night, he allowed himself to taste what they tasted.

Fernando poured him a glass, and another one for Bella. Fernando's hand was shaking, as if he'd already had a bit too much to drink.

'A word, for my doctor friend!' Fernando shouted. The small crowd turned to look at him – red-faced, white hair pointing in many directions and eyebrows the same, the personification of eccentricity and sincerity. He stood on a chair to be taller than Aday, and they all had a laugh as he mimicked measuring himself up for size.

'This man, he saved my life!' Fernando said. 'He knew the path for love needed some assistance. He was a stranger, but without him I would not be alive. I would be dead, from a broken heart.' He turned back to look at Christiana, who was sitting calmly near the cake. 'Today,' he continued, 'I am, how do you say? I overflow with happiness for these two. For him, to find such a beautiful, intelligent woman. A survivor ... and a nurse, she saves people too.

'She saved his life. Because he is a big man. Big heart, and had no one to love. But she loves him. And both of them have their chance for happiness. Right here, in London, in this café... So we raise a glass. In Spanish we say "*Salud!*" It means, to health. What do you say, Aday?'

Aday thought back to the lavish ceremonies at home, the colourful costumes, the ceremony and rituals with the bride's family. He couldn't describe these to them, the people in front of him with expectant faces. Just thinking about it took him away from this moment, when he just wanted to focus on no one but Bella: his unique, fragile, and fiercely proud bride.

'I think there is a Hebrew phrase for that,' he said, reaching for Bella's hand. 'What is it you say? It means "life", doesn't it?'

Bella smiled widely, her red lipstick perfectly setting off her skin and black hair. 'Of course: To life! *L'Chaim!*' She raised her glass and stood up tall.

'*L'Chaim!*' cheered the crowd, standing and clinking their glasses together. They were unfamiliar with the language, but the sentiment was shared and true.

Part II

Chapter Eleven

1954

Aday and Bella were walking, arm in arm, down Lewisham High Street in the early evening. It was one of Bella's good days, and both of them were in high spirits. Her small frame was wrapped in her wool coat, the same one she'd worn on the day when they'd first met. The growing bump prevented the buttons from closing, so it flapped as she walked. Her dark hair was shiny and smooth and wisps of it snuck out from under her small hat.

'You're a disgrace to your race!' someone shouted.

They turned. He was a squat man. Pale white skin, blotchy with some condition or anger patching his cheeks. He was backed up by a number of white friends. Unsteady on his feet, he had clearly been drinking. If the situation had been different, Aday could have felt sorry for him. If the man had come in as a patient, he would have been treated calmly and fairly. But this was not a clinical session. This was a direct threat to him and the woman he loved.

Aday's heart accelerated and he found it hard to breathe. Did the fool not see Aday's strength? He was more than a head taller than the man. But that didn't matter to him. The man had no coat, just an old army fatigue jacket that did nothing to repel the cold. Probably a desperate soul, but still a threat.

Bella spoke first. Aday had not expected that. She said, '*Excusez-moi?*'

The man pulled a face, clearly didn't speak French, but heard the anger in her voice.

'Disgrace to your race!' he shouted again. 'Going around with a gollywog, you oughtta be ashamed!' He was close enough now that they could see a string of spit connecting the top lip to the bottom.

Aday made a fist with his free hand, prepared to strike if he had to. But if there were witnesses, he could be arrested. He could lose his medical licence, lose everything he'd built. But he had to defend the woman he loved, the mother of his child. He had to protect her at all costs.

'And what race is that?' Bella said calmly. It was as if she was asking a simpleton about the weather.

The man ignored her words. He turned to Aday. 'You stupid, stupid ape!' he said. 'Why don't you bugger off back home?'

Bella was squarely in his face. 'Home? His home is with me, and my home is with him.' She wove her arm through Aday's.

The man stumbled on his reply. His friends mumbled and shifted their feet behind him, no one coming to his rescue.

'I am no race of yours,' she said, looking at him and all of his companions, who seemed to be retreating by inches as she spoke. 'I share none of your values, nor your likes. The Germans destroyed my home, and my family. So I am here, and he is my family now. If that offends your views, then ... that's in your twisted mind, not mine.'

She gently pulled Aday's arm to step away from the men, like avoiding excrement on the pavement. They crossed to the other side of the road. As they continued walking, Aday thought it was a risk, putting their backs to the men. They could still attack, like wounded dogs. His hearing was at heightened awareness, alert for any quick movements from behind, although he refused to grant them the satisfaction of a glance backwards.

He did not unclench his fist for several more streets. Only when it was time to grasp the handle of the door to Archibald's Café, then hold it open for Bella, could he relax slightly. Inside, they would try to put those men behind them and forget.

Three days later, Aday's mind was on the last patient he had seen in the clinic. A woman, pregnant with twins, struggling with increasing blood pressure. His thoughts were half with the woman, and half with his own wife, who was also pregnant, and not in danger, but she still occupied his mind.

He turned the corner and saw the broken window. At first, he was so stunned he convinced himself it wasn't their kitchen window at all; he must have turned onto the wrong street. But then his intellect caught up with the truth and he sprinted towards the house.

A large rock had been thrown through the window and was lying in the kitchen sink where it landed. Shards of glass had fallen haphazardly on the sill, in the sink, on the counter, on the dish towel beside, and onto the floor.

He called for Bella, frantic that she wouldn't be hurt or panicked. Then he remembered that tonight she was at the hospital to attend a talk about childbirth, even though she knew all about it from her time as a nurse.

But she would be devastated if she found it like this. He rushed inside to clean up as fast as he could. He would have to secure it for the night, and get a replacement fitted tomorrow as early as possible. He swept up the glass, crouching down to see whether tiny fragments were still underfoot. Then he found a hammer and nails, and some boards in the back of the shared garden. They would have to do.

Aday banged a nail in too hard, and it bent. He wanted to shout with frustration but that would only attract attention. But what else could he do? It was not his flat, and the landlord had already made it clear that they were lucky to have the place at all. It wasn't a good place. There was only one ring for cooking on, and the bath was shared with men upstairs who worked on the railway and left a black ring around the tub. The privy was outside. The place was ice-cold in the winter, and the smell of damp seeped into everything. Now a baby was coming. How could a child thrive in this place?

His brothers would be shocked to see where he was living. He would never be able to host any family members here, those who were used to the grand compounds and the extended family feasts. But no one had come to visit, so that at least was one problem he did not have. He wondered if they still thought about him. Their letters were less and less frequent these days. He did not know if he would ever be able to save up enough money to take Bella and the new baby home to see the places of his childhood and feel the sun on their faces. He wanted them to meet his mother and father, and brothers and sisters. Sometimes he felt like he would never fully warm up again, living in this flat where the draft whistled through the gaps in the windows.

He hadn't expected it to be so hard to find somewhere to live. After the College made it clear that doctors' housing was not for married men and their wives to stay long-term, it was nearly impossible to find a suitable place. So many doors closed in their faces. Once they saw that he was not an Englishman, even the fact that a baby was on the way did not help to persuade anybody.

Bella started going alone to visit flats, but as soon as she introduced herself as Mrs Falade, it was impossible to hide who they were. There were days when he wished his name did not identify him so obviously as an outsider. At low moments, he wished he was called something like Jonathan Roberts – a name that, on paper at least, could blend in with everyone else. If only he could somehow be invisible, just for a minute, while the rental agreement was signed, so that his wife and child could be assured warmth and safety.

The landlord here was charging more than double what was advertised; even on a doctor's salary, it hurt. He was finding it difficult to put aside the money he ought to have saved by now. The plan was to buy his own home someday, and to go back to Nigeria with the pride of having earned his wealth in Europe.

But plans fell aside with the urgency of the present. Everything seemed to narrow down to what was needed this month, this week, now. Whether Bella was able to get out of bed that morning, or whether her unexpected bouts of sadness kept her down. She hadn't told him about these low moods before they were married, seemed not very aware herself of where they came from, or how long they would last. Each time she did manage to lift herself out of it, but it took some days. And there were times when it wasn't clear if the hospital would pay his wages on time or not. As Bella had to stop working when they got married, it was all too tight. This short-sighted living left him nervous and short of breath much of the time.

And now this broken window. Someone had thrown a rock through, and it had landed in the kitchen sink. What if Bella had been there, washing the breakfast dishes? He hated to think of it. Even though they had not been home at the time, it was a shock.

He had no idea whether it was an accident, done in a burst of anger, or a planned act. It was hard to see how it could have been accidental. The window was visible from the main road; someone could have smashed it and dashed back to anonymity in just a moment. He sighed heavily. He could not change the perceptions and actions of strangers. This powerlessness made him shake with anger. The memory of the man shouting at them a few nights earlier loomed in his thoughts, but he brushed it away.

He continued again with the hammering, this time more gently to persuade the nails to take hold around the frame. That seemed to work better. It might have been just bad luck. Someone drunk or angry, not thinking about the consequences. Maybe it had nothing to do with them at all. Maybe someone just wanted to cause destruction and make a large crash, without regard to who was hurt. Or it could have been an accident. A speeding car, or a horse kicking up a rock just at the wrong angle. It was a possibility.

He could not let himself get angry. He would not be a victim. He was a strong man, a respected doctor in this community. Let us say it was an accident, he said to himself. But the landlord would not be happy with the damage. Aday would have to contact someone to replace the window discreetly, and as soon as possible.

'You can't live here, in this place.' Fernando said. The look on his face was one of disbelief, that a doctor could live in a place like this.

Aday had kept his friend away until now. Indeed, they did not have many close friends, and none had seen the flat. How do you explain that even with a genuine medical degree and a doctor's salary, this was all you could afford?

Fernando had been a carpenter in Spain, so he was quick to agree when Aday rang him to ask for some repairs on the house. He brought over his tools to have a look at the broken window. What he saw clearly did not impress him.

'This isn't good,' he said, running a finger over the putty holding the glass to the frame. It crumbled under his fingernail. 'Someone did it too fast, and not good material.'

'I do not own the house,' Aday said quietly. 'It's just where we are living, temporarily, until we find a better place.'

'Even for short time, my friend,' Fernando said, looking at the black mould coming from the drainpipe leading to the outside toilet, 'I wouldn't wish this on you.'

Aday could not disagree.

'Christiana, you know, she has big house. You have seen. Left to her by her husband, may he rest in peace. You should come live there, with us!'

'I couldn't do that,' Aday said. 'No, I could not ask that of you.'

'Nonsense, my friend! It's big! Too big for us. We are just two old people. There is a flat underground, how do you say? Down the stairs. But it is nice. Not like this.' He tapped the broken glass lightly with his hammer, and another piece fell with a small ping to the ground. 'Toilet is inside, and heating is in the walls. It's empty, no family living there. Have a look?'

'I could not impose on you, Fernando. You are a kind man, but…'

'What is that, *impose*? Is like suppose? You will think about it?'

'Ask Christiana, if you really insist. But I cannot assume that she wants us to move in. It is too much to ask.'

'No no no … she will love the idea. She loves children, you see. You are the one who needs to ask. Ask Bella. Ask Bella if she wants to stay here, with the broken glass, the toilet outside, and the baby coming. Or if she wants to live some place we can warm up with friendship. Ask her.'

Aday smiled for the first time since seeing the broken window that afternoon. Against his better judgement, he said, 'All right, I will ask Bella. But two conditions: one, that we pay an honest rent, just like any other respectable member of the community. And two, that you let me look after your health too. Your heart, your bouts with bronchitis…' Fernando tried to protest, but Aday waved away his exclamations. 'I'll offer my services to you as a doctor. It will just be for a short time, until we can save up for our own place.'

Fernando grinned widely and stuck out his hand. 'Shake on it, on your honour?'

Aday batted his hand away. 'You go talk to your Christiana, and I'll talk to Bella. And I need to buy some replacement glass and fix this window before the landlord finds out.'

Chapter Twelve

Gina turned the corner and saw an ambulance car in front of Nanna's house. She inhaled panic and sprang into a run.

The door was ajar and she flew inside. There was Oleg, his girlfriend, and a paramedic in the full green outfit all huddled around Nanna's chair.

'What happened?' Gina asked, and they all started talking at once.

'Suspected stroke,' Oleg said, nothing to soften the bluntness.

'We don't know that for sure,' his girlfriend said. Gina realised that she'd hardly heard her speak before. She had a soft Eastern European accent, less pronounced than Oleg's. 'She called out for you, for us, for anybody, and when we came upstairs she was sitting there with her head fallen forward. She was holding her collar like that. She seemed to be losing consciousness, and her vital signs were a bit worrying.' Gina looked at her quizzically. 'I'm a student nurse,' the girlfriend explained. 'We rang 999 and they came pretty quickly.'

'That's a relief,' Gina said, and knelt next to Nanna, holding her hand.

'The café, did I tell you my granddaughter works in the café on Manor Lane?' Nanna spoke more slowly than normal, as if it was difficult, but she was still determined. She was pretty coherent for someone who might have just had a stroke. Or a temporary stroke? She seemed okay now, although a little forgetful. Surely she knew that Oleg had already heard about Gina. Maybe Nanna thought the paramedic was interested.

'It wasn't always a café, you know,' Nanna continued telling the paramedic. Actually, she was telling the top of his bald head, as he leaned in closer to listen to her heart. He responded with repeated 'Uh-huh's' while trying to determine what was wrong.

'Nanna, shush. Don't bother him with local history.'

'That café, her grandfather used to go there every week.' She ignored Gina and kept going. 'We had our wedding reception there.' She looked up in the direction of the mantelpiece, with a framed picture of her and Grandfather, a photo more than sixty years old. Even though Gina was pretty sure Nanna could no longer make out the photo, she must have known it was still there. 'The café had cast-iron ceilings, and really lovely people running the place. The ceilings are still there, aren't they, *cherie*? The people keep changing though.'

'Should she be talking?' Gina asked the paramedic. There were so many things she didn't know about older people's health. She really should read up more, before it was too late. 'Nanna, maybe you should rest your voice.'

'No, that's okay,' the paramedic said, as he moved her gently forward to listen to her back. 'It's actually a good sign, that she can talk, and that she wants to talk.'

'Aday, you know, my husband – may he rest in peace – he loved that place. It was one of the few places where they always greeted him like a friend.' The paramedic murmured more encouraging noises so she kept talking. 'Everywhere else, you see, we faced such prejudice. People were so cruel, at times.

'Nanna, shush, don't get yourself upset.'

She patted her granddaughter's hand. 'You're right, you are. *Très intelligente*, this girl. Do you know what that means?' She looked in the direction of Oleg and the woman who might have saved her life, and continued. 'So intelligent. Not with the grades, though. She didn't do that well in school. Such a mind for poetry, art, culture, but not a head for figures or science. Never mind. Even in art school, where we were hoping people would understand her and her way of thinking, it didn't really work out, you know. Not academically.'

'Nanna, they don't want to hear about that....'

'But she's very intelligent. About people. How do they say it? Emotionally intelligent. This girl understands people, understands me, very well. Don't you, *cherie?*' She leaned back then in her recliner and closed her eyes.

Gina, alarmed, stood up abruptly but did not let go of Nanna's hand. 'Is she okay? What's going on? Is she having another one?'

'I think the worst has passed.' The medic stood up too. 'But just to be sure, I'd like to take her into Lewisham Hospital for some tests. Are you her next of kin?'

Gina nodded. She hated that phrase. It never meant anything good – it only meant being prepared for the worst. The label was the statement of a responsibility you never wanted to accept. They had talked about this scenario, with a hospital bag made up already. She knew she just needed to collect Nanna's regular medicine and check that her nightgown was inside, and a hot water bottle in case the ward was cold.

'It'll be okay.' Oleg's girlfriend gave Gina an unexpected hug around the shoulders. 'Here's my mobile.' She tore off a piece of paper and wrote down her number. 'I'm doing a shift at Lewisham next week. I can see if my friend is there tonight. I think she is.'

Gina couldn't say anything. Her worries wouldn't diminish so quickly, not after the sight of the ambulance in front of the house. She hoped that her nod sufficed for thanks.

'The name is Katarina, by the way.'

'Your friend?' Gina asked.

'No, sorry. My name is Katarina. My friend's name is Lucy, but text me and I'll get you in touch.'

. . .

'She was all right in the end,' Gina said when she next saw Tom. 'It wasn't a stroke, or one of those mini-strokes, what do they call them? A TIA. And there were no indications of a heart attack, other than her usual signs of arterial hardening and such. Apparently, there are markers in your blood that show when the heart as an apparatus is not working properly. I dunno, they measure your oxygen or something. Anyways, she had none of that. Maybe it was just her blood sugar got a bit low. So they let us come home.'

Gina had wanted to explain to him why she had missed their usual talks at the café. Although she owed him nothing, she had a strong sense that he would notice her absence, when she wasn't there for a few shifts in a row. One text led to another, and here he was, having a chat with Nanna. It was the first time he'd met her. Gina felt like she was twittering on a bit. But she wanted it to go well. If Nanna liked someone, then they could be a friend for life. If not, well ... best not to go there.

Tom sat on the footrest for some reason. Close to Nanna, his long legs were bent up at an angle like a stork's.

'They let us go, because they know I am an old woman, with an old heart,' Nanna said. 'It's nicer to be home.'

Gina wanted to argue, to say no, Nanna's heart was fine, that's why they let her come home, but she let the words go unsaid. It wasn't good to argue with the woman. Instead, she said, 'Cup of tea?'

Tom nodded.

'It's not like Archie's,' she said. 'No Americanos here,

I'm afraid.'

'No mum-and-toddler groups either, I presume?' He smiled at her. 'Maybe it will be nice to have a break from ABBA for a day.'

She made the tea, but with where Tom was sitting, it was difficult to know where to put the cup. His legs were at such an angle that he could not put it on his thigh, so he would have to balance it on his upturned knee. She reached over and placed it gently on the floor instead, so that Nanna didn't have to listen to the jangling noise of the spoon against the rim.

Nanna was telling him something about Gina's childhood. This could get embarrassing. 'And then when Drina was little, we went to the café, and it was a little bit like seeing her grandfather's friends again.'

'Wait, did you say Drina?' Tom asked.

'Yes, of course. Everyone calls her Gina, but that is not correct. Her name is Sandrine.' The way she said it, with the French pronunciation, it was a different name altogether. 'The English, they can't say it properly. So the poor child had to go by Gina.'

'It's not too bad, Nanna. I kind of like it now.'

'Oh, you were never a child who protested. It's your lovely disposition. You accept things how they are. Nothing like your *maman*. But sometimes I think you accept too much, *ma cherie*.'

She turned back to Tom. 'Sandrine, we named her. It was the name we were going to give our second daughter, if Aday and I ever had another. Aday, he used to play with names. Thumbelina, we used to say, because our Amara was born so small. Like that character in the story. So small she was a ballet dancer who slept in a – what do you call it? The thing for sewing, that protects the thumb.'

'A thimble?' Tom asked.

'When Amara was a baby, she was premature. So tiny, she could fit with her nappy in Aday's hand.'

'That's my mum,' Gina said. She hoped Tom wasn't getting bored.

'But not Drina. She had these long legs from an early age, like a horse or a dancer. She wasn't a Thumbelina.'

'Dumbellina, more like it,' Gina said. 'I didn't say anything for my first three years. At first, they thought I was deaf and mute. Or just that I heard French all day with Nanna, and my English wasn't formed yet. But really, no one knows why I didn't speak. One day, I just started.'

'And then it came out in full sentences, perfectly formed,' Nanna said.

'And you don't remember why?' Tom asked.

'Oh, God knows. I don't have any memories that far back.'

'It was the trauma, you see,' Nanna said.

'Trauma?' he asked.

'Oh Nanna, Tom doesn't want to hear about that.'

'Well, of losing her mother, so young. We didn't lose her, but … she didn't stay in England.' Nanna's eyes started to fill with the burden of tears, as they often did when Amara's departure came up.

Gina put a hand on her grandmother's shoulder and

changed the subject. 'Tom here is a structural engineer, like an architect, Nanna. I wish you could see his drawings.'

Nanna's face lifted to the ceiling, the tears receding back. She looked out the door towards the kitchen. 'Really? How lovely. We always wanted an architect around. To tell us how to get more light in here. This room,' she gestured around herself, 'it is always too dark. I would read in here, in the afternoon and into the evening. And then my eyes, they started to go. But you know, I can still see light. Light and shadows.'

'Can you?' Gina was surprised. She had assumed it was mostly dark.

'Of course, *cherie*. Shadows and shapes. Ill-defined shapes. Like the subject of nightmares as a child.' Nanna exhaled, then smiled. 'Or the feeling of sunshine coming through leaves. Yes, that's nicer. Let's say it's like that.'

'I could bring you some of my models sometime,' Tom offered. 'From my postgrad course. In addition to the 3-D drawings, we had to build things from fibre-glass tubes and such. You could feel them to get a sense of them by the touch. Would you like that?'

'Very much. That's very thoughtful of you. But also, I like to hear stories. Can you tell me about these buildings? Who do you build them for?' She leaned back, eyes closed in concentration.

Gina stood in the doorway to the kitchen and watched. She felt a little bit of heaviness lift off her back, for a moment. She hadn't known the weight was there, but as it rose off, she felt relief smooth into its place.

Chapter Thirteen

Alison and the mums were back at Archie's, and this time there were almost no other customers. Gina sat on the stool behind the counter and tried not to eavesdrop. She put her hand into the sugar bowl again, first time in a while. That session recently with her tools had got her thinking about finding a new project, but she wasn't sure what it should be. Shakespeare seemed juvenile now, part of her college past but not something new to look forward to. She wanted to grow, to change. To be someone different from who she was before. This would take some work, she knew, but she was excited about it, and actively trying to figure it out.

'Gina, come look!' Alison called.

Gina came out from behind the counter to see the mums on their feet, all looking down at Buddy, who was standing up in blue corduroy dungarees. He had a delighted open-mouthed smile, two bottom teeth showing. Alison stood behind him, his little fists wrapped around one finger on each of her hands.

'He's ready to walk!' Alison said. 'Just watch: stand there.' She pointed across the café.

'I dunno,' Gina said. 'Would he come to me?'

'Take this,' Alison handed her half of a croissant.

Gina crouched down with her back to the windows and held out the pastry. 'Wanna walk, Buddy?' she said.

'Go on, Buddy!' Alison gave him a little push. 'Show Gina how you can do it!'

Buddy's smile faltered a moment, as Alison shook free first one hand and then the other. He opened his mouth as if to protest, then changed his mind. He walked hesitantly at first, slapping each foot on the floor haphazardly before finding his rhythm. Then he sped up and approached running, his expression one of amazement at this new dimension in life. He crashed into Gina's arms, destroying the croissant, long forgotten, to the cheers of Alison and the other mums.

Gina held him to her chest a moment and felt his breathing and heartbeat. She was not around young children often; it was a new sensation to be trusted with someone so small. Then he twisted around to see his mother getting out her mobile phone to film it a second time.

'Do it again Buddy!' she called, and Gina turned him the right way forward to face his mother. He started back again, less hesitantly this time. With no knowledge of how to slow down, he collided with his mother and sent the mobile phone flying. Everyone was laughing, even Buddy, as

Alison crawled across the tiles to retrieve her phone and checked to see the screen wasn't cracked.

'I can't wait to show your dad that video,' she said. 'Thanks so much, Gina!'

'It's nothing,' Gina said, dusting the crumbs off her trousers. 'I'll get you another one.' She placed a new croissant on the table, where some of the other babies in highchairs were eyeing Buddy, perhaps next in line for walking.

'It's not nothing,' Alison said, finding the money in her purse. 'You're here for us, in this moment. This everyday but actually fairly remarkable moment. Buddy will never forget you.'

'I don't know about that.'

'Well, I won't be able to. You're in this video!' She held it out to Gina and it was really funny. Gina is in the far back of the short scene where the delighted boy stomps over to his mama; he grows faster and bigger by the moment until he knocks the phone out of her hands, like a baby Godzilla. You gotta love a kid who is learning to use his power like that.

The excitement came up from somewhere between Gina's sternum and her brain. She didn't want to like the art collective, not too much. What if it was an amazing place, but she didn't fit in?

Tom had talked her into it. She argued that she wasn't a real working artist, but he said she should see it. 'To give you some inspiration.' Typical of him, to get a bit cheesy like that. But he was right. She needed to get her artistic ideas going. He didn't even want to talk to her about the dues yet, wanted her to view the place first to see what she thought.

The collective didn't look like much. It was a large ramshackle house on one of the back streets between Lewisham and New Cross. Instead of a fence it had boarding along the pavement blocking the view of the front garden. Graffiti, not particularly artistic, was scribbled along the boards.

Tom reached through a carved hole up at the top of a makeshift door and lifted a latch. 'Welcome to Magnolia House,' he said.

The boarding moved on a hinge to open up and show a garden that was surprisingly well looked after. She hadn't expected the grass to be mowed in straight lines, with rows of lavender plants marking a path to the front door. There was a magnolia tree starting to think about budding into life, urged towards it by the early spring sun.

'Lovely tree,' she said.

'Hence the name,' he said. There were daffodils, too, reaching up in bunches of yellow. She smiled at the exuberance of colour. Someone should paint them.

The steps up to the door were crumbling; no one cared about the concrete foundations in the same way as they cared about the garden. The door opened into a hallway with murals that looked as if they were from another decade, the colour faded. Or maybe the colour was always those muted tones of khaki, pale blue, and grey. They were vaguely Picasso-esque, with figures made up of shapes, and faces not quite like faces. She tried to make out what they were trying to say, but then she gave up. Maybe they weren't supposed to mean anything.

'June's studio is up here,' Tom said, heading up the stairs. Gina followed, uneasy. Where was everybody? It was like being at a house party after the party was over. Or before anything happened. But it was a Saturday. Surely some people would be using their studios.

They walked onwards along a windowless landing. Every door blocked the light. There were signs on them with different names and symbols. One was in Chinese or Japanese, she didn't know which, kind of in block prints. Another was a collage, laminated, of eyes of different shapes and sizes, torn from fashion magazines or something. The corridor was long with lots of doors, but they reached the end with nowhere further to go.

'Up here.' Tom reached for the loft hatch and turned the key. It flapped down, missing his head by a tiny margin, but he seemed used to it and wasn't startled. The loft ladder groaned with the noise of springs disturbed from their fold.

'She's not here?'

'She doesn't mind.'

He stood back to let her climb first. She didn't like heights, and there wasn't anywhere to put her hands except on the rungs above. The ladder wobbled, unsteady on the floor. It was dark up there. She had no idea what to expect.

'There's a light there, pull the cord,' he said.

She ducked down so she wouldn't hit her head on where the eaves might be. But when she thought about it, Tom was much taller than she was, so she had the courage to straighten up. Her eyes adjusted to the gloom and she saw there were windows at opposite ends. They were dark with pollution or tree pollen, or whatever it was that gummed up old forgotten windows.

Her hands felt in the dark for a cord and she found the string. The light pinged into view with a line of naked bulbs across the beams. She saw a drafting table under one of the windows. It was large and covered with thick paper, curling at the edges. She moved closer and saw it was June's work in her signature black, white, and grey. She felt the thickness of the paper, and the weight of it brought back memories of Goldsmiths and the drawing modules. She was never that good at drawing, but she loved the different textures and weights and combinations of materials you could use.

There was dust on the artwork, and the water in the painting jar had dried up long ago. There were three dry and forgotten paintbrushes, leaning inside a lonely black ring. It looked like June hadn't touched the place in weeks.

'You okay up there?' Tom asked, his head coming into view.

'Sure, it's quite roomy once you have a look.'

He came up the ladder with a smile on his face. 'I know! That's what I was saying.'

She jiggled the handle of one of the windows. Spiders skidded away and made her feel like they were walking on her skin. 'It won't budge.'

'It will open, with some persuasion.' Tom came over in three strides. With a bit of effort it reluctantly moved, squealing as it pivoted on an old hinge. 'There you go.'

The flash of green from the trees outside changed the place inside completely. Instead of being dressed in browns and greys, the light danced around with the same energy as when it bounced off the magnolia tree.

'What do you think?' he asked.

'It's a great space. I can see why June likes it.'

'She wants you to think about, you know, being a part of it.'

She looked around the place. Under the open window was a folded table, up-ended against the slanted wall, ready to fall over. Several portfolios, A2 and A1 size, leaned against each other in a disorderly pile. A stool stood erect on its own, probably for a still life or a figure drawing. Gina ran her hands over her shoulders. It'd be a little chilly to work up here, this time of year. However, in the summer it was probably sweltering. Good thing her art was small and relatively portable, as long as she protected it from knocks and bumps (and thoughtless welders).

'But I need water, and access to a hob,' she said.

'There's a bathroom downstairs,' he said. 'And people share the communal kitchen.'

'Do they want another artist? Maybe they are full.'

'No, it's all fine.'

'But what about June, won't it cramp her style?'

'June needs you,' he said, as if that answered everything. 'It will be great, just great.'

Chapter Fourteen

1958

There should have been more descendants. He and Bella had talked about a large warm family with lots of children playing together and happy, but in the end, they had only Amara. Lord knows the reasons, but that was how it was. Maybe God knew that they needed to focus on caring for the one child, to keep her alive and close.

She was born premature, and tiny. That was a surprise, considering his stature. He seemed to remember that all the babies in his family made the women wait long weeks, until the mothers and grandmothers had their prayers heard. Still, in letters from family he was reminded by his older sister that their mother had borne seven children, and only four survived past infancy. He knew the facts; as a physician, he faced the reality every time he worked in the maternity wards. Some women had complications, some children were not made for breathing the air of this earth. Bella was a small woman, with a tiny frame. Her pelvis was narrow, compared to other women. It should not have surprised him.

When he first held Amara, and first felt her breaths, so weak under her thin skin, she reminded him of a small bird. Only then did he meet fear for the first time. Deep fear. The conviction that your heart could be broken by a small thing, and it could happen at any time. But you have no choice but to let the heart engage, and let it be broken, if need be.

In the first few weeks and months, that fear stayed with him and crested in Amara's moments of illness. Her breathing was often tight and had a wheeze like an eerie call, as if she was inviting predators to circle. Like a dance of worry in the night, he and Bella would hover around Amara's cot with steam and solutions to help her chest. Even with Bella's nursing training, and all of his medical knowledge, they were never fully sure what would make her better. They were none the wiser when she took a turn for the worse.

On the bad nights, her young airways sounded like a tiny accordion playing involuntarily. He and Bella took it in turns to administer medicines or steam and stay by the child's side, changing her pillowcases daily and searching for any tell-tale blood on the cotton. But so far, her condition had not proved consumptive. He wrestled with the relief that it was not too bad, and the frustration that she never quite got better. Whatever it was that gripped her lungs, she never seemed to fully break free. As he maintained the vigil by her bedside, he prayed for her protection. He also prayed for another child to come soon, and others behind that, so his worries could be divided somehow, and thus diminished in intensity.

The little bird-chest expanded and kept taking breaths, getting stronger and healthier. She was a fragile little thing but she grew into her genes and became bigger and bold. Her skin grew darker and sheened with a glow that came from his side of the family. What did she get from the Jewish side? It was always hard to know which parts of your legacy you give your child. Bella said maybe she had given her daughter a strong mind and a stubborn nature. He hoped so.

Amara brightened up when her father came home. If she was too breathless to run, she still hurried in her own way when he entered the house, and he would easily pick her up as he dropped his briefcase. She wanted to tell him stories about her dolls, or her imaginary friends Genviève and Jean-Jacques. Always these stories about these two, Genviève and Jean-Jacques; they were sometimes invisible, and often naughty. He listened attentively. In those moments he felt that he was born to be a father, and that she made him and Bella whole. He laughed and played along, unless her excitement made her contract into coughing spasms, and then he wished that he had not indulged the child.

Sometimes he thought they should move back home.

Where the air wasn't stained through, like it was here. Although he did remember that as a child, the heat sometimes used to press on his chest and make it hard to breathe, but it was different. The weather was a message from the seasons: telling you to slow down, to sleep in the shade and not to attempt anything too strenuous. It would be against nature to try to continue at the same level at the height of the dry season. England lacked an intensity that told you to slow down or step back.

The stories of the Notting Hill riots worried him. They took place near where Bella had lived when they were first courting. Bella was safe enough now, living in the basement flat under the kindness of Christiana and Fernando, but it felt fragile, this concept of safety. There was always the worry that it would prove to be temporary.

London was a tinderbox, the newspapers said. As if people were just matches, with a tendency to go up in flames from any stray spark. It was frightening to think about anger rising out of control. These were ordinary people, like the ones coming to his doctor's surgery, whipped up by hatred for other people. Despising people just for the fact that they had come here to work, were invited to come and serve the country and help it rebuild after the war. To live. To build a life. And this was not just shouting or threats. The racists were committing violence, even murdered a man. Just for the colour of his skin.

Aday wasn't afraid of much. As a tall, educated man, he had confidence in himself and his work. He trusted people in general to be fair, and to connect with him as a person.

He was a doctor and a family man. His patients knew that, and his colleagues respected him.

But crowds worried him. Crowds of people could not help but fail to see the attributes of the individual. Crowds acted mindlessly, like a pack of hyenas, or worse. At least hyenas killed for a reason. They attacked their food for survival. That made sense, in the nature of things. But these mobs of Teddy boys were a different breed. They acted, it was said, with a sense of pride, of injury to their way of life. This reasoning was irrational, and so no rational argument could persuade them otherwise. But why was it attractive? Did some young men need distraction now that there was no war to keep them occupied? Did they just need a sense of dominating or conquering? Or was it a sick kind of entertainment? Whatever it was, it swelled their ranks, and they used their strength in numbers to attack youths and businesses at the smallest provocation.

And the police, what about the police? He did not know what to make of the reports. He had confidence in the English authorities, but it seemed like something was not working as it should. The job of the police was to keep order and protect people and property, just as his job was to heal people, or to comfort the family if the patient was unlikely to recover. But for many people like him, their faith was shaken. They spoke in hushed tones to those they trusted, and looked over their shoulders when they worried out loud. They felt that the protection was not there. For the English people, and the white properties, yes. But for people like them—

He didn't like to think of it that way. It went against his nature to split people into separate and distinct categories. There were not just two types of people, but a huge range of characteristics and symptoms that people presented over a lifespan. As a doctor you were trained to discover the intrinsic causes of the problem. He could not split men into two groups at odds with each other, because that would mean there was no legitimate way to meet in the middle.

And he had come to the middle. He had fallen in love and crossed over a line that he had not realised was so impossible to others to fathom crossing. He didn't know why he and Bella seemed to have a capacity that others somehow lacked. To him, she was not a category. She was a radiantly beautiful and complicated woman that he was devoted to spending the rest of his life with. She changed with the seasons, with her moods, and with her smile.

He never fully knew her mind, but he knew he was her family now, and she was his. This was for life. In the years since they had met, she only grew more beautiful, the deeper he knew her. She was not perfect, and he welcomed her imperfections. Their lives were totally intertwined, as marriage should be. He loved her so intensely he knew now what people meant in the folk tales and the love stories. He would die for her and Amara, if he had to.

But would he kill for them? He did not like to think about it. He had hoped that this England he had migrated to was a land of law and order. If a doctor couldn't trust in that, well ... he didn't want to raise his family in that kind of place. Of course he would protect them. And to be fair, their home was nowhere near the riots. Their home was with Fernando and Christiana.

Gratitude spilled over him, thinking about the friendship that led to his family having a safe home. It was in sharp contrast with his worries about the news of the riots. It left him with divided sensations, like taking a cold shower on a hot day. How do you raise a child in times when anger flows on the streets? When it could be directed at her, with no rhyme or reason? How do you protect your wife and child in this kind of atmosphere?

He did not have anyone to ask. That's the problem with being the first in your family line to do the unexpected. When you live far away, you do not have anyone you can turn to, to ask for advice, like an older brother who had already tried a few different ways to approach a dilemma. You cannot share your worries. Or have a joke with an uncle to release the tension. You just had you, and your small and vulnerable family, in an atmosphere that could turn toxic.

He hadn't expected the heaviness of responsibility to be on him alone. He thought he knew everything about the weight some decisions laid on your shoulders. He was familiar with the moments when someone is close to death, but as a doctor you know of a procedure that might save them. Or when the window of treatment has closed, and it is the time to pass on your condolences to the next of kin. As a young man, unattached, living far from family, these decisions were clinical and practical. Emotional for those involved, yes, but he kept the distance of a scientist. He liked to think that he was a kind man and a good doctor, who would hold the hands of a dying woman or stroke the brow of a child. But his distance protected him, you see.

As a father, there was no distance, and no protection. You have to be the protector of yourself and the family, with no space to prepare. And when your daughter is struggling to breathe and sounds like a bad music-hall instrument, all out of tune; when she starts to laugh and you think at the same time 'Oh, yes indeed,' and 'Oh please God, no, not laughing', because you know what will happen next. And her throat gets raw with coughing and she vomits and you hold the bowl and rub her back because, along with tincture, there isn't anything else science can offer.

He never expected that, the end of the usefulness of science.

What else was there?

Chapter Fifteen

Gina looked around the attic space. It was a tad gloomy, that's for sure. She couldn't tell when June was last up there. Tom had said that she'd been having some of her low moods recently.

With some effort, she opened the back window, and saw the sky changing colour with sunset. The clouds were painted in slim streaks, burning pink and purple with the fading sun. She took a deep breath, ignoring the fusty smell of the wood beams, and tried to sense the magnolia tree below. She could create here, that's what it felt like. She wasn't sure what she'd make, but the possibility was alive.

She liked to look into the meaning of things. Art was like that. It wasn't just the materials used to make it, or the stroke of the graphite on the page. There was some reason behind it. There had to be, or else it was just random acts, no more significant than anything else.

She thought of Janine Antoni, who worked with

chocolate and soap. *Lick and Lather*, it was called. The show was in the States somewhere. It was a long time ago; Gina had studied it for her diploma. Fourteen busts, seven from chocolate and seven from soap. It was the same mould, the busts facing off in two lines like chess pieces. In the beginning you didn't know if the white side was stone or white chocolate or soap. If you were actually there, you would probably have been able to smell it in the air. You could walk through them and see them from every angle. Apparently at the opening the artist bit some of the chocolate ones and washed with the soapy ones (hope she chose the right ones). It was a statement about the female form and fighting back against the pressure to conform, or something like that.

Other artists worked with salt. Now that was a great medium. You had to mine it from mountainous places and caverns, like in Belarus and countries like that. It came up in these fantastic chunks, like rock only more fallible. Salt had a lot of hidden meaning for people. They used to sell it from the back of a wagon in the old days, before refrigeration. It was literally life-saving, killing the bacteria and everything. So people could still have their salted fish and pickled veggies and survive another winter.

Salt also means tears; salt water means someone has been crying. Or salt can symbolise the ocean, and the white crests of the waves. Or for Jews, the salt water you dip parsley in on Passover. But that symbolises tears too.

She had seen this guy work on big boulders of salt. He hammered away at it, like at an ice sculpture contest. He had to wear goggles in case the chips flew into his eyes. And he had a big wiry beard, a bald head, and these red-red cheeks. It was a hot day, outdoors at some summer festival one time. It was like ice or packed snow, white and opaque. She put her hand out to it, hovering just an inch away, and sensed that the heat of the day was there. It must have been formed under tremendous pressure. To pull together millions of grains of salt into a crystal taller than a man, one that holds up under different conditions and against hammering and travelling all the way from Eastern Europe, that takes strength. That's what those blocks of salt meant. Strength.

But Gina wasn't drawn to that as an art form. She couldn't get fine control with a hammer, and didn't think the brute strength angle was what she was about. She looked down at the shoebox she'd brought with her to the attic studio. Inside were some of the silicon moulds that she had used in the last foray into model-making. In her rucksack she had two kilos of sugar, golden syrup, some food colouring, and small pans to heat the concoction into a thickened, textured paste. She brought a sketchpad for new ideas. She didn't know what she was going to make, but even arriving here today alone – no Tom, no June – felt like an independent venture in a good direction.

She didn't know if she should introduce herself to people. It was a collective, that's what Tom had said, so perhaps people would want to come together and collaborate? Or maybe they just wanted their own private studio space. She went back and forth in her mind and felt a little less bold than when she had first walked in.

She had to poke around different doors on the first floor until she found the loo. It was a bit grotty in an undergrad-shared-flat sort of way, but not too horrible. She was going to go down to the kitchen to heat up some sugar, when she heard music coming from behind the door with the Chinese letters. Or Japanese. For God's sake, she really should learn more about the world. She decided to knock.

The person didn't respond. Maybe they didn't feel like socialising. Perhaps they were in the middle of something, inspired, and she was going to ruin the moment. Or maybe they weren't even in at all, just left the radio playing. She moved away and was halfway down the stairs, when the door opened and left her looking foolish, her head at the same level as the person's feet. Which were bare. And just a little bit hairy.

'Hullo?' a guy's voice said. She hurried back up the stairs, but with her hands full of her equipment, she realised too late she couldn't shake hands or anything.

'Hello, um... I'm new here, a friend of June's?' She didn't know why, when she was nervous, words came out like a question.

He looked at her with a half-smile. He was about her height, not that tall for a guy. He seemed to be East Asian, with brown skin. His hair was in short dreads, with a bandana tying it back. His round wire glasses made small circles around his eyes, like Harry Potter.

'Friend of June's?' he said.

'The artist, the black and white charcoals, works upstairs?'

'The depressed girl.' He said it straight, not like a question.

'Ah, well... Not for me to say, really.'

'So not a close friend then.'

'Actually, I know Tom better. Do you know Tom?'

He opened the door a little wider as he relaxed a bit. 'Nice guy. Tall.'

She nodded. That was a good short description of Tom. 'Is this your work?' She pointed to the collage on the front of the door, with the letters she couldn't read. 'Is that Japanese?'

'Cantonese,' he said.

'Are you Chinese then?'

'Boy, you're nosy, aren't you? My dad was from South Africa, my mum is from Hong Kong; the gene pool is all confused.'

'You sound like a real Londoner.'

'Yep.' He looked into her face then. Something in his look said that he was an open sort of person. 'Just like you, seems like.'

His name was Mason, and inside his studio she saw a clutter of paints and canvasses and strips of paper. He offered to help her carry her things, and show her where the kitchen was.

'Has June said anything about how it works, then?' He led the way down the stairs and to the back room, which was a 1970s kitchen. The cabinets were fake wood with pretend inlaid carvings, dust stuck to the ageing finish. The windows were single-glazed aluminium and cold, but the view of the back garden made it cheerful.

"Want some tea?" he asked. She nodded.

He moved with the grace of someone at ease in the space. He found two mugs – mismatched like from a charity shop – and laid them down on the counter without a clank. When he turned the kettle on, the roar was startling. He saw her jump and said, 'Needs a descaling.' He showed her an eclectic range of teas; some were generic from the Asda down the road, others were fancy organic and tied with a ribbon. Some were in plastic bags so you could see twisted dried leaves, with handwritten labels smudged with time. 'What do you fancy?' he asked. 'Breakfast, herbal, rooibos, hibiscus, Earl Grey ... or there's instant coffee too if you prefer.'

'No coffee, please. I work in a coffee shop. I think I've burned out on the stuff.'

'I get ya.'

They stood in silence as the kettle boiled, and then she chose a peppermint tea (Asda). He chose green (organic). 'No milk, sorry,' he said, gesturing to a fridge standing nearby, with Pizza Hut circulars and a notice for an art show last year pinned on by magnets from the seaside. 'It's gone off.'

'No worries. Peppermint doesn't need it anyways.' She blew over the top of hers until she could sip it. He did the same, and steam rose up to partially cloud his glasses. He didn't wipe it away, just let it fade.

She asked about his art, and he spoke with such a calm voice it was hard to imagine him getting worked up about anything. His work was 2-D and 3-D collage and other paper-based sculpture. Origami inspired him, as well as craft traditions such as weaving. 'I have kind of a loom I created, but for paper,' he said. 'It helps work different textures into a bigger picture. I'll show you sometime, if you'd like.'

There was a pause while he waited for her to say what she did. Suddenly she felt a rush of worry rise up her shoulders to her neck and she clenched her jaw. What if he laughed? What if these people didn't see her as a real artist? What if her sugar flopped again? She wasn't sure she could take being judged again by new eyes.

'I'm just playing around with ideas, me...' she said. He looked up, over the round frames of his glasses. His face was kind, no harsh angles. 'I got my degree with work around sugar, sugar granules, you know. But I'm thinking about branching out to other things.'

'Sugar,' he said, and then paused. After a moment he added, 'but you didn't take any with your tea?'

'No, I'm not a fan of it to drink. I sculpt with it. I heat it up, that's why I needed to know where the kitchen was. I make little dioramas and things. Trying to show something ... about how fragile it all is.'

'Sounds cool. Delicate... I'd like to see it sometime.'

She looked up at him and saw he was being genuine. She didn't know why she was surprised.

Her mobile rang in her back pocket. She didn't want to answer, but Mason was already walking out of the kitchen, motioning that he had to work. 'Nice to meet you,' she called to his back. She put her phone down on the counter. It was Javier. She watched it wriggle with the vibrations until the call went to voicemail.

Chapter Sixteen

1960

That winter, the sadness enveloped everything. Bella didn't know where it came from, and stopped torturing herself with the question of why. She just felt it when the covers were heavy and comforting, and too weighty to lift off her thin body. When tears ran down her face and she honestly could not say the reason. Food lost its taste, and words failed her.

Amara was stronger now, a six-year-old with energy and better health. Even though she still needed her inhaler and injections at times, her breathless nights and hospitalisations were a thing of the past. Bella heard her laughter in the corridor, as the child played loudly with imaginary Jean-Jacques and Geneviève. A small rock was used to jump hopscotch. Fast footsteps indicated races had begun, sprinting to the front door. Later, Bella could hear the sounds of the girl reading to her soft toys, using different voices for the various characters and species.

But noises were muffled in her ears, as if life was happening somewhere else. The feelings over Bella's body and mind were mainly numbness and distance from everything. It was as if the child was in another house, from another mother, at another time.

Occasionally there would be a quiet knock, and the light in the room would change with the door pushed slightly open.

'Mama?' Amara called.

Bella couldn't reply. It was too difficult to move her head, so she just watched the patterns and shadows change on the ceiling. How could she explain to the child about the sadness that weighed on her chest? She was again alone back in the bottom of the boat, drifting towards England from France, with an unknown future and no family left. While she fought through those first years by herself, the past was written and set.

The child didn't say anything more, and soon moved away.

As a professional, Aday knew the signs of depression, or melancholy, he would say. He couldn't get her to leave the house, not even to go to Archibald's. He confided in a colleague, who visited Bella and confirmed what Aday felt: it was depression, but not psychosis. There was no need at this point for hospitalisation or more forceful interventions.

They could try medications, although that could make the symptoms worse before they got better. Or they could wait it out.

Aday took a rare moment upstairs to share his concerns with Fernando and Christiana when Bella was resting. Amara was in their front room, watching a children's show on BBC, to give him a moment with his friends. Godparents to the child, they were the closest thing he and Bella had to family in London.

'It's the weather,' Fernando said, trying to assure him.

'Do you think so?' Aday wanted to believe that Bella's depression would pass, although he was reminded of the first lesson from medical school: 'Correlation does not prove causation'. This was the phrase the first-year students had to repeat until it was imprinted on their memory. He knew that other winters had not been so difficult, and could not understand why this one seemed to hit Bella harder.

'Nonsense.' Christiana cut off her husband's good-natured but meaningless assertions. She paused for a moment while she poured three cups of tea and placed the doctor's on the table first. 'It's about motherhood.'

Aday respected the woman highly, but didn't consider this to be a diagnosis. Millions of women had children without falling into a deep depression. He started to object but she held up her hand to stop him.

'As I see it,' she said, 'motherhood has provided Bella with family. Her only family, after the war. It is who she is today. But motherhood came at a cost. The hours and nights you lost, so worried about Amara's breathing.'

'That was years ago,' Aday interrupted. 'Lately it has been different—'

'Exactly, my friend.' Christiana would not be stopped. 'This winter is the first one – is it not? – where Bella has not needed to be on full alert, waiting for the child to have another crisis. While this is very good news for Amara, and we thank God for that, it is understandable that there has been a change for Bella.'

Aday sat back and held his tea with both hands. It was a little too hot, but he liked the feeling of it, as if holding onto it would help him feel some of Bella's pain, and transfer it away from her. 'Go on,' he said.

'The body has a way of holding onto echoes,' she said, staring at Fernando, daring him to disagree. 'I think it knows when you don't have time to deal with the pain, and when you do. For six years now, Bella has not had time to deal with the pain and worry of possibly losing Amara. Now that the threat is gone, the echo has a chance to come out. And even if you don't understand the language it speaks, the echo must be heard all the same.'

'I see what you mean,' Aday said, thinking it over. Amara's laugh came from the front room. He hoped that the show would continue a bit longer. 'But what can I do? She can't stay like this.'

'Give her time,' Christiana said. 'And love. You already give her love, just keep going.'

'But how much time?' he asked.

'You won't know until she returns to her senses. Literally, when she starts to look again and actually see you.

When she starts to say that some food tastes good. When you open the window and she notices the breeze on her face. Then you know that the echoes are dying away.'

'But in that time, what about the child?' Aday lowered his voice. 'The girl needs her mother, and it's like she is inaccessible.'

Christiana sighed, having no answer for that. 'Yes, that is the unfortunate thing. When a mother cannot love herself for a time, there is no extra love for the child. It may have a lasting impact, but I hope not.'

Fernando grunted and pushed his chair back. 'I think this will pass, doctor.' He patted Aday on the shoulder. 'And we have time. We take Amara to the park, tomorrow?'

Aday started to object, but saw there was no need. 'That would be kind,' he said, more into the teacup than out loud. He didn't know what he would do with a free Sunday, whether he should take a walk on his own, or try to coax Bella to the window to see that spring was in the air. Probably both. 'Thank you,' he whispered, as the sounds of Amara's running footsteps along the corridor signalled that the conversation had to be finished.

Chapter Seventeen

'You wouldn't believe how beautiful he was,' Nanna said.

Gina was surprised to find it was Katarina sitting on the footstool this time. She usually went straight into the basement flat. In fact, before Nanna's last episode, Gina was not sure she'd ever spoken directly with Katarina. But now she was looking at Nanna in that way people do when they want to hear more. Gina wondered if Nanna could sense how people looked at her. Or if she just assumed that she could keep on talking until she heard the signs of someone getting restless.

'*Bonjour, cherie,*' Nanna said, hearing Gina at the door. 'I was just telling Katarina here about the love of my life.'

'About Grandpa?' Gina kissed the top of Nanna's head. She smelled of Deep Heat and something softer, like lavender. 'Or someone else?'

Nanna batted her away. 'I never!'

Gina smiled and walked into the kitchen. 'Can I offer you a cup of tea, Katarina?'

She followed Gina into the kitchen. 'That's okay, I can get it,' Katarina said. 'You've been serving all day, haven't you?'

'It's no problem. Why are you up here? Did something go wrong again with Nanna?'

'No, I just like talking with your grandmother. We chat from time to time, when I come home from an overnight shift, mostly. I never knew my grandparents; they all passed away when I was very young.' She turned on the kettle and they waited in silence for it to boil. Then she helped herself to the mugs in the cupboard and chose a black tea (Tetley's). The girl fit in like family. 'And anyways,' she added, adding milk to cool it down, 'I want to specialise in gerontology. You know, medicine for older people.'

'My grandfather was a doctor, did she tell you?'

'Of course. Many times. So many delightful stories.' Her accent – was she Russian, like Oleg? Or something different? Polish, maybe? She seemed to have a gentleness about her that Oleg didn't bother with. Gina wondered what held them together, this couple that lived in the basement.

'*Cherie*, someone is coming to the door,' Nanna called from the front room. Gina was going to ask how she knew, but Nanna just knew these things. After she lost her sight, her other senses became stronger. Maybe someday she would go supersonic. But actually, it wouldn't take special talent to hear the heavy steps coming to the door a few seconds after the motorcycle engine cut off.

What was Javier doing, coming round? They hadn't spoken in days, had no plans. She inhaled sharply, trying to get courage before opening the door. Could she ignore it? Not with the other two there. She'd have to answer, or else he'd make a scene. She waited until he banged on the door. He didn't trust the doorbell.

'Hello,' she said as she opened it. She didn't lean forward for the automatic kiss.

'What's going on with you?' He was cross already. 'I called you, like, twenty times yesterday.'

'Did you?' She didn't feel like explaining herself. 'Sorry, maybe I didn't have good reception at the artists' collective.'

'Artists' collective? You're getting involved with something new? Why didn't you ask me?' He walked past her into the hall, ignoring Nanna in her chair.

'Ask you? I don't need to ask your permission to do art.'

Katarina came out of the kitchen, both hands holding the mug in front of her chest.

'No, not like that,' he said, changing his tone when he realised that other people were listening. 'Of course, you are an independent woman. That's what I love about you. It's just that, you know, as your boyfriend'—he searched the air for words—'I thought you would want some more time together, for us.'

'I'm starting a new project.'

His face curled into a snarl. 'It's not a sugar project, is it?'

She nodded, knowing what was coming next.

'That's so stupid. Couldn't you at least choose something that has a chance of working? You got destroyed at your last show. I saw it with my own eyes.'

'You saw what you wanted to see.'

'I'm not crazy.' He turned to Katarina. 'She works with sugar. Sugar that falls apart at the slightest tremble. How is anyone going to succeed in that?'

'That depends,' said Nanna, 'on how you define success.'

Javier looked around, but saw that there might be no one to take his side. 'Where is Oleg?'

'I don't know,' Katarina replied. 'He's his own person, as am I.'

Javier started to argue, but then changed his mind. He put an arm around Gina, conspiratorially. 'Gina, my love, is there a place where we can talk? Alone?'

She sighed. She didn't want to have a big confrontation in front of Katarina and Nanna. 'Let me get my coat.'

Javier looked down at the pub table while he spoke. His funding application had been rejected. He had worried that this was going to be the case, but as it was his last hope, he waited weeks before calling to confirm his fears. Yes, his application was denied. His PhD was no longer considered a viable investment for the university. If he was to finish, he would have to find funding on his own.

She had to lean closer. They had chosen the local and it

was loud. Thursday was quiz night, and a tall guy boomed into a microphone searching for nuggets of wisdom from British history (1966 World Cup, everyone knew that). She wanted to be anywhere but here.

Her mind wandered to how happy she had been yesterday afternoon, heating up sugar mixtures of different densities in the Magnolia House kitchen. With food colouring and some old moulds from uni she had created some creatures of different personalities. One had fire-red hair, coming out in all directions like a Scottish lass caught in a windstorm. Another one was all-over blue, like a Smurf, but thin. Maybe she should research Celtic history more. There were a lot of stories that could be brought to life. These creatures made her laugh, even though she didn't have a plan for them yet. She had gauzed them up like tiny mummies in toilet paper for their protection, and tucked them into a shoebox, hoping they might survive to see another day. Not wanting to risk them on public transport, she had left them in the far corner of the studio she shared with June. No one would bother them there. She had not yet seen any evidence of June coming, not recently anyway. But there could be mice up there. Why didn't she think of that? She hoped her creatures wouldn't get eaten. That would be tragic.

'Are you listening to me, Gina?'

She came back to the moment. He had a receipt that he was rolling between his thumb and forefinger. He was longing to smoke, she could tell, but he couldn't, not inside the pub.

'I was talking about commitment. Your commitment, and mine.' He dropped the rolled paper and took her hand. It was an awkward angle, turning her wrist to the side, and she wished he'd let go, but he had other plans.

'I need to know that I can count on your support. As my girlfriend, I'm entitled to that, no?'

'What are you getting at, Javier?'

He bit his lip, then the words came out in a rush. 'We should get married.'

'What?'

'Marriage. Commitment. You and me.'

'What are you talking about?'

He went on a bit, about opening a joint bank account, moving in together, all the while coming back to his PhD. 'If I could just be sure of your commitment, then I'm sure I could focus. I am so close, Gina. One, maybe two years, at most.'

She shook her head, searching for words. 'We are nowhere near ready to get married!'

'Why not? We've been together for years, and you know I love you like no one else. We're not getting any younger. And maybe once we get married, Nanna will accept me. You never know, maybe she could take out a loan with the equity on that big old house, and you and I could get our own place.'

'But I don't want to leave Nanna. Is that what this is about?'

'No, of course not. We wouldn't leave her out in the cold. It's just to tide things over, until I finish my degree and get a teaching position. You know, I would pay her back, honestly I would.'

Gina stood up. 'I can't believe this. Look, Javier, I am really sorry about your funding applications but maybe it's a sign. A sign that you have to finish sooner than you planned. Or to get a better job now, while you are finishing. We can't think about marriage now.'

'So you refuse me?' His face was sullen, like a frustrated child.

'You're out of your mind!' She left her drink there, half-drunk, and went out without looking back.

Chapter Eighteen

1962

It was a peculiar thing, having a growing daughter. Aday had expected other daughters to compare her to, and sons too. But in the end, they just had the one. And what a beauty Amara was too. She would grow taller than her mother – even at the age of eight that was certain. When he looked at her, he felt a strong pull of family pride. But other than Bella, he never had anyone he could share that with. He had posted photos to family when she was born and at the start of school, but it was expensive to post often, and things could get lost. He knew that Fernando and Christiana took notice of Amara's growth and progress, and that was something. But mostly he held the pride to himself, like a jewel on a chain tucked next to his heart.

But this pride was always edged with concern. Amara had them worried from her first breaths, and even now, with her regime of injections and tablets, particularly in the winter months, they had times where her life seemed so fragile. But when spring came, the grip of fear lost some of its power. Amara breathed more easily, and lost the wheeze and discomfort at night. She slept calmly, and that meant that they did too. They brought down her regime of injections from one per day to once a week. You could see the health and vibrancy in the child's face, and she was happier now. She was more comfortable 'in her own skin', as Bella liked to say – some French phrase from her childhood, translated.

Her curly hair was usually pulled tight into two braids. Bella asked some local Caribbean ladies what to do, once she got over her shyness. The women had large extended families, living together and supporting each other, while Bella had next to nothing like that. They sensed a difference between their families and the doctor's small cluster of three. Their families were people who came over with brothers and uncles, with wives and children, some born overseas, some born here. These families had plans. You could see their determination. They were getting jobs as porters, bus drivers, postmen, street cleaners. And the women, they were working as well. They were in the markets, and at the factories. The grandmothers or the aunties watched over the children if they weren't yet at school. Brothers and sisters stepped in if the elders were too busy or too frail. Each family member contributed to the purpose of the whole.

Aday felt it keenly that he and Bella had none of that. As

a young man he didn't set out with a plan to build a life and support a family in England. He was alone, just a medical student, due to head back home once he had earned his credentials. They didn't have the safety of a hive of active, talkative family members around them. Aday and Bella lacked that protection, and that socialisation. He couldn't figure out how to fix that, even though it vexed him and weighed on his thoughts whenever he was not working.

But Bella had an easier time than he did, in some ways. The women assumed she was English because of the colour of her skin, but once they heard her accent they knew that she, too, was a foreigner. And they could see that she had no extended family here to rely on. She had no one but the doctor, although that was something, because there were a lot of women with children who didn't even have a man. But still, their little family seemed to need something it lacked. So Bella reached out to these women. If her first attempt didn't lead to anything, she swallowed her pride and came back again. She bought her fruit or her fabrics from them in the market, and asked about their children. She brought Amara with her and talked to the women about what oils were best for the child's skin and hair, and the relationships grew from there, talking in different ways about the shared problems of raising a girl in this city. She started making the friendships that he, somehow, was not able to make.

She reported much to him over dinnertime, after Amara had gone to bed. She thought it was amusing, that she had access to a whole community of women that he could not know in the same way. Some even were his patients, but he could not say they were his friends. The 'women's world', she called it. He was glad for her that she made the friendships. It was not something he could help her with, but it gave him some relief from worry. She now had women to walk to the shops with. Women to talk to, to not feel so alone.

'Shouldn't she be in school?' he asked one morning, seeing Amara's shoes near the doorstep when he stopped home for lunch after his clinic.

'School's closed this week,' Bella said, with the local knowledge he'd missed. 'Influenza.'

He knew the figures were higher than last year. He had seen a number of patients with symptoms. But he hadn't heard of the outbreak that led to Amara's school being closed. This worried him.

'How is she?'

'Perfectly fine. Not a speck of illness. Lost in her *rêves*, as usual. She doesn't seem upset in the slightest about school being closed. You would think she'd rather live in her books than be with children her age.'

He knocked on the door to her room, and she called to him to come in. It was a small room made for an infant. Still, there were no complaints; in that basement flat the walls were clean and the heating was warm. Her room was decorated to suit her. Photos from magazine adverts for films were pinned to the walls – Rock Hudson, Sidney

Poitier, Doris Day. She was lying on her chest, chin in her hand, reading a book. She looked like a sculpture of childhood, frozen in a moment.

'*Famous Five*, is it?' He didn't know why she loved those stories, but it was clear that she did. Although she had little in common with the characters living in rural England, surrounded by siblings, something about them had her reading the tales again and again.

'Hello, Papa,' she said, not lifting her eyes from the page.

'No school today?'

'No, not this week. Didn't Mama tell you? Sickness, closing all the classes. Some teachers have it too.'

'Are you unwell?'

'No, I feel fine.'

He put his hand to her head. Her skin felt cool and unbothered. 'What about your old nemesis? It's not back, is it?'

'No, Papa, no wheeziness.'

'And you don't mind, missing classes?'

'I don't mind.' She said no more, resting her smallest finger in the corner of her mouth, like she did when she was younger.

'You don't like school anymore?'

'Oh Papa, it's not that.' She pulled her eyes away from the page reluctantly. 'It's just the children, you know. They are mean to me. They say I'm different.'

He lifted some magazines and set them on his lap as he sat down on the child's bed. It groaned with the weight of an old man, or so he felt. 'What do you mean, different?'

'You know.' She did not want to explain.

He looked in her eyes, those beautiful perfect brown irises flecked with yellow that he could never lie to. He left her space to expand, if she wanted to.

'The coloured kids sit with the coloured kids, and the white kids sit with the same. They pretend to be my friend at times, but really they don't like me. Neither side wants me. I don't fit.'

He put his arm around her and rubbed her shoulder. It was a small round joint, too frail to hold the weight of bigger problems.

He waited for her to say more, but it did not come. His experience of childhood was so different, any advice he could offer was meaningless. Where he grew up there wasn't this division of people by colour, so no one felt they were worth less. Or that's how he remembered it. He continued to rub her shoulder without saying anything. He took some comfort in the fact that the bird bones underneath were getting stronger over the years. Her gaze went back to the book. She turned a page, sighing a little.

He wished he could conjure up more children for her to play with. Brothers and sisters or cousins, that was what a child like her needed. Some children just like her, but unique in their own way, wearing their dual heritage with pride and a sense of sureness. She was born here and London was her home. She had a right to be here and have a happy childhood, just like any other child raised here with love and intent.

But he couldn't say any of that, not to a child. Her eighth birthday was coming up, but she said there were no close friends to invite. She'd asked for Bella to make her favourite lemon cake, and to go for a ride on the merry-go-round in the park. Her requests were so simple it made his heart ache sometimes. Important things were not requested, and were not available to give.

Later, when the lights were out and Bella's breath was even, sleeping beside him, he thought of what he should have said. Sometimes his mind needed time to digest the words before the right ones came to his lips. He regretted that, the time delay. He got out of bed and felt around the side table for paper and a pencil. In the low light coming from a streetlamp outside the window, he wrote:

Dearest Amara,

You are the best of your mama and your papa combined. You are more beautiful than we ever imagined. Do not be bothered by the small-mindedness of others. You will make your friendships when you, and they, are ready.

As long as I am near you, my dearest, you will always have somewhere you belong.

He would remember to give it to her tomorrow.

Chapter Nineteen

'So there are just these boxes full of blocks of the stuff. Piled up to the ceiling!' Tom had gone on his first visit to Costco, and it left him stunned. He said the first thing he thought of was telling Gina at the café. He wanted to see what her imagination would do with the idea of huge quantities and different versions of sugar: sugar cubes, sugar syrup, molasses, candy floss... They had a laugh about imagining moving through the piles with a forklift.

It felt good to laugh when she had a chance to sit down with him at the end of her shift. She rubbed the heel of her hand over her eyes. She wasn't sure why they were so heavy lately. Maybe she needed glasses? Or she wasn't reading in the right light? She moved her hand in small circles around the bony ridges. Eyes closed, she enjoyed the patterns of light and sensations behind the massage.

'You okay?'

She opened her eyes again to see him looking at her with

a concerned expression. 'I'm fine, totally fine. Just not been getting enough sleep maybe.'

'June too,' he said. It was the first time he'd said her name that afternoon. He stopped to take a sip from his coffee cup, but they both knew it was empty.

'Want another one?' She moved to get up, but he put out a hand to stop her.

'She's getting worse,' he said.

'Worse?'

'The depression. The blues. The Winter SADs, whatever you want to call it. I've never seen her so bad, or for it to last so long.' He turned to gesture out the window. 'Nothing I do changes anything.'

'It's not you, you know.'

'I'm an idiot. I keep suggesting things that don't work.'

'You're there for her, that's what matters.'

He blew out his breath in disdain. 'It's March, the daffodils are out. Winter is in retreat. You would think she would be able to see that.'

'Sometimes, maybe…' She tried to think of the right thing to say. 'Sometimes we can't see the good in things, even if we want to.'

'I don't know. It's so hard. She knows I don't understand it. How can I understand it? I've never had depression. You can't know what it's like if you haven't had it. That's what she says, and she's probably right. She doesn't mean to be unkind, but…' He trailed off, looking forlornly at the empty cup.

She paused a moment, then took the cup away. 'One more Americano, on the house.'

'On the house?' He changed gear with a smile. 'Only if I can get you to try out this forklift I saw…'

'It's a deal. But I don't have a driver's licence. Failed twice, couldn't bring myself to try again.'

'Wasn't it Samuel Beckett who once said, "If you fail once, next time, try to fail better"?'

'Something like that. Or maybe it was "fail faster"? I was always rubbish with quotations.'

'Anyway, driving tests are tricky. My brother failed three times. My sister twice. I embarrassed my whole family by passing on my first go.'

The bells rang, and Gina knew without looking that Javier had walked in, although he rarely came into the café unless he wanted something.

Wearing his full black leather motorcycle outfit, he refused to take off the helmet as he walked up to the counter. He did not look at Tom or the other customers. 'Gina,' he said. 'What time do you finish?'

'You know what time I finish. Same as always.'

'Couldn't you be a little earlier today? I have an interview. Can you help me? Coach me for it, like last time? And I need you to iron my shirt.'

'I'm working.' She gestured to the café, which should have been obvious. 'Can't you work the iron yourself?'

'I don't have one; we always use yours, remember?'

Gina hated it, but Javier was right. She always did his

ironing, didn't she? Lucky he didn't have a job in the City or else she would be doing it all the time.

'What's the interview?'

'A research job. Think-tank sort of thing. I need to look the part.'

She nodded. 'I'll try to finish up earlier.'

Only then did Javier look at Tom. He paused, then turned back to Gina. 'So not a lot of chats with your little buddies here, all right?'

Tom pushed back his chair and stood up to his full height. On his face was a complicated mix of emotions. Gina couldn't imagine what was going through his mind. Sure, he was proving he was taller than Javier. But there was sadness too, like he couldn't think of anything that would make the situation easier for her, and that sobered him.

He wrapped his scarf around his unkempt beard and swung his rucksack on his shoulder. 'See you later, Gina,' he said slowly, emphasising each word. 'We will catch up another time...' The last words were a promise; he could be relied on.

Javier walked into the house, and without a word dashed up to her room, where he kept his clothes. Gina went into the cupboard under the stairs looking for the iron and board.

'*Cherie, c'est toi?*' Nanna didn't usually speak French

with other people around. She should have known it was Gina, anyways, by the sound of the footsteps.

'Oui Nanna... Ça va?' Gina approached her in the armchair. Something didn't look right. If anything, Nanna was shrinking. Her delicate frame seemed to sink into the fabric of the old chair even further, and she didn't bother to open her eyes. She didn't seem at all well.

'Are you okay?' Gina put down the cold iron and took her grandmother's hand in hers. It felt hot. 'Do you have a fever?'

Nanna didn't answer.

'Gina!' Javier called from upstairs. 'Where are you?'

Where was her phone? Should she call the ambulance again? She started to panic. What if she was losing Nanna?

But what would she say to the doctor? 'My nanna looks a bit ill?' How vague is that?

She remembered Katarina and Oleg downstairs. She banged hard, too hard, on their door. Nanna winced a little, so her hearing was still working. Gina was relieved to hear light footsteps coming up. Katarina opened the door and read the worry on Gina's face.

The words came out in a rush. 'It's Nanna, I'm worried, but I don't know why. Can you come see her?'

Katarina quickly came to Nanna's side. 'Bella, are you all right?'

Nanna pulled back a little, as if the sounds hurt her. Katarina reached for Nanna's pulse, and with the other hand felt her forehead. Her hair was damp with sweat.

'Pulse is fast. She has a temperature, probably making

her uncomfortable,' she said. 'Something is going on. I've got the car. I think we should take her in.'

'I'll just get her hospital bag, and her medicines.' Gina ran into Nanna's room on the ground floor, and found what she needed by the bedside and in the medicine cabinet.

'Something to eat too, and a water bottle.' Katarina was systematic in her thinking. 'Sleepwear, and a change of clothes as she might be there for a few days. Some slippers.'

Javier came down the stairs, too loudly, and started to speak until he saw Katarina and Gina rushing around.

'Nanna's sick,' Gina said, without looking at him. 'Iron your own fucking shirt!'

'Of course, my love, no problem.' He looked like he was going to say more, but she had no time for that.

Labyrinthitis. What a name for a condition that basically just means an ear infection. Deep in the inner ear, in the tiny caverns with these delicate moving parts that have to work together to ensure that you hear correctly. Poor Nanna, relying on her ears, and then they go and get inflamed from the inside. Must have been like torture. No wonder she was grimacing with every noise. And she had said she felt dizzy in the days before; that explained it.

Katarina had been brilliant. She drove Gina and Nanna to Lewisham Hospital, and dropped them off at the entrance to A&E while she found a place to park. She told them just what to say to the reception desk to get the red flags waving and get Nanna seen earlier. There was a bit of waiting around, but it wasn't bad. Once they decided to admit her and gave her some painkillers and antibiotics and fluids, it was wonderful to see Nanna's face sort of plump up again, and relax. You could tell that she was fighting something, but hopefully they had found the source of the problem.

She was admitted to hospital overnight as a precaution. When an older person gets a fever, the doctor explained, it's to fight the infection, but it can cause other problems.

'Like leaving your laptop in the sun,' the doctor said to Gina, as if that would help her understand. Once the doctor left, she and Katarina had a laugh at that. Nanna as a computer. There was nothing less like Nanna, with her love of people and radio and changing moods. Nothing was automatic about her. The doctor should have said something like 'It's like leaving a plant without water.' That would have suited her better.

'I used to come here often, when Aday was working.' Bella was in a talkative mood. The antibiotics were making her feel so much better. The impossible pain in her ear, which had made it difficult to concentrate, was so improved. She had her thoughts back, and they were working themselves out, no longer jumbled. She was alert, present, clear-minded once more. What a relief.

Katarina came back the following day, which was lovely. She was such a kind girl, and you could tell she had the brains and caring nature to be a good nurse, when she finished her studies. She brought her friend Lucy, who had already qualified and was working in the hospital.

'You see, it was a blessing to have my husband work close to home,' Bella continued. 'Some other doctors we knew had to take the train across London, or if they worked in the country they spent long hours on rural roads doing home visits. Can you imagine rural people when faced with a doctor from West Africa? No, we were grateful that he could stay nearby, where the families got to know him and accepted him, accepted us. But usually he worked so hard I didn't want to visit. I'd get in the way.' Her gaze was on the window of the door, where she sensed the moving shapes and shadows in the corridor outside.

'Sometimes we would meet at the café after work. You know, the one where Gina works? It was a café back then, too. We got married there. Did you know that, *cherie*?'

Gina nodded, having heard the story many times.

'Lewisham was a quieter place back then, not so many people... I remember the week of Passover, that's when I would see a lot of the hospital.' She turned back to Katarina. 'Because we are Jewish, didn't you know? Or rather I am, and Aday wanted us to hold onto that. He wasn't religious himself, but it was important for him that we made some effort for my culture. Because, you know...' Her voice got softer. 'We lost a lot of my culture. My family. In the war.'

Bella fell into sadness. Katarina reached over to squeeze her hand. She perked up again after a moment. It cheered her to think of the little rituals they had had as a tiny family of three. 'We didn't keep Kosher during most of the year, just during the main Jewish holidays. It was too much trouble, and since we were not part of a Jewish community or anything, there was really no one to be offended. We thought it was more important to make sure that Amara got a healthy dose of red meat and milk at all times, to build up her strength. She had so many infections, so many problems with her weak lungs, you know. I've told you about that, no?'

'Yes, Bella,' Katarina said.

'But on Rosh Hashana,' she continued, 'and the week of Passover, that's when I would make his lunch and bring it to him. When he was in the GP surgery, it was easy. I just gave it to the receptionist. But here, on his hospital shifts, that was more challenging.'

She leaned back into her pillow, leaving behind the small audience of two. She inhaled deeply and smiled.

Chapter Twenty

1964

When Bella saw him from a distance, she had to remind herself that he had chosen to marry her. Of all the women in the world, he had seen something special in her. And she felt the same about him. In a country where each of them had no other, they were unique but not alone.

Her visits to the hospital were not usually like other people's, full of worry. No, after Amara's lungs grew stronger, the hospital was always rather a pleasure. She was just a woman trying to find her husband to deliver his lunch. The fact that the lunch was odd (Kosher) and that he was unusual (the only Black doctor in the building) didn't matter in the slightest. His colleagues would laugh and tease him, because it was a special thing, having your wife deliver your lunch for eight days a year. And then they would peer at the matzah that she had taken the train to

North London for, and they would swallow their questions. They were kind, his colleagues, but they knew nothing about Jews. Or about a Jew like her.

She didn't know any other Jews in London, and she had lost touch with everyone she knew from before. She didn't really know why. It wasn't ever a decision she made, perhaps it wasn't even conscious. But she was Sephardi, when many of the Jews she saw on the occasional visits to North London were Orthodox Ashkenazi. She felt that they were not much closer to understanding her culture than the doctor colleagues back in Lewisham chuckling at the matzah.

And there was the added risk: that she could approach these Jews, but once they learned about her, she might not be welcomed. For leaving her family behind? She'd had no choice in that. But for marrying a non-Jew, definitely the Orthodox would not accept that. For marrying a Black man? Well, she had never heard of a Jew doing such a thing. Not that their opinions mattered to her in the slightest.

When she was first in England, she had been desperate to find out what happened to the people from the Vélodrome d'Hiver. She made long-distance calls, and sent letters to Paris, tried to contact anyone who knew the family, but it was too late. About eight months after her safe arrival, she found they were held at Drancy for some weeks, and then sent to Auschwitz. Not a single survivor.

She spoke to no one about it, except for the one time she told Aday. Otherwise, she remained silent. She hadn't been there to bear witness, but perhaps that was a blessing. She supposed other people had to see what happened with their own eyes, and it slashed through their dreams for ever.

She faced forward, choosing life. And she chose Aday. He was her way, her only. And her devotion to him, and his to her, gave her the strength to create a future, totally unlike the past she had lost.

So it gave her great pleasure to call him her husband. Even though English people could be quite rude. Things were shouted at them sometimes, when the two of them were together. One woman even tried to spit at her from a moving tram. But Bella found, if she kept to her normal patterns of home, Amara's school, Aday's work, they were safe. They were okay.

She liked it when she saw him before he saw her. When she came to the hospital reception, he would be wearing the doctor's uniform with a stethoscope around his neck. He was taller than most people, and his skin had a vibrant shine. Everyone else was so pale in comparison. He looked like the only truly healthy man there.

And of course, he was the only Black doctor there for years. After more colonies gained independence, some others managed to study and come, but they were very rare. She heard that the government made it very difficult to transfer your training from another country to here. So it was fortunate that Aday had come so young, and finished his training here. But it was sad that it cut him off from his childhood and his culture. He never returned home, not even for his father's funeral, due to Amara's precarious health at the time. Aday sent money to the family, to look after extended cousins and elderly, but he and Bella never managed to visit where he grew up.

They were together in that as well. As their ancestors fell into their graves, it was just their small family of three that clung to each other, and chose to live.

Chapter Twenty-One

Gina was feeling grateful: to Lewisham Hospital, to Katarina, and even to Javier for getting her home earlier than usual from the café. Maybe she should call him later to see how his interview went yesterday. Or text. Yes, texting would be better. She felt bad about how the conversation went the other day, about his problems with his PhD and the whole marriage thing.

If he had said it in a different way, she could have maybe been open to working on a solution, finding a loan or something. But that was just like Javier. He acted on impulse and didn't think things through. He would argue that he was a true romantic, but he was oblivious to the impact of his moods on other people. He was very passionate about his work, she knew. He just assumed that his passion could drive everything else too.

She needed some space, that's what the conversation about marriage highlighted for her. Because without space, she became wrapped around by his ideas and his plans, and there was no room to breathe. She needed to follow her own passions, even if they were, well, a bit silly and still being formed. Works in progress. She hadn't had enough time to find out what they were, not really.

Her phone vibrated, and she was going to ignore it when she saw it was a text from Tom.

> Have you heard from June?

That's odd. He should have known that June didn't have her number. She wrote back:

> Is something wrong?

> Can I call?

She looked at Nanna, napping in the hospital bed, her slippers tucked up underneath. She looked calm and cared for. Hopefully when she woke up, she wouldn't be alarmed by the strange noises of the hospital. At least Lewisham gave her a private room; that was a blessing.

She stepped outside the room and rang his number. He picked up on the first ring.

'It's June. She's gone.'

'She said it would be better without her... That I would be better off without her.' Tom had come round to see Gina, after hearing that she was in the hospital with Nanna. His hands were shaking even though he was still wearing his hat and scarf. The coffee cup rattled on the saucer when he put it down.

The hospital cafeteria was painted a 1970s green that unfortunately made you think of sick. Or the contents of a baby's nappy. Or both. Who approved that colour? It took your appetite away, anyway. Couldn't be good for revenues.

'She didn't mean it,' Gina said. She had the urge to take his hand to show support, but she hesitated.

'People who are depressed say things like that. Right before, you know...'

'But she's not ... in that way, is she?' Gina didn't know how to talk about these things. She wished she had more experience. All the words were jumbled in her head and she could only think of what not to say. She didn't want to say the wrong thing. But maybe there wasn't a wrong thing, if you wanted to stop something bad from happening.

'It's happened before, a few years ago. Same pattern. She gets really down in the winter, and then for some reason she gets this clarity about her, and seems a bit better. But actually, it's just when she's decided to go through with it. As luck would have it, on that day I came home earlier than I had planned. There was a drinks party at work, and she knew I was supposed to be out. But I didn't stay late, didn't feel like it, for some reason. That's when I found her, passed out already from the pills. The doctors said it was lucky I got there when I did. They pumped her stomach.'

'But that was years ago, you said.'

'Yes, and I thought she was better. Even though she lost

that flat share; her friends said she couldn't live there anymore. They couldn't handle it, and sort of cut her off. But she pulled herself together and by the summertime it was like she was a different person. A new version of June, with only the vague shadows from before. That's what I thought, I really did. But now I don't know. Do people ever really change?' He was so sad, like a child who had lost something precious. She reached out and held his hand cupped in both of hers.

'Let's think, the two of us, together. My nanna's well looked after here, and Katarina says she'll keep an eye on her. She'll stay another night as a precaution, that's what the doctor said. The sun won't set for hours. You and me, we'll find June. Okay?'

He nodded. 'But I don't know where she is. She's taken her normal bag, not a suitcase or anything, and actually she left her pills behind.'

'Anything else? Sketchpad? Passport?'

'Don't think so…'

'Is there anywhere she likes to go when she's feeling down? Home?'

He shook his head. 'No. It's just her mum at home in Milton Keynes, and they kind of hate each other.'

'She hasn't been to Magnolia House?'

He shook his head.

'Where else? Where does she go when she really can't take it anymore?'

He looked out the window, going through memories.

'Actually, I don't know why I didn't think of it before.' He smiled, for the first time. 'The water.'

'The coast?'

'Riverside.'

They paid the fare and walked the plank onto the commuter boat. Boarding at the front, they looked at each row of sheltered passenger seats as they walked through to the open-air seating at the back. There were not many people on the boat, as it was a grey day with mist and a threat of rain.

No sign of June, but there was a feeling, like they were following her scent. Almost no one was outside, so they had rows to choose from. As the engines started up, it was too loud and windy to talk, but that was fine. They could just sit together, bundled against the spray off the water.

The boat pulled away from Greenwich pier and Gina looked back. The dome of the Greenwich Tunnel and the columns of the Royal Naval College disappeared into the distance. When they turned the U-bend in the river, she could no longer see the observatory or the hills of Greenwich Park. She felt the gentle vibration from the engines through her body and in the corner of her jaw. It was soothing. Announcements about the riverboat service circled in a recorded loop, and the passengers and crew said little. It was a safe space, where you could observe the water and think, without having to answer difficult questions.

She got up to stand next to the railing. The grey water blurred underneath as the boat cut through. She liked the old-fashioned orange doughnut life ring hanging there on a peg. Was that really enough to save someone's life?

The water was opaque. Sediment and old treasures, that's what she'd been told make the Thames grey. Not pollution. Apparently, they had cleaned it up a while ago, but due to the tide coming in from the mouth of the river, the sand and debris never quite settled down and away. You had to take the expert's word for it, really. Looking at it, you wouldn't believe it was clean. And you still wouldn't let it touch your mouth. That would be mad.

'It's low tide,' Tom said. 'June would know that this was the perfect time.'

'For what?'

'Mudlarking.'

They passed under Tower Bridge, and Tom indicated they should get off at Bankside.

'She'll be here,' he said, a sense of certainty on his face.

The wind was fierce, even off the boat. As it pulled away and left them standing on the pier, she felt the absence of sound, as the boat's vibrations dissipated. The air was fresh, even though they were in central London. Shakespeare's Globe Theatre stood round and cheerful in front of them, the black and white details reminding Gina of the time she went with her uni friends and watched *The Tempest* for a fiver. Someone a girl knew was in the cast. What they hadn't known was that £5 got you the right to stand up and watch the play, no seats. She remembered the sore feet, and sitting right down on the ground during the interval, drinking from bottles of wine that cost only a bit more than the ticket. But it was a laugh, seeing Shakespeare at the Globe. The memory reminded her of those friends – why did she lose touch with them? They had been fun, creative, tested out new ideas. One time she and three friends danced across the concourse at Waterloo after seeing some third years do an experimental performance dance thing in the vaults under the station. Several bottles of wine had been shared.

She'd like that back again, having friends you could do anything with, try things out. What happened to them? That was a time before Javier – or, actually, she remembered now that they had met him and hadn't liked him. He knew it, and didn't hide the fact that he resented them for taking her out without him. No, it was deeper than that – for knowing her before him, and in ways that he could never know. They had tried to tell her to save some space independent from him, but she didn't listen. She found it easier to not fight him, and his tendency to dominate. It made her angry, thinking of it now. Why had she let him take over that way?

Something was changing in her, and she didn't think Javier was going to take it well. But for some reason, his opinions were no longer so high on her list of priorities. Her independence, and everything that might come from that –

friendships, art, and beyond – that was more important, surely?

Tom was walking a few steps ahead, as they went in front of the artists' studios and shops that were part of the OXO complex. She would love to stop and window-shop to see what people were up to. Many were textile artists, or working with silver and gems. Others went in different directions – some went big and dramatic, with large abstract canvases; others went commercial, with humour or sweary-mottos to make people laugh and buy souvenir T-shirts.

Tom went down steps near the disused pier in front of the Oxo Tower. He was right, it was low tide, and the exposed beach was a complicated mix of gravel, pebbles and discarded pieces linked to the sea and its industrial past: old bricks with rounded corners, crockery, cement underlay of some kind, a tyre. There was something beautiful about it, in a grey and muddy sort of way.

The sun would be setting soon. They walked west, squinting into a hazy sun that could give them a colourful finale, or could just fall away unnoticed. It was that kind of day. They crossed paths with a couple walking in the opposite direction, holding hands. The woman's cheeks were reddened, hair a mess with the wind. The man's face was relaxed and happy, his free hand clutching the strap of a rucksack on one shoulder. They seemed to belong to each other, and to the place.

A lone man in a knitted cap was out as far as the tide would let him. He wore simple trainers, standing on low slabs that could have been concrete or stone. Another man with a long grey beard was in the Thames in full fisherman's waders. The water was up to his waist, and it must have been cold. It was only March. Maybe the waders were lined.

A woman approached slowly and then passed by, not looking up. She had a metal detector in her hand and headphones on. Intensely scanning the ground, she looked like someone who really needed a lucky break, and soon. Her movements were jerks and starts, in response to whatever the machine was telling her. She didn't stop, so nothing seemed like the jackpot, not yet.

'Some people take this larking quite seriously,' Tom said. His voice changed as he looked away towards the east. 'Not June, though. Look.'

In the distance, they saw a figure dressed all in black. Her short hair was hidden under a cap, but flicks of it broke free in the wind. She wore wellies and crouched down to look at something more closely. She reached into the sand and moved something precious through her fingers.

'June!' Gina shouted, but the wind took the sound away and it didn't reach. She started to run, not looking back as Tom's footsteps failed to keep pace with hers.

June stood up slowly, intent on a small piece of something from the Thames in her hand.

Gina was out of breath, suddenly worried about startling her, but she couldn't go back now. 'June,' she exhaled, closer now. There was more to say, about how they were worried about her, about how they took the boat, about Nanna in hospital, but all she could say was her name.

June turned to her, as if she had been expecting them. She was smiling, and her cheerfulness spilled over as if they were continuing a conversation she had already started in her head. 'Isn't it marvellous? Dutch, I think. Must be seventeenth or eighteenth century.' She held out a ceramic shard, no bigger than a 50p coin. The colours on it were faded blue and grey. She let Gina hold it. It was rough with sand and age, but with a thickness that felt robust.

'You haven't seen my collection, have you?' June took it back and pocketed it, looking out at the grey river running past. 'I took some old 3D frames, used to hold model trains, and turned them into my own little museum. I have a lot of things from the eighteenth century, but not much before. Except I have one that I think is a piece of a Roman shoe, with some real leather attached. Can you imagine? Very rare.'

She looked up at Gina. 'Oh, I need to give it all to the Museum of London someday. That's the deal, with the mudlarking license. And I will. But not just yet. I like having my own little museum of history for a while.'

Tom came up behind her and slipped his arms around June's waist. She rubbed her hands over his, sand coming off on his sleeves. It was as if this is what she had expected all along. Then she reached out to Gina too. They stood there, a triangle of friends, and were complete.

. . .

Although it wasn't Gina's day to work, Lizl let them come into the café just before closing. It was nice to have a manager like that, who gave you a bit of space to feel at home. Gina put a five pound note in the till and made three hot chocolates, bringing them out together to June and Tom, who were sitting by the fogged-up front window.

They examined June's discoveries from her day by the river. What at first glance were crumbled pieces of rubbish took on new meaning when you saw how they had the potential to be pieces that told you about the Thames. Together, the bits and pieces of broken ceramics, rounded beads, and river-brushed glass made a nice little collection.

Tom rubbed a hole in the steam on the window, and then settled back to watch June from a relaxed stance. He was so much more at ease now that his worries had proven unfounded. It was as if he was meant to be with these two, and now that they had found June, their contentment was settled.

'Did you see that woman with the metal detector?' Gina asked.

'She's there all the time,' June said, her mouth trying to smile and drink her hot chocolate same time. 'She never finds anything.'

'What would happen, do you think, if we plugged her headphones into some heavy metal instead?' Gina said. 'Would she change her path? Start digging uncontrollably?'

'Maybe she just finds it soothing to be out there,' Tom said. 'Like a meditation. Perhaps she's not actually looking for anything at all.'

'Oh, I think everyone's looking for something,' June said, but she didn't expand.

'Who knows? Maybe she's struck gold by now, while we are just drinking hot cocoa at a café and having a laugh,' Gina said.

'Maybe, but this life isn't so bad.' Tom reached over to June and kissed her on top of her head. 'Is it?'

June nuzzled into the embrace but didn't answer.

Chapter Twenty-Two

1966

The girl was unreachable at times. She was twelve, in secondary school, and sometimes seemed like a foreign creature.

'Be patient with her,' Aday said to Bella. 'She is not like you, or like me. She is growing up as a Londoner, in different times.'

'Thank God,' Bella replied, in a rare moment of acknowledging the difficulties of her childhood, one evening when they had been invited upstairs to eat with Fernando and Christiana. Amara had already excused herself – a bit rudely, Bella thought – to go downstairs to read a book.

'I don't know what she has to complain about,' Bella continued.

Fernando brought out a Spanish red wine, and offered some to both Aday and Bella.

'Not on a work night,' Aday said, out of habit more than anything else.

Bella accepted more in her glass, despite already having finished one earlier. She knew that two was her limit, or she might say something that could offend their old friends. Not that she ever had, but there was always that worry.

Christiana sat at the top of the table, near the cooker, looking regal and calm. At the age of sixty-six, she liked to say she was as old as the century. When she experienced a grey London day, she would laugh and twist a lock of her hair around her finger and compare it to the colour of the sky. 'Same, same,' she said with a wistful laugh.

'Amara wants to fight the big fights,' Bella continued. 'About Rhodesia. Vietnam. Civil rights in America. But what has that got to do with us? I don't know why she wants to debate everything, like even what to have for dinner or what to watch on the TV. Everything is an argument with that girl.'

Aday gave her the look he often did, that said that although Bella had a point, he wished she felt differently. 'She's just a girl, working things through,' he offered.

'What do you know about what it's like to be a girl? To be an adolescent girl?' Bella goaded him, as she did only rarely, when her nerves were frayed.

'You are right; I do not know,' Aday said. He moved his water glass back and forth from one hand to the other. 'But I do observe.'

Bella sighed. That was always Aday's trump card, the doctor, a dispassionate observer.

'And what I see is a girl whose mother loves her very much.' He reached out for Bella's hand, resting on the dining table.

She didn't pull it away. 'But,' she said, pre-empting him, 'there always is a "but".'

'No ... no but. However—', at this, Fernando laughed, as he had heard the couple go down this road before. 'However,' Aday continued, 'she is going to have her own path. Neither of us grew up black in 1960s London. Where I grew up, I didn't feel black. I was a member of the kingdom, no more, no less. A kingdom without much money, but still we were accepted and loved. You, you tell me you didn't feel white, growing up as a Jew in Nazi-occupied France. But our daughter, she is both, and neither. She'll have to find her own way.'

'And unfortunately,' Christiana said as she stood up to clear the dishes, 'she may have some fights to fight.' She put the dishes in the sink, where Fernando would tackle them after the guests left, as was their way. 'So the girl, she is practising at home her arguments and passions. Because it is a safe space, you see? Before she has to do them out there.' She gestured to the window, where a police siren was sounding not too far away.

Bella said, more to her glass than to them, 'But she doesn't listen. When you are learning about the world, about life, you need to listen, no?'

'There's time for that.' Christiana put her hand on Bella's

shoulder for a moment. 'My boys, they didn't listen either, when they were going through things. But they come back, in a way. They do, once they are ready.'

'I don't know,' Bella said. A sadness settled upon her shoulders that made her feel like the sound of the ocean was in her ears. 'I don't think she'll reach for me, when the time comes. When she needs someone.' She looked at Aday. 'She's her daddy's girl, that's for sure.'

Aday opened his mouth to argue, but he had nothing wise to say, so he closed it again.

Chapter Twenty-Three

'Mason knows about these things,' June said.
They were all sitting on the floor in Mason's small studio. They had found some cocktail mix in the communal kitchen and decided a little unwisely to improvise drinks with tonic and vodka. There weren't proper cocktail glasses, just old jam jars that could be used for drinking or painting or whatever. Just hope that the painters had cleaned them properly; you don't want to ingest some of those vibrant colours or else you'll be sick in a moment (cadmium yellow – one to avoid).

Mason's art was stacked against the wall to make some space for socialising. They had to cross their legs like schoolchildren to fit in the small space. Tom's legs were too long and he wasn't comfortable until he stretched them out. A heavy plan chest took up much of the floor in one corner, with long flat drawers for protecting Mason's work.

'June talks to me, sometimes,' Mason said. He was

wearing a flat cap turned backwards. The black leather matched his hair and dark eyes exactly. 'I understand a bit about how it is.'

'How what is?' Tom said, sounding rather defensive.

'You know, depression.'

'I don't like to put a label on it,' June said. 'But if you've experienced it yourself, you kind of get it.'

'I had bouts of it before I moved to Lewisham,' Mason said. 'Where I grew up, in Essex, people could be quite nasty to "Oriental" kids, as we were called then. You had it really bad if you were mixed race. The Asian kids didn't like me because of the African side, and the black kids made fun of the way I talked, because I had a different accent, coming from the Chinese-speaking community. I was a mess.'

'And here, in southeast London, it's not a mess?' Tom said.

'Oh, it is. Nowhere is perfect. But you don't feel like there's just one group of people, and you're an outsider. Or even just two groups of people, going at each other, and you're supposed to choose sides. Here, there's such a mix, and many people, like Gina here, and me, we are the mix. But you know what? We are London too. And this city, well … it lets you be whoever you want. Most of the time, it just lets you be.'

They were quiet a moment. Each of their cocktails was at a different depth, depending on their enthusiasm for the drink. June's was almost gone; Gina's and Mason's were halfway. Tom's was barely touched. He probably would have preferred a coffee.

'So Gina and I, we aren't capable of understanding depression?' Tom uncrossed his outstretched legs and hugged them in towards his chest. 'Because we haven't had it? I don't think that's fair.'

'No, love,' June came in. 'You've been there with me in the dark times.' She threaded her arm through his. 'You are empathetic, to the core. That's what's special about you.'

Tom grunted, chin into his knees.

'And Gina here, well, I can't speak for you, obviously.' June looked up, as if asking to be interrupted, but no break came. 'You seem resilient. You have a core about you that seems to hold it together. Like you won't lose your shit, because if you did, no one else would be able to manage either. I don't know what it is, but it's there, and people can sense it. It draws people to you.'

'Really?' Gina wasn't sure if this was an accurate description. 'I don't think I'm all that special.'

'No, you are,' June said. 'That's what we love about you.'

'We?' Gina said, starting to laugh. The cocktail was stronger than it looked.

'Speak for yourself,' Mason said, his eyes smiling at the corners. 'I barely know the girl.'

'Well, we do. Me and Tom. We've already talked about adopting her.'

'You have?' Gina found that really funny, and couldn't stop laughing. 'I'm not a puppy!'

'No, you know what I mean.' June let go of Tom and was hugging Gina now. 'Couples need that, you know. They need friendships. It makes a good kind of balance.'

'I dunno,' Mason said, finishing his drink. 'I think it sounds a bit complicated.'

'No, it's simple. Just follow your instincts and you'll be fine.'

'What about Gina here, doesn't she get a say? You said she had a boyfriend. Spanish guy.' Mason rolled his jam jar back and forth in both hands.

'How is Javier?' June asked. 'Does he want to hang out sometime?'

'No, he's okay.' Gina didn't like being under the spotlight. 'He just has a lot of stress at the moment. He lost his academic grants…'

'That doesn't mean he should be rude to you,' Tom said. After a pause, he said, more to his drink than to his friends, 'Or to your grandmother.'

'Bella? Did she say something?'

'You can just tell, Gina. Guys like that, there's a word for it. What is it?' He searched his mind a moment. 'Narcissist.'

'You don't know him that well. We've been through a lot together.' Gina tried to think what she should tell them. It was hard to say that when they got together, she was floundering in art school, and he made her feel like someone worth something. He made her complete. He was loyal, and there for her. And she should be there for him, through the bad patches. 'When we got together, I was really alone. He was there for me, made up for what I'd missed. I know he's a bit self-centred ... but you don't see the good sides...'

Gina suddenly wasn't enjoying the conversation anymore. She felt acid in her throat, coming up from her stomach. Was she going to throw up? She shook her head. God no, not in Mason's studio. 'I need the loo,' she said, getting up. She knocked over her glass on the floor, but thankfully it was already empty.

She got to the door, then stopped and looked back at them when it was half-open. 'He asked me to marry him, you know.'

June looked alarmed. Tom didn't say anything, although he probably wanted to.

Mason said, 'What did you say?'

'He's out of his mind,' she said. She left the door open as she walked down the hall.

'I've never met the guy,' she heard Mason say. 'But all I can say, is that as soon as anyone talks about him, you all go grey. It's like the mere mention of him saps all the colour from the room.'

Gina sat fully clothed on the lid of the loo for a while, door shut. Her head was spinning and it wasn't good. Those drinks were too strong. Trust June to not pay attention to how much vodka went in. Gina needed some water, soon, to dilute the drunken feeling.

The inside of the loo door was covered in graffiti, as you might expect in an artist's co-op. Some were simple pen marks saying 'JP wuz here' and 'Ben & Lara 4EVA'. Others were more intricate. How long did people spend in here? Too long, probably. One was quite a detailed drawing of a girl with a huge head and wide eyes, but a tiny body, kind of like a manga drawing. Someone else had taken to carving into the door, like lino art. Funny what artists will do when no one is looking.

'You okay in there?' June knocked on the door.

'Just a sec,' she said.

'We're going to the kitchen to see if there's anything to eat,' she heard June say, and then the sounds of people going down the wooden stairs.

She took a few breaths, then flushed the toilet and came out. The light was still on in Mason's studio. She reached to turn it off, but she stopped when she saw he was still there.

'Sorry, I thought you were with them,' she said.

'I wanted to show you something.' He was looking at his phone. She came closer and put a hand on his arm to steady herself, or steady the screen, she wasn't sure which. He smelled of aftershave, and a bit like acrylic paints too.

On his screen was a YouTube video with Chinese characters. It opened to a street market in China somewhere.

'What the…' she said.

'Shh … watch. It's about sugar.'

The camera came closer to a lady with a market stall. She was stirring an opaque white mixture in a hot steel pot, steam rising up. Then she took a ball of it in her hands, blowing on it and transferring it from hand to hand, moving quickly so it wouldn't burn. She formed a ball and kept rolling it into more of a tube, then pressed her thumb in to make it hollow. She pulled out one long string like a tail, blew on it a few more times, then broke off the end and put it in her mouth. She blew into it slowly, and the lump started to expand. Not dramatically, but in a concentrated way that showed she knew what she was doing.

Onlookers onscreen said something in Chinese. The subtitles said, *'It's beautiful, like a flower.'* Another person replied: *'But would you eat a flower?'*

The lady pulled out at the edges as she blew, and an animal form started to take shape. She pulled out ears, a snout and four legs, while the belly got rounder and more transparent. The sugar was making a glass-like sculpture, small and surprisingly beautiful. Then the lady stopped blowing, spinning the blow tube into a springy tail for a piglet.

A crowd around her cheered and applauded as she lifted it up. She held it carefully, like a precious ornament. Then she came back to her hot bowl and spun a wooden stick in the sugar solution. With precise aim she pressed the wooden stick, softened with a glob of sugar, into the belly of the animal, so that she could hold it without the risk of crushing it in her grip.

'Pig on a stick,' Gina said.

'Yeah, it was the Year of the Pig, a few years back,' Mason said.

The lady finished up with painting on some eyes and some stripes.

'I hope that's edible paint,' Gina said.

Mason nodded. 'They've been doing this for centuries. The kids love it.'

The market lady handed over the finished pig to a very happy child. 'Apparently so,' Gina said. 'But why…' She didn't finish her question.

'I was thinking about you, and your sugar.' Mason said, putting his phone into his back pocket. He seemed a bit embarrassed all of a sudden. 'You don't have to do animals, but I thought you'd like to see other people working with the medium.'

'Yeah, no, thanks so much. I didn't know about that … tradition.'

'It's kind of like glassblowing, although a lot less dangerous. And you can do it at home, not hard at all.'

'Don't you need special equipment?'

'We could try to set something up. I think it would take two pans together, a double-burner, like wax, for candles.'

'In the kitchen? You don't think the others would mind?'

'No, no one minds. We know that you need to experiment, to find your form.'

They started out of the room to join the others downstairs. 'It could be interesting,' she thought out loud. 'Maybe combining the texture of blown sugar with spun sugar, and then the granules … but I don't know what I'd do with it. I work small, you see.'

'You'll figure it out,' he said. 'I have faith in you.'

Chapter Twenty-Four

Passover came late that year. April was already feeling the wisps of summer, with the heat of the sunny days making people shocked when the spring rains washed in again. The Jewish holiday seemed over-ripe and overdue. They should have done it already. Which they had, Bella and Gina, every year since the child was old enough to sit at the table.

Bella didn't hold onto many rituals. She knew that she would not be allowed as a member in the Orthodox synagogues, and she didn't know how to approach others. She had heard about the Liberal one in St John's Wood; maybe that could be a place for people like her. But the other side of London was like the other side of the world, if you didn't drive, and she'd never learned how.

In any case, she didn't feel like she needed to find or make a Jewish community here. Her life was a break with everything that came before. It would have felt false. Like shaving your head, and then wearing a wig on top. Better just to let the new skin breathe.

But, like any Jew, Bella had contradictions within her. On the Jewish New Year and on Passover, she always felt that she should do something. For Gina's sake, really. Especially now that Amara had left she felt that some pattern of ritual might be helpful somehow.

How do you raise a grandchild on your own? No one ever expects it, and no one can explain it. There weren't radio programmes dedicated to it like there are about motherhood. Goodness, women these days could learn anything they wanted about babies in utero, breastfeeding, every minuscule detail. It wasn't like that when she was pregnant with Amara. But something about being a grandparent was a lot easier than being a parent. It was as if the rules could be looser because you had the perspective that this too shall pass. This problem, this phase, it would pass. Too quickly, if you didn't take care.

Maybe there were some support groups now for grandmothers, but it was too late. Gina mentioned something she had seen online. The girl tried to get Bella to use the internet, using something called 'voice recognition' – dragon-something – but it was too fiddly and didn't understand her French-accented English very well. In any case, Bella believed that there was such a thing as information inundation, and that's what computers offered. Too much information could lead to despair. When you saw all the grief in the world, and you couldn't find in yourself enough joy to balance it, that did no one any good at all.

But today wasn't a day for thinking such thoughts. She was going to have a proper Passover Seder, and she had asked Gina to invite people. The new friends she had made, the artist-girl and that nice boy Tom. Gina hadn't mentioned Javier, so neither had she. It was just as well; he was a prickly person, you never knew how he would act. And Tom, well, he had such a different disposition. You could tell in an instant that a room was calm with him in it. He was that type of boy. A man, really, but to Bella anyone who was Amara's or Gina's age would always be young. A young man, then. You could say that about people, couldn't you? Without being told off for being condescending or impolite? She hoped so.

And she had insisted on inviting Oleg and Katarina. Such a nice girl; Bella really liked her. She should have sensed her warmth long before that time when she had labyrinthitis. Katarina would make an excellent nurse when she finished her training. Bella really was just so grateful that they had lodgers. The income, that was appreciated. But it was more about presence. Gina, bless her, had her own life and an irregular schedule, with the café and this new artists' cooperative. It was nice to know that other people might be around to help, if needed.

Passover Seder made more work for Gina, of course. She insisted on cooking the big dinner, when to be truthful the girl was not a good cook. She even burnt toast much of the time. Lord knows how she held down the job at the café. But she was a good person, deeply good. She still had that sweet look on her face, half-scared of doing the wrong thing. Nothing Bella could do would take that look away. It stayed with her, like a birthmark.

And in any case, you could order in lots of food now. That wasn't possible before. Time was when you had to go to the East End or further, Golders Green, for proper challah during the normal months, and matzah during Passover. These days you could just order it with a service, like Ocado or Sainsburys. They all deliver now, if you get on the computer, which Bella didn't. So, again, she depended on Gina.

Hopefully, the girl would realise what was needed for the Seder plate. The only Passover Haggadah Bella had was in French and Hebrew; Gina really struggled with that one. However, it also gave them a chance to spend time together planning, as Gina read out the passages in the best French she could muster, and Bella translated it, reciting the Hebrew prayers memorised decades ago. She wished she had taught Gina more of the traditions, but there never seemed to be the chance. Maybe she still could learn some Hebrew now. It's never too late. Bella had even heard of an older woman, a retired lady with grandchildren, learning the prayers and going for a Bat-Mitzvah. She recited the Torah and Haftarah in front of the whole congregation, just like a Rabbi. Nothing was impossible for women now.

It wasn't like that when Amara was young. Bella remembered trying to explain the traditions to her, but it was like talking to a glass plane; the words just went straight through. They didn't know any other families like them: mixed in race, religion, traditions. They were improvising all the time.

There was something about Amara that never absorbed Jewishness. Maybe Bella herself was not demonstrative enough, having left it all behind in France. She should have tried harder, to give Amara half of her identity.

After Aday died, it was even more difficult. She couldn't share with Amara much about West Africa; they had never been to where he grew up, and he didn't speak much about his childhood and traditions. He only had one or two photographs from his childhood, and a few postcards that were more recent. And he never had a chance to write anything down. That was one of Bella's biggest regrets, that she didn't get him to write his stories down or record them somehow. About his childhood, about his clan. To her, the family tree, on his side, was a mystery.

And on her side, well … it had been chopped down. The whole tree, as far as she knew. With nothing left, it was too painful to talk about the stories and traditions. She could only go so deep in the stories before feeling a hard wall inside herself. If she pressed against that wall, tried to break through it herself, there was a huge fear about what lay behind. She had a hint of a feeling, and it scared her. The emotions would just be a flood. Something unstoppable, like the time of Noah and the Ark. She couldn't let that happen.

Bella was a practical woman. She always had been. Even after all the horrors she had experienced, she knew she had to keep working and keep raising the child. She would catch herself humming songs from childhood, thinking they were in French. When the words surfaced, however, they were Hebrew prayers from long ago.

'And you want me to do what? With the afi-what?' Tom asked, holding a piece of matzah in a cloth napkin.

'The *afikoman*.' Gina giggled. The words sounded so funny when you explained it to a newcomer. 'I dunno. Bella always used to hide it, and I would go find it. It's a tradition for kids, really. But if there are no kids around...' She looked to Bella who sat firmly at the head of the table.

'You still hide it, Tom,' Nanna said. 'And later whoever finds it will get a prize.'

'What prize?' June asked.

'You'll see,' Nanna smiled.

Gina liked the feeling around the table. Oleg and Katarina were a bit shy at first, but after the second glass of wine was drunk, everyone got rosier. Even Nanna, who normally only sipped her wine, looked slightly tipsy and very merry about it. It was nice to see.

'I feel funny, rummaging around someone else's house,' Tom grumbled, standing up with the *afikoman* in his hand, wrapped in a cloth napkin. 'But all right, I'll hide it somewhere in the kitchen.'

'Don't tell us!' June said.

'And isn't there another tradition, about the stranger coming to the door?' Oleg asked.

'Elijah,' Gina said. 'You pour a glass and leave it, in case a stranger comes. Over the course of the meal, you see if the level has gone down. If so, then...'

'A ghost?' June asked.

'Not a ghost, I dunno.' Gina looked at Nanna, who didn't seem to be listening. 'Nanna, what is it again?'

'Oh, it's a bit complicated. But in its essence, it's about being open to strangers in need.' Nanna reached out her hands. To one side was Gina, the other side Tom, who had just sat down again. Both took hold.

Gina looked at the frail thing in her hand. Her grandmother's years were etched across the ligaments, veins and bone. It felt as fragile as a bird fallen from a tree. The skin was so thin as to be translucent, with the wrinkles and pores there for all to see. As a child, Gina used to trace the blue lines, expanding into an arrangement. She thought they looked like thin rivers, moving and shifting as Nanna wiggled her fingers. Although Nanna used to tell her not to poke too hard, she never scolded her.

'It is the Tree of Life, we used to say,' Nanna continued. 'In Hebrew, *Etz chayim hi*. It gives you life, connecting to tradition.' She took her hand back from Tom and patted the one in Gina's grasp. 'I hope you feel that, *ma cherie*.'

'I do, Nanna.' Gina wanted to reassure her grandmother; there was a risk she could become distressed, talking about tradition.

Gina jumped at a sharp knock at the door.

'It's Elijah!' June giggled, reaching to pour herself another glass of wine.

The knocks came again, in rapid succession. Tom moved his chair back. 'Do you want me to see who it is?'

'Yeah, no, I'll get it,' Gina said. Tom followed her to the door in any case.

Javier stood there, in a foul mood. 'Why didn't you respond to my texts?' he shouted at her. 'I've been trying to get you for hours! I need the papers in your room. You've got my degree transcript, and the deadline for this grant is midnight!'

'Hello, Javier,' Tom said. 'We're having Passover with Gina's grandmother.'

Javier belatedly saw him, then shifted his gaze into the front room, which had been rearranged for the dinner. When he saw that there was an audience, his tone shifted, just slightly. 'A dinner party? With guests?'

'Yeah, Javier, you see...' Gina lost her words. 'It's a Jewish holiday. I thought you were busy.'

'Right. And I need that transcript. I'm really late!' He pushed past Tom and half-ran up the stairs to Gina's room.

She watched the blank space where his body had been. The others at the table didn't say anything. Should she go with him? No, his filing was a mess, in folders stashed under her bed. She shouldn't get involved; it would only lead to an argument.

'It's all right,' she said to no one in particular. 'He'll find it.'

'Such a hurry,' Nanna said. 'That boy is always in such a hurry.'

'Too much of a hurry to say hello,' June said.

'Or to wish you a happy Passover,' Tom said, sitting down again.

They stayed quiet, finishing off the last of the main course. The meal wasn't very good. She had burned the roast trying to make sure it wasn't still raw inside. She couldn't risk that with Nanna's health. But no one had told her to cover it in foil, not until too late. Oh well. At least the salmon, from M&S, was presented ready-made from the store and it looked the part. Shame about the sprouts, though.

'What about dessert?' Nanna said suddenly. 'I think we have dessert, *non*?'

Gina felt relief at being given something to do. 'Right, guys. Pass over your plates.'

'I'll help,' Katarina said. She picked up the dishes from the others with a grace that showed she had practised this somehow. Maybe she gave lavish dinner parties where she came from. Or maybe she had to work in a café too, at some point. Nursing students also needed money.

In the kitchen, Gina clattered the dishes and cutlery in the sink. Katarina reached for the sponge and soap, but Gina stopped her. 'Leave the washing up,' she said.

'Are you sure? There's a lot to do. And you cooked for everyone.'

'It's no problem. Here, help me with the sorbet.'

They went into the freezer. 'Hope people like raspberry or lemon,' Gina said. 'Or there are the lovely chocolates you brought. The heart-healthy kind. Really thoughtful of you.'

'It's the least we could do, with you having us for

dinner,' Katarina said. 'Listen, if you ever want someone to talk to … someone neutral…'

Javier's steps pounded down the stairs again.

'Found it!' he said, a huge grin on his face. 'My system, it's chaotic, but it always comes through in the end!' He got to the door and turned back. 'Sorry I can't stay. But you see, I am trying to get funding to stay in this country. To stay near Gina, my love.' He opened the door dramatically, but before he closed it, he couldn't stop himself. 'This is what a man does for true love. But maybe you wouldn't recognise what love looks like,' he said. 'Raised unconventionally, you know. No father, no mother here in this dysfunctional place.'

Gina was frozen at the door of the kitchen as he left. She couldn't think fast enough to contradict him or brush him out the door. Nanna would have heard every word.

Chapter Twenty-Five

The sun was bright, heating up the skin in that way it can do in late spring. It transformed Londoners into sun-worshippers – and burnt lobsters, many of them. Unless you had your own healthy way of absorbing the sun. It was one thing that Gina was happy with, the colour of her skin. She felt that the bronze tone connected her to her mum and her grandfather. Set her apart from Nanna, but not too much. There was Mediterranean blood in her Jewish line as well.

In the garden of Magnolia House with the others, Gina had an urge to climb the tree in the back garden. It wasn't tall, looking more like a gnarled old man than a robust specimen of tree. But it seemed like it could hold you. It had probably been climbed by generations of children. It was just too tempting, the lower branches right within reach.

'Go on then,' Mason said, as she was already moving that way. 'People do it all the time.'

'Something about it,' she said, already climbing into the branches. 'Can't resist.'

'Just don't fall on Tom!' June called out as she came from the kitchen with an armful of drinks.

Tom was stretched out below the tree, far from the angle of drop. 'No worries,' he said. 'Not a problem.'

Gina looked down at him from above. Tom was never a problem. As long as he knew June was okay, he was at ease. She really liked them as a couple. They seemed to love each other, but also allow the other space to be themselves. There was contentment in that.

From above, you could see that Tom's hair had started to thin out in the back in a little circle, like a flesh-coloured skull cap. It was funny; he was so tall, no one would notice until it was much further gone. She wondered if he knew it was there. He probably felt it, if he noticed things like that at all. She wouldn't mention it.

'How long are you going to stay up there?' June wagged a bottle of Victorian Lemonade at Gina. 'I got your favourite! Just like you serve in that posh café!'

'Oh please,' Gina said. 'It's my day off! Don't remind me.'

She looked into the branches overhead and watched the wind shift through the leaves. It was a subtle thing today, the change in the air. The sun was the dominant feeling; that's what got people out of the house, taking a break from their work. But once you were up here, sheltered from the warmth, you noticed other things. Like the leaves, they were always moving. Maybe from her weight? She shifted to rest more on her bum than her crouched legs, which were growing tired. No, it wasn't her. It came from the atmosphere, this vibrating tension in the green.

'Stay as long as you like,' Mason said, not looking up. 'It's nearly summer.'

'But there's chocolate!' June said, and with that, Gina decided to come down.

June liked little details and little gifts. She was like a kid sometimes. She loved chocolate, especially the special ones with an artistic flair. It cheered her up. And she was generous, June was. If she loved something, she immediately wanted to show it to you and share.

She had a bag of different chocolates and treats. Some were ordinary – the typical Cadbury's Creme Eggs. But she also showed off some sweet designs she'd bought from a market stall in Brockley on the weekend.

Gina picked one of the special ones up and held it in her hand. It was made of sugar, pressed tight somehow, probably with a heat mould. It was like a little fence made up of tiny eggs, complete with lines of grass and flower bits. It was minuscule. 'Wonder how they did it?'

Mason sat up. 'Maybe they have tiny moulds and then press it together at different times. It could be machine-made, you know.'

'Naw, not this one. Machines are more for the mass-marketed ones. Otherwise, the scale doesn't pay off.'

'You're the expert.'

'I've been thinking of branching out,' she said.

'Sugar blowing?'

'Maybe ... and other things. Maybe chocolate?' She reached into June's bag and found a Cadbury's bar.

'Sticking with a sweet theme then?'

'Yes, but I was thinking of making it ironic. Moving further into tragedy. Shakespeare is so overdone.'

'What are you thinking?'

'I dunno ... the history of chocolate, you know, it's pretty bad. Sugar too, obviously. The slave trade and all that.'

'You could do something interesting with it...' Mason seemed to go into himself, making mental notes. 'You could tell that story ... I think I've seen something. I'll have a look in my files.'

Chapter Twenty-Six

1968

Aday knew that Christiana had been disappointed about the summer. As a Spaniard, the lady always craved the hot dry days of her childhood. She and Fernando spoke a lot about Albalario on the coast, where they used to go as children to the pier. But they never went back. It was as if it was preserved in memory, but was inaccessible now.

Amara's asthma came back. That was a surprise, as usually they had a stay over the warm months. That summer, though, the wheeziness never fully subsided. Aday listened to her breaths and tried to figure out the triggers. Bella fretted over any dust in the girl's bedroom and made her refrain from sports. It just drove the child deeper into her books.

Aday understood her much better than her mother did. He was surprised that was how it had worked out, but he didn't try to undo it. He didn't know what was going through the mind of either his wife or his daughter, but he seemed to be able to keep the peace between them, most of the time.

One summer night they had the windows closed against the rain. Bella told him that she had a feeling that something was going to happen. She held him close, her tension transmitting her worries and unfinished conclusions.

Aday's instincts made him concerned. He insisted on a close examination of Amara. The child sat on a stool in the kitchen while he listened at length to her lungs, examined her for rashes or the tell-tale signs of something threatening.

It was not their daughter, not that time. But you could not give thanks to God for sparing your child, when He left someone else bereft. However, we all are bereft at one time or another, are we not? Just that summer, it was Christiana's turn. No, all of them were broken up about it. But none as much as her.

Aday, Bella and Amara were eating dinner in the basement flat, when a loud thud came from the ceiling above. Then another noise, like a chair scraping across the wood, and the crash of dishes hitting the floor.

Bella looked at Aday, whose fork was frozen in midair.

'Fernando fell,' Amara said. How she knew with such certainty, Aday could never explain.

He ran up the stairs, taking two at a time. They could already hear Christiana wailing, and some other noises too. Murmurs from Fernando, they realised. Amara was at

Aday's heels, so Bella was the last to see what they did: Fernando down on one knee, a smashed dinner plate fallen off the table, food slopped onto the floor. Both of his hands were cupped over his heart, and his face was grey.

'Get her back!' Aday spoke sharply to Bella, and gestured for Amara to be shielded from the scene, but she had already absorbed it all. Bella tried to pull the child away, but she was a tall girl, and stubborn, not be moved.

'Call an ambulance!' he said.

Aday quickly assessed his dear friend, and what he saw was alarming. The man was clutching at his shirt-collar, as if he could not get it loose fast enough. His lips were turning a grey-blue, and his face was twisted in pain.

Fernando quietly whispered: '*El dolor, mi querido amigo ... mi corazón...*'

Bella came back from phoning the ambulance as soon as she could and wrapped her arms around Christiana, who was reaching for Fernando but risked getting in the way.

Aday lay his friend on the floor and put his feet up on a chair. He loosened his shirt buttons and urged his friend to be still. 'Help is on the way. Bella called, and the ambulance is coming.'

Fernando continued to hold his chest, looking with increased horror at the pain he felt inside but could not express. The dear man they knew was being torn away from them, and it was clear that death was not coming peacefully.

'Hold onto life, my friend,' Aday said. He rubbed his hands together then put them on either side of Fernando's face. His skin looked so pale, embraced between Aday's dark brown powerful hands. 'Hold on!'

Fernando said nothing, but the fear made every mark and wrinkle in that face seem deeper and more strained.

'We're losing him,' Aday said. Later, he told Bella, when he wept over the man, that those words were his biggest regret. Because Christiana ripped herself out of Bella's embrace and pushed to Fernando's side. 'No!' she screamed, and the noise was so loud it hurt their ears. *'No no no! No, mi amor, no puede estar pasando, no me dejes!'*

Aday had to push her away, in order to start heart compressions and breathing into his mouth. There was silence then, or close to silence. Amara was still as a watching spirit in the background. Aday's rhythm held his concentration and he could think of nothing else.

Christiana continued to weep, but very quietly. *'No me dejes,'* she repeated, but no one could prevent her from being alone for the rest of her life. By the time the ambulance came, he was gone.

Part III

Chapter Twenty-Seven

2011

It was hot for June. Everyone said so. The radio talked about drought and the risk of water rationing and standpipes. They compared it to the summer of 1976, when half the people listening weren't even born yet. Probably more than half. Sometimes they got it wrong, those weather people.

The heat agreed with Gina more than the cold. Maybe that was something she got from her mum. And Nanna's health was better in the summer. Her arthritis eased, and she had less to bother her. Gina felt better too, if she had to go out and leave Nanna on her own.

Archie's had a back garden. It was a bit of a faff to take food and drinks out there, but it was all right. Alison, Buddy and the mums were out there now, the babies all toddling around like bumper cars in a safe place. Alison's mum was there again too and came up to order.

'Something cool?' she asked.

'Iced tea?' Gina said.

'Lord no!' The woman shuddered as she looked over the menu again. 'Couldn't take my tea cold. I'm just not made for that. What about the elderflower drink?' When she looked up, behind her glasses her eyes were the same hazel-flecked colour as her grandson's.

'People like that one. With ice?'

'That'd be lovely, two of those. Thank you.'

'And something for Buddy?'

'Yes, one of those baby vegetable squeezies? Thanks so much.'

It was a nice perk, that garden. Inside, the kitchen got a bit overheated in this weather. You had to be careful with the cappuccino machine; if you weren't exact in the steps, it would spray the steam out in all directions and you could get scalded. You'd only have yourself to blame if you were absent-minded with that thing. Lord knows she had used it thousands of times by now.

Lizl had tried to get her to talk about the future. Did she want more hours, more responsibility? Gina didn't know. She didn't think so. She didn't have any great passion for café life. She didn't harbour big ambitions to run her own place, to be a successful businesswoman. That was what Amara was doing, apparently. Not that Gina had ever seen the hotels that she heard about. Once or twice a year she would get a postcard with a new picture of the hotel on the beach. It always looked more or less the same.

Lizl had probably wanted to hear more enthusiasm from her longest-serving staff member. Something more like a partnership, stepping up to a stronger role. But Gina didn't have it in her for that. She didn't know why she daydreamed. Concentration just seemed really hard, like she was living in a fog.

It didn't help that Javier was so angry all the time. She had to ask him not to come to the café anymore. Lizl said he was turning off some customers. He walked around with a permanent frown, almost like a caricature of himself. He used to be a good laugh, didn't he? She tried to remember how they got together, when she was still in uni. More than three years together now, she realised.

It was obvious, wasn't it? Javier was angry with her because she couldn't be the person he wanted her to be. She should be massaging away his defeats. She needed to find a job that paid more money. She should have let him move in with them. Given him the space and time to finish his PhD. Protected him from the rejections from the outside world. But she was not a normal girlfriend. She was responsible for an old woman who was quite fixed in her ways. Nanna had raised her, when no one else was up for the job. They were connected, forever. If Javier couldn't handle that, then … screw him.

There was an energy coming up from her, an angry one. Why was it that he was the only one allowed to be angry?

She was a person too, had a right to feelings and opinions. Even if he didn't like it, that was who she was.

Sometimes he called her spineless. 'You don't know who you are yet,' he said. Just because he was five years older, he felt justified with the condescending tone.

She should have said something clever back to shut him up. At least she didn't get thrown out of cafés for being an arsehole. At least she had friends, even if there weren't many. She was connected to people and didn't feel the need to lash out and attack. But she hadn't thought of any of that. Just mumbled something to his back.

However, that was changing. Her irritation was turning into something else. Yes, she had a spine. She was fed up. With him, with his dramas about the funding, with all of it. If this was love, the kind of love he wanted to demonstrate, then she was finished with it. It didn't feel right anymore. She wanted out.

She had a feeling that there was another way. Another kind of love that didn't have sharp edges and angry fights. There had to be, didn't there?

She started going to Magnolia House more often, even if June and Tom were busy. She felt at home there, with the squeaky floorboards and the bannister that wobbled more than it supported as she went up the stairs. She always listened at Mason's door to see if he was in, although today his door was locked, and no light escaped from underneath.

She stood on tiptoe to reach for the loft latch and shuttled the ladder down.

It was hot up there. Stale air from the closed windows in the eaves made her grimace. She'd have to open it up for a few minutes before starting work.

She had new energy, and a new idea. It was a bit tragic; she was wondering if she could make it more palatable. But she really wanted to do it. She imagined the whole thing, but it would take some planning. What she wanted to do was a big model slave ship. A chocolate one, complete with different levels. And the people, they would be made of sugar. She would have to do hundreds of them. Thousands maybe. She'd have to get her moulds just right, so she could make the same shapes over and over, and put them in different positions. And the sepia colouring she usually did, that would have to be darker for the skin tone. These were going to be West Africans, crossing the Atlantic. It would be a powerful statement, and yet ephemeral. Because chocolate doesn't last, wouldn't last, and slavery, too, couldn't last. Not in that form, anyways.

She had talked the idea over with Mason, and he was really helpful. It was he who said she should approach Tate Britain or the Museum of London. Tate had made their money from the sugar trade, after all. And the Museum of London in the Docklands had some permanent exhibits about the slave trade. She should talk to them, he insisted. See if they had any funding.

She faltered at that. She had never done any kind of grant application. She was sure she wouldn't be any good at it. But there was something about Mason that radiated confidence. The kind of confidence that gave it to other people at the same time. If he had enthusiasm for your ideas, then maybe they were worth something.

So she bought a big sketchpad, A3 size, and went to work drawing ideas. The first ones were kind of fanciful, as everything had to come way down in scale. You had to think about what would support the chocolate in the bowed shape of the bottom of a boat. She might need something to make up the ribs of the bow – shortbread maybe. How would the different levels work? Would the people be lying down, or labouring? She had to learn more.

Suddenly, she was heading back to the library. She hadn't been since she was working on essays for uni. She was now going into the history section, trying to find books with sketches to show the boats from the seventeenth and eighteenth centuries. Also heading to museums, proper museums. The British Museum, the Horniman. How long had it been since she had stepped into a history museum with any interest? Hadn't happened since school, and even then she couldn't remember ever being excited about history. But now, she wanted to know it all.

She heard a 'Hello' from downstairs and was happy to see Mason coming up the ladder. 'You all right?' he said.

'Sure, you?'

'It's hot up here,' he said.

'I was just about to take my sketchpad to the garden.'

'I have some newspaper cuttings I found for you. Come down and take a look?'

She opened the windows on both sides and the hot air chased its way out. Grabbing her sketchpad, and a couple of favourite pens, she managed the ladder one-handed. Halfway down she realised she had left her phone up top, but she couldn't be bothered to go back.

Mason turned the key in the lock of his studio and held the door open behind him. He pulled a shoebox out of his bag. 'This is how I hatch some early ideas,' he said.

Inside there were some envelopes. They were labelled with different things, but he flicked through them so fast she couldn't make out the writing. 'Here's the one,' he said. Onto the floor he tumbled out a range of clippings, some folded and big, others tiny, just a snippet of a column. She sat down and started reading. They were articles and photos from newspapers talking about the anniversary of the end of slavery in 1807. There were a lot of events a few years back in 2007. Some events seemed big and ceremonial, others were small and barely noted.

But what caught her attention most were the pieces from the Museum of London. There were lithographs of slave ships, and the people packed on board. Reproductions of newspapers from the abolitionist movement. As this was before photography, they were just sketches, but very effective in giving the sense of cramped terror. They were mass coffins on the sea, with living people struggling inside.

The evidence was so useful for her project, and she was

about to say so when she was hit by a big emotion, too large to name. The awful sadness of these people, not so different from her grandfather, but packed into these ships. The cruelty of it all. Tears came to her eyes. She tried not to show him, but he saw anyway.

He reached out to her. 'I know, it's a heavy subject.' His arm was around her shoulders and stayed there. 'I've started looking into work about the anti-apartheid movement, and what was happening at the time when my dad left South Africa. Sometimes it gets too much. I have to put it down.'

She nodded.

'I think it's when it strikes something personal, you know?' he continued. 'You're not affected as an individual, in the space and time you inhabit. But you know it is painful, and it has caused pain to someone who looks like you, or who shares something with you. Some attributes, or some history. And it was pain on a huge scale, for millions of people. That can be painful, physically.'

'And there's no one I can talk to.' She was crying then. 'All I have is Nanna. I'm alone, you see.'

He held her close. Didn't have to say more for a moment, just let her cry.

Her breath came out in jagged waves, humid against his neck. She didn't know why she was thinking about her grandfather. How much he didn't have a chance to tell her. How other children had grandparents and fathers and mothers who could talk about these things to their kids. She didn't have a mum, not present, anyways. Gina was alone.

Nanna didn't know either. She was brilliant and meant everything to her. But this wasn't her history.

'You're not alone,' he said after a while. 'You make your own community, you know?'

'But I don't fit in with any crowd.'

'Me neither,' he said. 'I'll be your crowd, if you want.'

'You get what I'm talking about?'

'I'd like to think so,' he said. 'But I need to do a lot more listening.'

'You're perfect at it.'

'Thank you.' He said it like he hadn't been complimented in a long time.

She kissed him then, first on the cheek. It was wet, and she couldn't tell if it was from her tears or her breath or his. But it didn't matter.

He moved back an inch to look at her face. 'What was that for?'

'For being you.'

His eyes flicked from one of her eyes to the other. 'Are you sure?'

'Sure you're perfect? Yes.'

'No, thanks, but ... sure you want to do this?'

'Do what?' She kissed his other cheek this time. She smiled. This was fun.

He laughed. 'You're being cheeky!'

'I hope so!' She laughed too. It felt good to laugh.

'What about, you know ... the Spanish guy?'

'Who?' she said, nuzzling back into that space between

his chin and his shoulder. 'Don't want to think about him right now.'

'Right. Shall we talk about slavery then?'

'Let's not talk,' she said, and put her hands on either side of his face.

The kiss was soft, tentative at first and then more confident. She held him there and enjoyed kissing him more than she had in a long time. It didn't matter how hot it was in the room, or that they were sitting on some of the clippings he had gathered for her. She could hear her phone ringing up in the attic, and she couldn't care less. Mason was kissing her, and nothing else mattered.

Chapter Twenty-Eight

1969

Bella reached out to fold the silk blouse in tissue paper. She couldn't believe, after so many years, that Christiana would think about leaving London.

'It's just not the same,' Christiana had said. 'I've outlived two husbands. I simply won't feel the joy that I used to feel.'

'It takes time,' Bella said, not really knowing what it would be like to lose a husband, but guessing. 'Time, and friendship. We can give you that, surely?'

Christiana reached over and put her hand over Bella's for a moment. A sad smile rested on her lips, and then she pretended to fuss over a crease in the blouse. 'This was my mother's,' she said, pressing it gently on top of others in her trunk. 'I think I'd like to give it to my son's wife for their anniversary.'

'I just can't imagine it here without you,' Bella said, knowing that she wasn't making this any easier. 'Who am I going to talk to about Amara's teenage antics?'

Christiana let out a little laugh. 'I will miss those tricks,' she said. 'But you can tell me on the phone.' She stood up and looked at herself in her round mirror on the wall. It had an ornate silver frame, with an elegance that matched her own.

'It's not the same... It's your house, and it just feels so natural, visiting you up here, with Fernando—' Bella stopped herself.

'*Exactamente*,' Christiana said, locking eyes with her in the mirror for a moment. 'That is what I feel.' She reached to take the mirror from its hook on the wall, but then stopped. She dropped her hands to her sides. 'Without Fernando, it does not feel like my home.'

She turned to Bella. 'But it is yours, the whole thing. As I told Aday, but I don't think he believed me. It is a home for your family, for your Amara to grow into, to be a teenager and then a woman. And for you, maybe one day to be a grandmother!'

At that, Bella laughed out loud in objection. Nothing could be further from her mind. 'But your boys,' Bella said. She did not want to get in the middle of any family feud.

'They have their own houses, their own families. They do not know London. It would never be their home.'

'It is too generous,' Bella said. 'I wish we could repay you somehow.'

'Have Amara write me letters,' Christiana said, and she

smoothed back her grey hair and smiled at her reflection. 'Tell her to write to me about anything on her mind. The books she is reading, the latest cause she is trying out. She is a brilliant girl, Bella. She is still forming, but when she chooses her direction, nothing will hold her back.'

Chapter Twenty-Nine

Gina shouldn't have done it over the phone. But with Javier, there was just no knowing when he would be around and be in the right mood to talk. And anyway, she didn't want to get caught up in an argument. He would get angry and run circles around her if they spoke. He had that uncanny way of jumping to offence, and showering insults on anyone and anything, trying to deflect from whatever it was he objected to.

So she sent a text message. She wasn't proud of it, but what could you do, with a guy like that? He tried to control her in so many small ways, that in the end, she just wanted to get out.

She talked it over with Mason; she could tell he was quietly pleased that she was bringing it up, but he wanted to stay out of it.

'He's your history, Gina,' Mason said, tracing his hand

gently over the underside of her forearm. 'I can't tell you what to do with your history.'

So she sent the text. Something simple, although she agonised over it for hours. How do you detach yourself from someone like Javier? His clothes and files in her bedroom, three years of memories, some of them good. There was a strange attraction to him, all wrapped up around a fiery passion. What is it that brought people into his web and kept them there? Actually, he didn't have a lot of friends or a lot of exes. There was just him, and that's how he wanted to have her, as well. Alone, no connections, depending on him for emotional guidance.

She typed:

> Javier, this relationship is over. We don't make each other happy. I let you go.

There was no reply.

It was time for her to start a shift at Archie's, and she didn't want to be late. She tried to put it out of her head, hoping the café would be busy and the time would pass quickly.

Mason didn't have anywhere else to be that afternoon, so he stayed with her at the café. Sitting in the corner, reading yesterday's papers, he seemed content. She made him a latte and he insisted on paying. She looked over at him every so often, and when she caught his eye, it made her smile to herself. She had never met anyone like him. He was so calm. And his approach to life, his way of sharing creative ideas and inspiration made it double what it might have been. But it was more than that, potentially much more.

Joanne was there, as usual, waiting for the last orders for croissants. Alison, Buddy and the other mums were there too. Gina should've been concentrating more on the customers, rather than gazing at Mason, when she was startled by a violent jangle of the bells on the door being pushed too hard. Javier stormed in, ripping off his motorcycle helmet mid-stride.

'What the fuck, Gina?' he shouted. He marched up to the counter with the helmet still in his hand. 'You fucking "let me go"?! You think you can end it, just like that?'

His face was red and blotchy, his hair flattened from being under the helmet and falling into one eye. He swung around to face the rest of the café, like he was giving a performance. 'More than three years I've loved this woman!' It wasn't clear who he thought gave the final judgement. 'Three years of sacrifices! Slaving away to try to make ends meet!'

The customers at the café were not used to such high drama, and no one said anything. This reaction was not enough for Javier. He turned back around to face Gina, his helmet swinging dangerously like a wrecking ball.

'And she just says I don't make her "happy".' His tone grew sarcastic and he did the little quotation marks with his free hand. 'Does she ever think about me? My happiness?'

He dropped the helmet then, and the noise on the floor made Gina jump. There was a counter between them, but it seemed like he might vault over it. What should she do?

She reached to the side. Could she find something to defend herself with? That would be terrible, blood everywhere, on Lizl's kitchen. Everyone would hate her then, blame her for spoiling a local café with a lovers' spat. Without looking, her hand found a long metal spoon, and she closed her fingers around it.

Mason got up then. It was subtle; he didn't make a noise in leaving the table, but as he moved into Javier's peripheral vision, the man jerked around.

'What are you looking at?' Javier snapped at him. 'This doesn't concern you.'

'Gina, do you want me to call someone?' Mason said, ignoring Javier.

'Piss off, she's my girlfriend.'

'She's not, actually. She ended it this afternoon. I saw the text.'

Mason shouldn't have said that. But perhaps he felt that Javier was getting too close, and wanted to bring him down a notch. Hard to know what he was thinking beneath the surface. But it was clear that Mason was not leaving the scene, and Javier was not going to get his way, whatever that was.

'For him? You're leaving me for him?' Javier spun back to Gina, spitting as he spoke. 'For the Chinese guy? A mixed-up kid, like you?'

Mason made a fist, she could see. This was terrible, and it was all her fault. She stepped out from the counter to try to stop it, still holding the long spoon.

'Javier, stop! I'm sorry I sent the text. I'm sorry you had

to meet Mason this way. But it's over. I can't do this. You're too angry all the time. I don't think you like it either. I'm not even sure if you like me, anymore. You're not happy. And there's no joy for me.'

'Joy? All you think about is your own selfish, selfish self. Such a selfish bitch, you know that? For three years I have worked so hard, never getting any real love from you or your family or friends.'

'You cut me off from any friends I ever had!' Gina was getting angrier. 'No one was good enough, so I had to drop them. You never understood friendship, or community.' She gestured around her. 'This is my café, my place. And I'm sick of your high drama. I deserve better than this, than you.'

His eyes narrowed. 'You were just a shy nobody when we met. I elevated you; put you on a pedestal. You remember, how you were so down before me?'

'No, actually.' Gina's voice grew more confident as her vision cleared. 'I don't remember it that way. I remember being an art student, playing with ideas like all creative people do.' She looked again at Mason and tried not to smile. 'And then you came into my life, like a hurricane. I let you do that to me, whip up the winds and chase my friends away. I take some responsibility for that. But no longer, Javier. I've had enough.'

His voice dropped as he squared his jaw against her. 'You don't mean that,' he said. 'After all I've done for you, to be with you.'

'I do mean it, Javier. It's over.'

'You stupid woman. You'll regret this ... and I've worked so hard, sacrificing myself to stay in this country ... I could kill you...' He looked at her then with real venom in his eyes.

'Shut it, you creep!' Joanne's voice was surprisingly loud and made him jump.

'Yeah, you can't come in here, threatening our Gina,' Alison joined in. She was standing, holding Buddy on her hip, with a look of real determination on her face.

'That's enough.' Lizl's voice sounded from behind, as she came in from the storage shed in the back garden. 'Javier, you are banned from this place. And Gina should get a restraining order against you. I'd support her.'

'You all, you were always against me. You always have been...' Javier was whining now, like a dog, beaten.

'Get the fuck out of here, Javier, or I'll call the police right now,' Lizl said. 'In fact, I think somebody already did.'

He looked alarmed then. He picked up his helmet, glared at Mason, and stomped out the door. Once outside he shout-screamed like someone who had lost something valuable. Then he kicked over the bins with a vengeance, and they rumbled to the ground in a series of muted bumps. From inside the café they heard the motorcycle start, then he moved off and the noise drifted away.

'Sorry, folks,' Lizl said with a forced cheerfulness. 'I don't usually swear.'

Gina grabbed her by the shoulder. 'Lizl, I'm so sorry. What should I do?'

'You need to be rid of him. That's all you can do.' Lizl

found the stereo remote and pumped up the Heart 80s a few notches. 'Go take a cigarette break outside back.'

'I don't smoke, you know that.'

'Go anyways. And take that handsome new guy with you.'

'If you're going to do a project on slavery,' Nanna said, 'you really might call Amara.'

Gina wished Nanna hadn't said that. Mason was there, along with Katarina and Oleg, June and Tom. Bella had wanted to invite people for a Bastille day party, it was July 14th after all. But it was so hot a day that the afternoon's energy had evaporated and they were just slumped into chairs with G&Ts. Not very French, perhaps. At least Bella was drinking some rosé.

Bella hadn't said anything about Javier's absence. Now that he had moved his papers and stuff out of her room, Gina felt a new sense of space. She had opened all the windows and pushed back the curtains, despite the sun's heat pouring in. She changed the sheets, aired the pillows, dusted the forgotten corners, swept under the bed, and felt free.

'I might not do it about Jamaica,' Gina said, in response to Nanna. 'I might focus on Brazil, with the big sugar plantations. Or the American colonies. I'm still doing my research.'

'But you'd be mad to miss the connection with Jamaica,' Bella said. 'I've never had the chance to go, but from what

Amara tells me...' Her voice trailed off in the way it did when she spoke of her daughter. Katarina and Oleg were used to it, but Mason was so new that his eyebrows perked up in confusion.

'Who's Amara?' he asked.

'My mum,' Gina said softly, more to the G&T than to him. Before any more questions could come, she got up to see how Katarina and Oleg were doing in the kitchen.

She caught them in a moment – Katarina had her hands in oven gloves, holding the skillet to flip the crêpes, in nearly circular shapes. Not perfect, but authentic; that was what homemade crêpes should look like. Oleg stood behind her, arms wrapped around her waist, probably hindering the movements, but from the look on her face the embrace was welcome. She was laughing at something he whispered in her ear. In watching that moment Gina she saw them both in a new way, something usually hidden from view. They had a tenderness between them that lingered. And people who could be sweet like that to each other also radiated a kind of joy to others, that's what it felt like.

'Oh Gina, you surprised me.' Katarina pushed away from Oleg's embrace to focus on the crêpes again.

'Sorry! Just seeking another drink. How are the crêpes?

'Well, I don't know if it's the French way,' Oleg said, 'and it's definitely not Russian. Maybe a kind of Polish improvisation going on.'

Gina looked at the new stack, and the one in the pan. 'Looks fine.'

'Well, you're an uncritical crowd,' Oleg said. He had a

funny way of smiling with a frown, as if his face was built to be sarcastic. 'I'll wait for the taste-test.'

When she turned to go back to the sitting room, Mason was standing in the doorway. 'Sorry,' he said.

She still wasn't used to him being close to her. His face was so handsome, she had to blink sometimes to believe it. He kept it shaved and smooth. His hair was held back with a band, not touching his shoulders. His eyes held a natural neutral expression with a tinge of sadness. But usually, in her company, he looked happy.

'What do you have to be sorry for?' she said.

'Asking about your mum... I don't mean to pry.'

'No, it's not that. It's just that Nanna always gets sad when she thinks about my mum. They never talk, it's not like a normal relationship. And when she does call us, she always forgets what it's like here.' She lowered her voice so Nanna wouldn't hear. 'She missed everything about my childhood. Missed my first steps, first day at school, everything. And she calls me "baby girl" on the rare times when I speak with her, like she's forgotten that twenty years have gone by since she lived in England. She doesn't know anything about us, really. It's a bit painful.'

She realised that she was bringing the mood down, and that wasn't what she wanted to do. Not on Bastille Day, for God's sake. 'Anyway, she's a queen of all these hotels. Probably what she's really worried about is that I'll bring some motley crew like you lot out to Jamaica and try to move in!'

'To the top suite!' Katarina said with a grin.

'Ocean views!' Oleg added.

'With our own private cruise ship, that we pirated away from some blue-haired old ladies playing bridge!' Mason said. She liked that about him, and the others, too. They could acknowledge that it was tough; yet they were able to dance around it in a way that made it feel less heavy. It was still there, this thing about Mum; they couldn't erase it. But they made it smaller, somehow, with their presence.

Nanna might have had too much to drink. Her cheeks were rosy and her eyelids were lowering. She wore a thin yellow cotton dress, one from the 70s that still looked nice with her black hair, streaked with grey. It was usually up in a bun, but today it was down in a long plait roped past her shoulder blades.

Gina came back into the sitting room to see Nanna patting Tom's hand on the arm of her sitting chair. Nanna's eyes were red-rimmed and looked like they might well over.

'The last time I remember it this hot,' she said, and Gina knew what was coming next. She wished she had intervened earlier, had some segue from the conversation that always unfurled when Nanna brought up the summer of 1976.

'My dear late husband, taken too soon. It was such a hot summer. And hospitals then, you know, had no kind of air conditioning. The ventilation was inadequate.' She let go of Tom's hand a moment to press back some imaginary stray hairs behind her ears. 'I was working too, in the maternity ward. The babies, the mothers ... you worried about heatstroke. Sometimes we had to put a wet flannel on those little babies' chests, just to keep them cool. And we'd fan them like this.' She demonstrated with her free hand, like she had a small baby on her lap.

She smiled then. 'My girl was grown by then, so both Aday and I spent all our hours at work. Amara was finishing her degree at SOAS, saving up money to travel the world, you see. My husband, he was going to go with her to Africa, to meet his family after all those years, but it didn't happen. You see, the heat...' She stopped.

Gina felt obligated to finish the sentence, it was unfair to the people listening not to. 'He died that summer,' she said.

'Of heatstroke?' asked June.

'No, just stroke,' Nanna said. 'He was working too hard. I should have got him to slow down.'

No one knew what to say then, so it was a relief when Katarina and Oleg came in with a plate piled high with crêpes of different shapes and sizes. They put them on the table and people could decorate them as they liked, sweet or savoury, whatever they pleased.

Nanna fell asleep in her chair, but the night was still young and clear, so the rest of them took the party outside into the small garden. It wasn't much, and Gina never took the time to cut back the hedges and make it into a properly nice garden, but there were benches and these old rose bushes planted by the Spanish couple who had gifted the house to Nanna. The smell of the roses in the July heat was strong, like someone had spilled perfume around the place. If you closed your eyes, you didn't have to be in London. You could be in Morocco, or Turkey, or anywhere. Except the sound of sirens brought you back, and you remembered you lived in Lewisham after all.

June had found some sparklers at a high street shop, and Gina went to get the Shabbat matches from the kitchen windowsill. They lit them and laughed like kids. Holding them together at first, it made a big ball of light in the middle.

Gina looked around at the faces around the lit-up flares, shaped by sparks and shadow, each delighted in their own way. Then they pulled apart and drew patterns and swirls in the air before the sparklers started to die away.

'What am I writing? See if you can guess,' Mason said.

She looked at his shapes in the air. 'Sparkler?'

'Summer!' he said and kept writing more in the air like a kid with a magic wand.

'How 'bout this one?' June asked.

'Life?' ventured Gina.

'Love,' said Tom, certainty in his voice.

'How cheesy,' said Oleg.

'He always guesses,' June said, sounding almost disappointed. 'I can never catch him out.'

Chapter Thirty

1977

Working at the hospital never felt the same after Aday died. Or probably Bella herself changed, and the hospital, being made out of concrete and glass, did not bend to soothe her mind. It remained the same geometrically planned, static place where people with their hopes and worries and worst nightmares came in and out of the revolving doors. But she was not the same. Her broken heart never regained its strong beat after that. Funny what people say about hearts. After you lose the one you love, it really does feel like it is going to break. Like something is so fragile inside you, something you never knew was fragile, and it will crack like the shell of an egg and beat no more. And you are shocked, because despite the folk tales and the warnings, you never expected the protective membrane to be that fragile, for something so important.

But you have life still. You are breathing and have your child and your community and your work … and somehow you live. But it is a mystery, how the heart continues to beat when it has been broken.

In Lewisham Hospital, it was a different feeling than when she was no longer the wife of the prominent doctor. By the time Aday died, there were many more people from different countries around. No one talked about the colonies anymore. Bella started working again as a nurse, and she had friends from Jamaica, India, Ghana, Brazil, Portugal, Ireland … the list was long. It changed the texture of the place and made her feel less like an outsider and not so alone. After Aday died, and suddenly Christiana's large house was just for her and Amara, she would have felt lost without the friendship of other women. People who knew her from before, whom she didn't have to explain herself to. That's probably what saved her sanity, when she had lost half of herself.

Bella was too caught up in the dark clouds of despair those first few months to be a good mother. It is hard to pay attention to others when your heart has been wrenched from your body, when all your plans for the future had come to a sudden halt. She found that she fell back into thinking in French, something that had been banished to the back of her mind for many years, as she didn't share that language with Aday.

Irrational thoughts whirled through her mind at night. She kept thinking about her mother and father. Were they somewhere with Aday? Did they know each other? Were they watching her? Were they close by, near enough to touch? At times when London descended into fog, it was almost believable that the spirits were still there, whispering at the edges. You couldn't quite believe that the people who had been so vibrant, part of your every day, were just suddenly gone.

She woke up at night, reached over to his side of the bed, and was frightened and saddened once again that he was not there, would never be there again. She tried to hide her sobs from her daughter over mealtimes, but when that effort became too much she retreated to her bedroom.

She heard the outside door close. She realised that Amara, mourning her father in her own way, had started walking the streets at night.

She always returned, sometimes in the early morning hours, sometimes after dawn. Bella, a light sleeper, would wake to hear the key turn in the lock. But Amara was a young woman now, she didn't have to explain herself to her mother or anyone. In fact, she was nearly the age when Bella met Aday. Bella couldn't stop her from wandering, couldn't admonish her for doing so.

But as the weeks passed and Bella started to come out of her deep moments of sadness, there were cracks where curiosity seeped in. Where did the girl go? Should she be concerned? Surely a mother should know these things, *non*?

One night, Bella went to her bedroom early, and heard Amara go out the door as usual. It was summer, and only just past sunset. Bella quickly put on her mac and shoes and ran out behind her daughter. She saw Amara turn the corner and walk towards Lewisham High Street. She followed at a distance, praying that Amara wouldn't turn around. The girl looked left and right at the crossroads, but never behind; she didn't expect to be followed, and that brought Bella some comfort. Amara was confident walking the streets of southeast London. Bella and Aday had raised a proud girl who knew she had the right to be there.

Bella was a little mixed up in the different back streets. In evening walks she always used to have Aday with her, trusting his sense of direction over her own. And there was still a feeling that a small woman of her generation shouldn't walk at night by herself. But there was her daughter, tall and unafraid, going wherever she wanted. Bella took courage from that.

Amara turned onto the main street and stopped under the awning of a 1950s building. Bella realised it was the Lewisham Library. It was closed at this hour, surely? In any case, that did not seem to deter Amara. She folded up a jumper and put it under her bum, then sat on the sidewalk. She took out a book and started to read in the streetlamps coming from under the awning. It couldn't have been good for her eyes; if Aday was here he would have scolded her for not looking after her vision. In fact, Bella nearly walked up to her to say the same, but she stopped herself.

For some reason, her grown daughter was more content reading out here in the open, in the semi-darkness, than in her own home. Was this from sadness, missing her father? Was it the sense of his absence in every room of the house? Or was it something else? A chance to claim her own space, away from her mother and father, her late godparents, and everyone that came before?

Amara was her own girl now. No, Bella corrected herself, as she watched Amara twirl a plait around her finger while she read. Amara was a woman who would decide her own story.

Amara felt like she was being watched, but when she looked back, no one was there. Probably just her imagination. She didn't know why she was drawn to this spot, sitting in front of the library after dark, reading by the light of a streetlamp not far away. She just couldn't stay in that house. The weight of sadness pulled down at her shoulders, her scalp, her muscles and bones. Bone-tired. She understood why Mama went to bed so early, and sometimes stayed there all day. That was what older people did. But not younger people. That felt all wrong, when what she wanted to do was just get up, get out, throw off this sadness and replace it with something else. Something that suited her age, and her times.

'Hey,' a man's voice called out to her, calm and quiet. He stepped forward. He was slim and wearing jeans and a jumper, despite the summer months.

'I've seen you before,' he said.

She didn't know how to respond to that, even though she wanted to say something clever. 'You have?'

'You like books.' He came up and sat down beside her. 'That's cool.'

'Do you like to read?' She shuffled a bit so that their hips wouldn't touch in the small space afforded by the steps of the library.

'I'm a student at UCL,' he said. 'You?'

'I'm at SOAS.'

'Where all the smartest kids go. Why don't you study at the library there?'

'I'm not studying.' She waved the book at him. 'I read fiction to escape.'

'I would too, if I had time.'

'You're too busy?'

'I'm an organiser. Against the racists. Do you know what they are trying to do here?'

She listened to what he had to say and took a leaflet about the big anti-racist rally in August. She wanted to be part of the movement, but what would Papa say? He had been her compass. All his life he'd steered well clear of riots and protests. He would see it as people causing trouble or putting themselves in harm's way. He wouldn't approve of her joining in.

But Papa was gone now. She had to find her own direction and decide on her own.

Chapter Thirty-One

1978

What was just supposed to be a short trip to Jamaica to celebrate Amara finishing her degree stretched into a longer stay, then a job. She called home every week, with news of sunshine, promotions, new friendships. She sounded like a new person, breezy and hopeful. She bore little resemblance to the moody teenager, nose in the books, who'd lost her father two years before.

Bella didn't fight it. She hid her loneliness and let her only child share bits of news over a scratchy phone line. She sent Amara traveller's cheques through special post and supported her bid to buy into a hotel business with the money they recovered from Aday's life insurance. Bella received a postcard with a profile of the hotel at sunset, a beach scene with palm trees and silhouettes of a couple holding hands. It was all utterly foreign to her, but of course she could not object.

She asked Nellie what she thought. Nellie was a nurse too, from Ghana. She had the confidence of a woman who had fought for recognition all her life and earned it. She was taller and physically stronger than Bella, and sometimes they worked together if there was a larger patient or someone Bella couldn't manage on her own. In fact, Bella often had no problems, as she was persuasive and direct, and the drunks or belligerents were stunned to be told off and put in their place by the little lady with a French accent. But sometimes it was just a question of sheer might, and then Bella asked for help from the taller nurses or the porters.

Nellie was very matter-of-fact about Amara's travels. 'She's found herself,' she said. 'She was lost in London, never made her way, never found her community. You raised her well, with Aday, but the three of you were like boats tied to each other's anchor. Or he was the anchor, and now it leaves you and Amara to drift.' Nellie ran her tongue behind her teeth to click. 'You can't fight that. You can't fight a grown woman, even if she is your daughter.'

Bella knew her friend was right, although something in her still wanted to object.

'But what about you?' Nellie said, reaching out to touch Bella's unwashed curls. 'You are letting yourself go.'

'What do I care what I look like?' Bella said. 'There's no one around to see me now.'

'*You* are here to see you, don't you care?' Nellie's

expression softened. 'You have such pretty hair, and your eyes behind those glasses too, it's no wonder why that man was smitten. But you have to go on living with yourself, so keep on living!'

'This is what you are gonna do,' Nellie continued. 'You are going to go home after this shift, and clean yourself up. Treat yourself to a couple of magazines, *Vogue* or something. Take a long bath. Then go to the salon and make a change. Maybe paint your nails too.' Bella looked down at her ragged hands, wrinkled before her time, nails chipped and uneven.

'You're going to come to our house for dinner one night, and then on the weekend we'll go to the cinema. What do you say?' Nellie's face was suddenly sweet and hopeful, like a friend from childhood.

Bella was surprised at how forceful the woman was being. But something in her liked being told what to do at that moment. She nodded and reached forward to put her hand on Nellie's. While she still had life in her, she had to keep living. But with Aday gone and Amara so far away, it was hard to see the reasons why. Better not to examine things closely. Just accept the kindness and keep going.

'I can't breathe here, Mama,' Amara had said on one of her rare trips back to London. 'You know that.'

Bella tried to understand. 'Your asthma, is that it?'

'It's more than that. I wish you would come to Jamaica. The air is cleaner, and the pace is slower.'

'But the pollution here, it's not so bad. I don't cough anymore.'

'Mama, you know I have to live on the inhalers when I am here. The air's no good for me. You and Papa tried everything, I know you did.'

'But this is home; this is where you grew up!' Bella felt tears coming to the surface whenever she reached this point in conversations with her daughter. She didn't know why. Even just the mention of the word 'home' was enough to make her feel like she had personally failed. She had started with less than nothing. No family support, just admission to a nursing school based on false papers, that was all. And a good head on her shoulders. But Amara didn't see that they'd made a home, this family legacy was hers. It was all her mother and father had to give her. No, it was just too painful.

'Mama, don't cry. Please don't cry. You know, I have tried. When Papa was alive'—Amara's voice failed then, as it often did when talking about Aday—'it was better. But it's so different in Jamaica. I can be me there. I have the hotel we bought, the staff. People give me respect. No one judges me by the colour of my skin, or my south London accent. They don't decide who you are on first glance. They see me for being me, not just a member of a category they don't like.'

Bella never had an answer for that. She couldn't control what other people did, or what they saw. She only knew that her beautiful, majestic, tall daughter, with her father's royal lineage, felt like she could not come back to London.

Something about the political work she did in the year after Aday's death foreshadowed this decision, but that wasn't all.

She never made a home here. She didn't put down roots, and the ones her parents tried to plant for her proved too shallow. She didn't have the friendships or the community, for some reason. Bella had to admit that London had failed their daughter.

Chapter Thirty-Two

1989

There was little mention of the father, but Amara couldn't hide her condition when she came to visit in the spring before the baby was due. Bella stroked her daughter's hand, trying to understand what was going on in her mind.

The baby was about to arrive, kicking and turning inside. The child changed everything about their conversations about home, about work. The child needed somewhere to live, and a family. But there Amara was, a thirty-five-year-old woman, unmarried, and rootless.

'I don't know, Mama.' Suddenly Amara's face looked like the child she had been, or the teenager. When she was searching for an explanation for what bullies did in the playground. Things she told only Aday, never Bella. Bella was left to intuit the gist of the stories and imagine the rest.

It made her heart ache when her daughter looked at her with those perfect brown eyes, with flecks of yellow like the tiger's eye stones. They would always be the most beautiful eyes Bella had ever seen.

'Don't worry. We will figure it out, my love.' Bella changed her tone and took charge. She would midwife this child into the world. 'We will do it together.'

The birth was easy, with no complications. Bella hoped the experience was what Amara wanted, but there wasn't really time to check. There was no man there, to be fair. Some women did want the father to be at the birth, but Bella thought that was unnecessary. Men had their strengths, but most of them—Aday excepted, of course—did not have the temperament to be that close to the moment of birth.

When Sandrine was born, little Drina, there was only one parent on the birth certificate. That made Bella so sad, she wanted to put her own name in the second spot. Just to show that family was there. She would make sure that this child would have family, even if it was not the conventional kind.

But Amara didn't seem to have the normal feelings of a mother when the newborn was placed in her arms. She held the child, if she had to. But she had a look about her, like a bird who finds an imposter chick in its nest. Bella knew from experience as a nurse that childbirth can change a woman, at that moment, or over the following days and weeks. But there was something unexpected about Amara, how she first held that child with a blank look in her eyes. How she pushed the baby to Bella to give her a bottle, didn't hold her to her breast despite urging.

Over the first weeks and months, Amara seemed to have lost the capacity for delight or any emotion. Bella tried to help Amara play the role of mother. She brought mother and baby home and set up a cot alongside Amara's childhood bed. She bought packs of disposable nappies, so Amara wouldn't be tied up with boiling and hanging out linen. She heard the baby cry in the night and made bottles, letting Amara sleep. But her grown daughter seemed to sink into sadness and couldn't surface from the depths. It was deeper than after Aday's death. Like she was hollowed out from the inside, nothing left but a fragile casing.

Amara didn't get out of bed unless physically pulled. She did not look in the mirror; her beautiful thick hair grew matted and knotted. Bella did not know what to do. She was still working shifts at the hospital and hoped that the baby wouldn't be trouble for the hours when she was away. Amara seemed not to notice when a nappy was dirty, or the child needed to be held. Her mind remained at a distance, never attached to the child or the present moment.

'*Cherie*, I understand how you can have low moods.' Bella tried to talk about it. 'I used to have them too. Do you remember, when you were a child? But I managed to pull myself out of it. You have a child now, something to live for, non?'

'I don't want to talk about it, Mama,' Amara replied in a monotone. 'You wouldn't understand.'

They couldn't continue like that. Bella asked Nellie what to do. Nellie had raised her children in New Cross. She had her children and her children's children under one roof and seemed to manage well. When Bella described the state that Amara was in, Nellie didn't hesitate.

'She needs help, Bella. Not everyone is born to be a mother. Sometimes the shock is too great. Not everyone has that caring instinct. Sometimes women lose it.'

Once it had been stated so plainly, Bella saw it, of course. But she felt a deep shame. How could she have failed so badly? To have a daughter who could not care for her own child. She wished again for the thousandth time that Aday had lived longer. He had been the only one who Amara confided in, and his guidance tethered the girl to community and to home. There was nothing Bella could do or say that helped and held onto Amara in the same way.

Nellie promised that her teenage granddaughter could come and look after the baby in the afternoons. And she gave Bella the number of a lady who would come to the house and sort out Amara's hair. 'Let see what we can do to make her feel better about herself,' Nellie said. 'Maybe she's missing who she was in Jamaica, you know. An independent businesswoman, the world at her feet. I've heard the water there is so good for the hair and the skin. She might feel like she's not herself here.'

Nellie was right, and the lady who came to tackle Amara's hair was the first person to coax a smile from her in a long time. She was from Jamaica herself and had heard of Amara's hotels. Over the course of a few hours, sitting at the kitchen table, the woman massaged conditioner into Amara's long, tangled hair. She picked her way through the knots and found the shape of the curls again, all the while talking about home.

The baby, now two months old, lay on a blanket in the living room. Bella looked over and saw her eyes wide open, fists tight around a small toy. The baby moved her head as if she was listening to the different women's voices in the kitchen. She hadn't heard much of her mother's voice so far. Bella picked her up and brought her closer, so she could watch what was happening.

The woman moved into cornrowing the hair, 'to keep it tidy here, where the air is so dry,' she said. Amara complained slightly about the pulling, but in a way that made clear she was here in the moment, paying attention to something for the first time in weeks. As she relaxed and let the other woman's fingers twist across her scalp, she let the words flow about Jamaica. Her hotels – she owned two, and hoped to buy another two next year. She spoke about the staff she had left in charge of the places, and their personalities and stories. They were trustworthy, she was sure. But when you are not there for long, there could be difficulties later. Decisions you need to take, on a monthly basis, maintenance and choices. If you're not there to take them, well … you could lose control. You might lose everything you had built.

As the lady finished with the plaits, she asked if Amara wanted beads on the ends.

Amara smiled then, a broad smile. 'Like the market girls, you mean?'

'It's not just for the girls. You can have it any way you want.'

'Okay. Let's have it the Jamaican way,' she said. She looked in the mirror and seemed pleased with the results.

Bella watched her daughter, this girl grown into a woman, and was struck again by how beautiful she was. She looked so much like Aday, and yet was her own woman, with a female grace that she could claim all to herself. But it was also a mystery, and a painful one at that, how deeply she as a mother knew her child, but how opaque Amara remained. A child, once so close to her breast, had always been and will always be separate and free to make her own choices and mistakes.

What was she thinking, this woman who buys hotels but who could not embrace her new baby?

What was she going to do?

Bella finished a long day shift, ready to head home. When the baby couldn't be with Nellie's granddaughter, she was watched over by an old neighbour who was good with children. But it would be better to get home as soon as possible. Poor thing, it wasn't much of a life being shuttled between a teenager and old women for your care while Amara was having a short visit home to check on her businesses.

She went to the nurse's station to tell Nellie she was

done for the day. However, Nellie was waving her arms to urge her to the phone.

'It's a call from Jamaica,' she said.

She rushed over. 'Is something wrong?'

'No, it is just Amara. Here.'

Bella held onto the receiver, and Amara asked her how she was, but she didn't listen to the answer. Amara rushed into a long speech, and Bella realised that her daughter had been preparing this. She had only been away for a week; it was supposed to be a short stop, to make sure that her affairs were in order and the hotels were running smoothly in her absence. She didn't take the baby, of course, because, well … four months was too young to travel. It can be torture on the ears, the poor things, to take babies on a plane. And Amara was still not very good with Drina's crying. She was a bit better than before, but no matter how patient Bella was in teaching her the basics, Amara didn't seem to know how to soothe the child. They would wind each other up, a new mother and an increasingly frantic little one.

On the phone, Bella listened to what was not being said. It was clear that Amara had made up her mind.

'You're not coming back,' Bella interrupted. Her heart felt alarmed and that was no good for anyone. She needed to sit down. She gestured to Nellie to give her the stool and was able to perch while she listened to her daughter plead her absence.

Amara hesitated a moment then carried on. 'There are so many things I need to take care of here, Mama. If I take my eyes off of it, the business could be at a disadvantage. Everything I've built could come crumbling down.'

'But what about Sandrine? You have a child now.'

'That's what I'm talking about, Mama. That's why I need you to say that she can stay with you.'

'Stay with me, for how long?'

'I'll send you money, Mama, don't worry about that.'

'It's not about money, *ma cherie*. It's about...' Bella stopped. How do you explain the maternal instinct to someone who seemed to lack it entirely? 'It's about taking care.'

'Mama,' Amara let out a long sigh. 'Please don't make it difficult. This is hard for me. You know I hate London. It's not a good place for me. And I'm not good with babies. I'm not good with her. I don't have it in me, that magic touch. I'm not like you.'

'I raised you. I learned it.'

'You are brilliant with her, Mama. You always are.'

Bella wanted to contradict her. To tell her all the reasons why she should come back. To say that she's an old woman and had already lost a husband. She wanted to stop working soon, put her feet up. Maybe travel with Nellie or some other friends. Go to Jamaica herself, on a cruise, like a lady of leisure.

But what she said was, 'If that's what you want.' She felt heavy on the wooden NHS stool. *'Comme tu veux.'*

Amara gushed thanks and rang off quickly, saying she would call again soon to talk more. There would be no chance to change her mind.

Bella heard the relief in her daughter's voice, and remembered how low Amara was in her days in London. It was right, she couldn't breathe here. She wouldn't thrive. Like a plant, she had to find a habitat that suited her. But that left behind a child, a child now entrusted to Bella alone.

Chapter Thirty-Three

August 2011

A London double-decker bus was on fire on the BBC. Gina wouldn't have believed it if it hadn't been for the headline beneath: 'London in Flames: Tottenham riots.'

'What's going on?' She came closer to Bella's chair, both of them leaning towards the television. She could tell that Bella was listening intently.

'There is some trouble in north London,' Bella said. 'The police went and killed a boy, and when their family marched for justice, riots broke out.'

Gina looked at the scenes playing out in front of her. Rows of shops with broken glass, spilt piles of produce or trainers or electronics stomped on, destroyed or looted. A woman in a nightdress jumping from a first-floor balcony above a shop on fire. This was London?

'I'm worried, *cherie*. It could be like before, when Amara first left London.'

Gina patted Nanna's hand. She didn't know what to say to make her feel better. A man's face came up in a photograph, the guy shot by police. Underneath the headline said: 'Mark Duggan's death to be investigated.' He wasn't a boy, really, but she could see why Nanna felt that way. To a woman in her eighties, everyone was a boy. It was clear that the Duggan family deserved answers, that it could be another case of police brutality and cover-ups. When the TV just kept repeating the same videos over and over, Gina turned it off.

They were surprised by the ringing phone. No one ever used the landline, except if they were looking for lodging, or if it was a call from Jamaica.

'Are you okay?' Amara's voice was breathy and light, an ocean away. 'I saw the news, about the riots.'

'Oh, that's not here,' Gina said. 'You remember, north London is like another country.'

'But you know, they could spread. Look at history, these things can spark problems in other places.'

'That's kind of jumping to conclusions, don't you think?'

'Baby girl, I lived there my whole life until I was twenty-two.'

'I'm twenty-two.' Gina paused a moment to see if her mum remembered. 'Anyway, it was different back then. And you know, I don't need to be called "baby girl". I've graduated from uni now.'

'Yes, course you have. But, you know, England has never

been that great in how it treats black people.' She sounded resentful and distant. '1977 – the Battle of Lewisham. Did they teach you that in school?'

'I did art, remember? Not history.'

'History lessons haven't changed much since the times when it was all Henry VIII and the Blitz and that's about it. I was there in 1977. The police brutality would leave you speechless.' Amara gave a sour laugh.

'Why are you laughing? London is my home, our home!' Gina felt tension rise in her throat. She didn't like these phone calls from far away, throwing blame around but not actually living near enough to experience it. 'Don't go rubbishing London.'

'No, babyg— I mean Gina. Honey, that's not what I'm saying.'

'I don't know what you're trying to say. Why do you even bother calling, when you haven't visited in years? Where were you when Nanna was in hospital? Or when my friend went missing?'

'Your friend went missing?'

'No, we found her...' Gina's thoughts jumbled in her head but then grew more clear. 'The point is, Nanna and me, this is our home. If it has problems, we have to deal with them. Together, with the people around us. We try to find good people around us, because ... well, family just aren't here.'

'You know I'd be there if I could, my asthma....'

'Yeah, I know. Your asthma. You miss everything, Mum. If you don't understand that, then I can't explain it to you. It's like art.' She thought of June's dark paintings hanging in the Royal Drawing School show, Mason's collages made on his loom, and her own figures, playing out the different scenarios for the next piece in her mind. 'If you don't see it for yourself, you'll never really have the experience. You missed my first steps, my first boyfriend, all my art shows. It's too late, Mum, to be worried about us now.'

'If that's the way you feel.' She sounded offended. 'Just forget it. Can you pass me to Nanna?'

Gina looked over at Bella, about to give her the phone, but then stopped. Perhaps it was the worry from the TV, but she had nodded off. 'Sorry, she's asleep in her chair.'

'Tell her she can call me anytime. And you know, you could always come out here to visit, spend some time here. You both could.'

'No, thanks though.' Gina looked over at Bella, her small frame sinking into the corner of the worn armchair. Eighty-two was too old to fly, Amara should know that. 'This is where I belong.'

'Think about it. And Gina?'

'Hmmm?'

'I'm sorry.' Amara's voice was low now, and the sirens outside threatened to drown out her words. 'I am so sorry with how I've missed so much. Some people just aren't capable of certain things, even though they should be. I was pretty broken down when you were born; I needed to put myself back together and build my life here. And whenever I saw you, you were so happy with Nanna. You seemed to be thriving in a way I never did. So I didn't see a reason to change things, to uproot you.'

'I'm glad you didn't,' Gina said without thinking. 'I would have hated to leave Nanna, to leave London.'

'That's what I thought.' Amara hung up without saying goodbye.

Gina took a deep breath. She didn't know what made her speak so plainly to Amara, but it felt right to do it today. And Amara was a grown woman, she should be able to hear the truth.

Just then, footsteps came up from the basement flat. Katarina emerged and saw Gina standing in the doorway of the kitchen.

'Cup of tea?' Gina asked, hoping she would say yes.

Katarina had her nurse's uniform on already. 'Sorry, lovely, I have to get to the hospital. It's my shift tonight and they are worried about these riots.' She moved towards the door.

'Wait,' Gina said, surprising them both. Katarina turned, hand on the doorknob, and looked back at her.

In a rush, Gina came over and hugged her. 'Be careful,' she said.

'I'll be fine,' Katarina replied, with a look of confidence on her face that said she could handle anything.

It should have been a normal August day, but the air was different. There was a horrible smell, of burnt tyres and pollution and something rotten you never wanted to be close to. From listening to the news again this morning, the riots had spread. There was looting and fires in a few more places, and people were worried about Brixton, Croydon, and Lewisham too.

At home, there were more calls from concerned people – mainly Nanna's retired nurse friends wanting to make sure everything was all right. Some lived in London, but others had moved to the countryside or abroad. Still, they cared about Nanna and the lives they used to live, entwined in each other's day through work and community. To each of them Gina gave reassurances, while still keeping one ear listening to the radio or TV. Even French radio was now reporting on the London riots. It was eerie to be in the centre of world attention for all the wrong reasons.

There were none of the regulars at the café that day. Alison and the other mums' groups didn't show. Joanne stopped by, but didn't stay. Lizl came around two and said they should close early.

'There could be more trouble tonight,' Lizl said. The news services and the Blackberries and Twitter were getting alarmed about messages spreading, violence being orchestrated in different places across the city. Other cities too – there were rumours about Manchester, Birmingham, Nottingham. It wasn't clear why, what was the reason why one incident had sparked so much violence and anger, and why there were so many people caught up in it all. Lizl asked for help with putting some boarding over the windows. She worried it might draw attention to the café, rather than protect it, but she didn't want to risk the glass shattering.

'We'll just have to cross our fingers and hope for the best,' Lizl said with false cheerfulness, but she did take away all the money from the till at 3pm and left a large new sign saying: NO MONEY OR VALUABLES LEFT OVERNIGHT ON THE PREMISES.

As Gina walked home early, she wondered if there was something she could do. Shouldn't she be volunteering to help somebody, the firefighters or some orphans or something? Of course, she needed to take care of Nanna and make sure nothing worried her. She sped up, but just then she heard a motorcycle coming around the corner. The engine noise made her shoulders rise defensively, as it pulled up next to her.

It was Javier. She hadn't seen him in over a month, and she realised that she hadn't thought of him in nearly as long. It was peculiar, that someone could occupy your mind to such a dramatic extent, and then, somehow, just evaporate. She steeled herself for a confrontation.

'Hey,' he said, much more gentle than she had expected. He put his feet down and turned off the engine, taking his helmet off too. He was sweaty with all the bike gear on, and looked tired. Maybe the heat was tiring some people out, while it wound other people up.

'Hey,' she said.

'How are you?' he asked, in a way that she hadn't heard in a long time. Like he actually wanted to know the answer.

'I'm okay,' she said, wondering what was coming next.

'You and Bella, are you all right with these riots? I wanted to check on you.'

'Oh.' She relaxed her shoulders. 'We're fine. It's not near us, not at the moment, anyway. Lizl's more worried about the café, to be honest.' She remembered Javier kicking the bins over, and wished she hadn't mentioned it.

'Ah, Lizl and the café…' He didn't go on.

'How are you, and the research?'

'I got some funding through … I wanted to tell you. I'm not so stressed anymore.'

'That's great news, Javier. I'm really happy for you. Truly.'

There was an awkward moment, and then he let it out in a rush: 'I just wanted to say I'm sorry, about everything,' he said. 'I was an arsehole, blaming everything on you. You know what they say, mean people are actually unhappy people. I wasn't happy, you were right … I know you deserve more, but I can be a better man, so much better … if you wanted to give me another chance—'

She cut him off. 'No, it's over now. I've moved on.'

He winced, but when his face relaxed he just looked sad.

'Anyway.' He started the engine again. 'I thought … if you or Bella need anything in the next few days or weeks, you know you can always ring.'

She nodded, wondering if she would ever see him again.

'Ciao,' he said, then put on his helmet and she couldn't see his expression anymore.

. . .

That night the sirens went wild, wailing all the time. The news was confusing and contradictory. The family of the man who was killed appealed for calm, but everything seemed to be out of control.

Mason came over to watch the news with them, but not much could be said. They could tell from the smell of the heat and the pollution in the air that the riots were near. But without going out into the night, they had no idea how close, or what was happening. It was a terrible feeling, not knowing.

Nanna fell asleep again in front of the TV. It was happening more often now. Gina hoped it wasn't a sign of her health going downhill. When was the last time she had seen the GP or health visitor? Gina would have to ring soon.

Mason helped; together they carried Bella to bed. She was so light that he could have done it alone, but Nanna wouldn't have liked that. She didn't know him that well, not yet.

They laid her down fully clothed on top of the sheet. It was hot, and with the window closed against the smoke outside it was nearly unbearable. Gina pulled off Nanna's slippers and turned on a fan. Nanna sometimes said she didn't like the vibrations – she felt them even when she wasn't bothered by the noise. But tonight there was no objection and no waking her. She slept with a worried expression on her face.

Mason stayed over that night. He slipped behind Gina when they both were pretending they were asleep. They stayed like that for most of the night. There wasn't anything to say that hadn't already been said. They were worried for their city, but they had little information. Not quite brave enough to go see it for themselves with their own eyes in the darkness, they needed day to break.

But the night held on. The sky was disturbed, with flashes of light pollution and blue lights circling round, even when the sirens grew quieter after midnight. At one point, Gina's mind went to Jamaica and she wondered why she had never taken up Amara's offer of spending some time in the Caribbean. It was mainly because of Bella, but Gina wasn't too bothered about going. In the back of her mind, she didn't know who Amara was. She had been a depressing character in the few times when they had spent Christmas together, hard to understand, especially when Gina was young. Most of the time, Amara was just an absence. And about Gina's father, there was a resounding silence. Gina had never known about him, and probably never would.

And anyway, she didn't feel a pull towards the sea. She was so used to London, after all. Even when it was burning, it was home.

Chapter Thirty-Four

1977

'Fuck off back to Africa!' The racists screamed.
One of them lost hold of their banner and it fluttered over the shoulders and heads of the police. A woman in Amara's line reached up, and before the policeman swung a baton she managed to grab the banner by the corner. She was an older white lady with grey-streaked hair in a bun falling out at the sides. Her bottom front teeth were missing, so her chin had that look like it was curling in on itself. Pure delight splashed across her face. Amara had never seen her before, and probably never would again, but in that moment, they were on the same side, the right side.

There was more shouting and pushing, and then she heard, 'We broke through!' All heads craned to the middle, where the protestors had pressed against the police lines and unexpectedly found a weak link. Like a sandbank being breached, the anti-racists flowed in at the same time as peaches, tomatoes, rocks and other projectiles were launched. The police split into two, and the fascists cowered in both directions.

A murmur went through the protesting crowd. "We broke the lines, the police lines!' Whistles rang out louder than before, cheering rising up with shouting. The pandemonium grew, and the racists were pushed apart and back. Amara had never heard of this happening before, and it felt like no one knew what to do next.

'We can stop them before the clock tower!'

With the others, she started to run down towards the high street. 'They can't keep going!' someone shouted. 'Send them cowering back!' The mood was jubilant. There was music playing out of the flat windows above the shops, Bob Marley pumping from the speakers. Amara was laughing and wishing she had someone to be there with. Someone who understood what this all meant.

When she reached the clock tower on the high street, it was a real celebration. Justice had won, and the racists had been defeated by sheer people power. Protestors stopped traffic and there was dancing in the streets. People were hugging each other, strangers acting like old friends. Amara had long lost track of the Quaker guy and the French couple. Her eyes searched for the student from the library or anyone she knew. No matter. She was hugged and given high-fives from a number of random people, feeling part of it all.

She could see up the road to the intersection leading to New Cross, and she wondered if the fascists were going to try to keep marching, or if they would turn back. She imagined they were humiliated by now. She started thinking about how she would describe it to Mama. About the looks on their faces, about the shred of the banner that the old lady got to keep. Mama wouldn't approve, of course, but if she was told after the fact, she could probably see its importance, and how Amara simply had to be part of it.

'Defeated! They're abandoning their course!' The call came out from a man with a megaphone, and the crowd cheered and hollered. The racists, still protected by lines of police despite their numbers diminishing, turned to retreat from the high street. The atmosphere around the clock tower was something special: there were people still trying to give out the *Socialist Worker* free flyers, talking politics despite no one really listening, while groups of people shared cigarettes and laughed. You could tell from the accents that they were from the Caribbean or the States or from up North and other places, but they shared some common roots or beliefs. The Irish nuns were there in habits with large crosses dangling from chains around their necks; the hippies had their tie-dyes; the Indians and the Sikhs, and the students from Goldsmiths up the road, they were all there too.

Amara moved back into the centre of everything. For a

moment she closed her eyes and just held out her hands, people brushing up against her good-naturedly. She turned around to absorb all of the energy, music and sound, and thought to herself: *Yes! This is London.*

No one noticed the change in police tactics, until they were nearly upon them.

'What the hell?' Amara opened her eyes, but she couldn't see through the crowd. She heard the sound of hooves moving in concert. People started to panic and tried to run in all directions. Others stood where they were, with stiffened shoulders. You could no longer hear the music or feel the mood of the celebration.

'We ain't doin' nothing wrong!' a man called out with a megaphone from the second floor of a flat above the shops. 'We ain't the racists!'

The noise of the hooves grew louder, and faster. Then Amara saw them, the mounted police that had the advantage of height. Other police were advancing on foot on the pavement, with riot shields held in formation. They had cut off the roads to the north and the west. The marchers were hemmed in by the shopping streets and the market.

'CLEAR THE AREA!' the police bellowed, and the horses were kicked into a gallop. The crowd went into distress. Amara saw that she had to flee or she might be trampled. She came up against the clock tower itself. Made of stone, it had sloping sides that were slick with green lichen. She moved around to the back, wondering if it would protect her. There was a wooden door there, ancient-looking but probably only a few decades old. It was locked. She pressed herself against the wood and watched the crowd fleeing. There was chaos in people's movements. What one moment ago was a party celebrating justice was now a hurried dash in all directions, without any plan, without victory.

She could hear the mounted police galloping into the crowd. There were screams and shouts, swearing and cries. Some people stood their ground and threw whatever was to hand – rubbish, rocks, any remaining rotten fruit. Newspapers and flyers flapped in the wind and were crumpled in the stampede. A young man's foot was crushed under a horse's hoof and he screamed out in pain; the policeman took no notice as the man clutched his limp leg and half-hopped, half-stumbled away. People were screaming at the police to stop, even as they ran and pushed to get out of the way.

A policeman on horseback came right past the clock tower, looking ahead, not underfoot. Then he swung the horse around and saw Amara there, huddled in the small archway in front of that historic door. She still had the carrier bag of rotten fruit around her wrist. If she had been a practised protestor, she would have lobbed it at him there and then, and run. It was clear that the police and the racists were the same, in it together. Why else would they gallop straight into the peaceful crowds, no longer with the aim of keeping the National Front and the anti-racists apart? They were there to punish them, punish black people and their allies.

The horse snorted as it chewed the bit, and the rider had a choice. He could have recognised her as an unarmed young woman, and let her be, or he could treat her like the enemy.

He had sunglasses on, so she could not see his eyes. The police were no longer working together to a rhythm; with the shouts and screams all around she could tell that their formation was breaking and falling into disarray. He had to make up his own mind.

He lifted the reins and kicked the horse to run again into the crowd. As he passed her, he said, 'Black bitch!' He smashed her hard on the back with his baton, and a crack resonated through her ribcage as pain shot through her. She screamed and crumpled. One arm cradled her broken ribs, the other shielded her head from the horse's hooves. She failed to break her own fall, and no one was there to catch her. She landed hard, the bag of rotten fruit smashed underneath. She curled into a ball while other feet and screams were pounding around her.

Lying tight in the foetal position, she closed her eyes and wished for Papa to be there, anywhere, near to her at that moment. She knew it was too late, but that didn't stop her praying for it to be.

Chapter Thirty-Five

Gina woke next to Mason, and watched his sleeping face marked by the shapes and shadows coming through the blinds in her room. He looked peaceful, thoughts somewhere beyond London and the fires and the riots. His hair was tied back, but one dreadlock had fallen out and was lying on his forehead. She wanted to brush it back, to touch him and feel his warmth, but she thought it would be selfish to wake him up just for that. Instead, she got up as quietly as she could and slipped on her robe. She hoped the click of the door wouldn't make him stir as she went downstairs.

She followed the sound of classical music, and found Nanna standing in the kitchen, looking out at the garden in its lush August bloom. Roses and peonies and all the other flowers that Gina couldn't name crowded out of the corners and pushed into the sunlight. Every summer she thought that she should focus more on tidying the garden, nurturing the plants, and every autumn came and she did no such thing. They grew anyway, and more or less seemed to be happy and robust in their own way.

Nanna was stirring her tea, and took out the bag. 'Did you sleep all right, *cherie*? Or did the sirens bother you?'

'Slept okay, thanks, Nanna.' Gina went over and held her elbow. 'Can I help you to your chair?'

'Not yet, thank you, dear. I wanted to be near the garden another minute.'

Gina followed her gaze and saw the intense green. She could smell the roses through the open window. The table and chairs were where they left them after the Bastille Day party not long ago. Was that the last time she'd used the garden? She wondered what Nanna saw, if the shapes and shadows that made up her vision had colour, or if that was depleted long ago. She couldn't bring herself to ask.

The music ended, and the radio switched to the news on the hour. The announcer listed the places where there had been riots the previous night: Battersea, Brixton, Bromley, Camden, Croydon, Ealing, East Ham, Hackney, Harrow, Lewisham, Peckham, Stratford, Waltham Forest, Woolwich, Wood Green. Lewisham was on the list.

There was Birmingham, Bristol, Gloucester, Gillingham, and Nottingham too. It was tragic; these were all communities where people were living, babies were crying, grannies were watching the telly, and people would be worried about who didn't come home that night. The crowds didn't believe the official announcements about Mark Duggan, and the police lost people's trust with their heavy-handed tactics. A man was shot in Croydon, the news said. Another was assaulted in Ealing, left in critical condition in the hospital. Hundreds were arrested, many of them underage. Dozens of policemen were injured. All London firefighters had their leave cancelled and had been working double shifts. And what was it all for? Gina didn't know.

The world felt upside-down. Their house, with its little overgrown garden, was home. It was safe, with Mason upstairs. She heard him open the bedroom door and use the bathroom. He was awake now and would hear the news. At least it seemed like Essex wasn't in the riots, so his family would be okay.

Nanna smiled and put her arm around Gina's waist. 'Your young man, he stayed over?'

Gina blushed a little. Nanna could tell, even though she couldn't see. 'Yes, but...' She couldn't think of what to say.

'I'm glad,' Nana said simply. 'He is nice to you, and kind to me. He can stay anytime, as far as I'm concerned.' She took her tea with her to the chair in the living room and sat down with a sigh.

Mason came down the stairs, dressed in the same clothes as the night before. Gina had a passing wish that Nanna could see just how handsome he was, unusual, and unique. She couldn't imagine another man like him anywhere, in London or beyond.

. . .

After reassuring Nanna that she would be sensible, had her phone and it was charged up, they had to go out. They both needed to see what had happened to the city.

Travelling on foot, it was obvious something was going on, but there was an eerie calm. The air was humid and still, with a terrible tinge to it like a ripe sewer. Smells combined in the back of the throat and stayed on your tongue as the taste of something burnt and a bit rotten. They held hands as they walked the streets towards Lewisham town centre. They didn't talk, but they both knew they had to see what state everything was in.

They could hear sirens going again, but the roads were strangely quiet. Then a text came in from June.

> The café! Come quick!

Gina tried to ring her but couldn't get through. What had happened to the café? Was it caught up in the riots? They dropped hands and broke into a run.

The smell was worse the closer you got to the high street. The roads were devoid of traffic, which felt so odd in itself. Where was everyone? Gina didn't know why she wanted to see people. Not a riot, of course, but just the ordinary people you always saw. People you didn't know but recognised, because they came into the café sometimes, or they took the 261 bus at the same time you did. People who never quite looked you in the eye, might not know your name. Maybe you felt sorry for them because they had a toddler who was screaming a monumental meltdown. Or they were old and struggling with a cane, and made you think about Nanna and how you didn't want her to be alone.

These were the Londoners that she was used to. And of course June, Tom, Lizl, even Javier – she would have been happy to see anyone she recognised at that moment, just to reaffirm that this was still home.

They turned the corner of the street where the café was, and it felt different. The bins were all knocked over and many were kicked in. Rubbish was all over the street. A cat with mange was scratching inside a KFC box, and some pigeons fought over another one nearby. A few cars had shattered windows and looked ransacked. Pools of glass collected; they trailed away and crinkled underfoot, even if you tried not to step in it.

Closer to the café, Gina saw June standing out front, holding a broom in one hand, leaning into Tom. A big black scar loomed on the boarding that Lizl had nailed in the afternoon before. It looked like someone had tried to set fire to the plywood. The shape was large and menacing, taller than Tom and wider than a car. But it wasn't lit now. As she came closer, she could smell the scorched plywood.

'Any damage inside?' she asked.

'Don't think so,' June said. 'It seems like they couldn't reach the glass, and the boards didn't catch fire like they wanted to, so they moved on.' She gave Mason a quick hug, then held Gina a little longer. 'Sorry if my text was dramatic. I was trying to ring you to say I over-reacted, but I couldn't get through.'

'No worries,' Gina said. 'The network might be jammed. We were heading here anyway.'

'It looks bad, though, doesn't it?' Tom said, his hand tracing an outline around the charred shape.

They went inside, just to confirm that the place was okay. It was preserved as if nothing had happened. Gina texted Lizl to tell her the news. The sixty-year-old café was still standing, despite everything.

Gina wanted to get moving again. There was something in her that couldn't stand still, needed to keep going.

'Wait, where's the broom closet?' June asked. Gina pointed to the back hallway, and June came back with an odd assortment of brooms and dustpans. 'Let's go see what we can do,' she said.

'What do you mean?' Gina asked.

'I saw it on Twitter: #riotcleanup. Looks like anyone with a broom who wants to pitch in can meet on Lewisham High Street at noon.'

The smell was terrible this close. It was a mix of burnt plastic and dumped rubbish and piss. But they had a purpose now, and it felt right to be heading towards the epicentre.

Shattered glass littered the streets in waves, as car windows and shop fronts alike had been attacked with no respite. There didn't seem to be much reason as to what was hit and what wasn't. The street with the market was uncharacteristically quiet, with none of the colour and shouting normally found on a weekend morning. The shop keepers had kept their wares off the street last night, and the aluminium poles stood empty with nothing to sell underneath. Some of the awnings had been set alight, and were left charred and torn at the sides.

They were not alone. June was right – the call had been made and people heard from Twitter or on their Blackberrys or whatever that there was a job to do and they needed to pitch in. People came from all directions – from the side streets, from inside the shopping centre itself, even off the DLR. They joined the waves of people already there, and held their brooms high with pride. With a dustpan in one hand, broom in another, Gina felt a sense of belonging that had escaped her for the last few days.

People were chanting Labour songs and protest songs and other things. Someone set up a sound system out of a second-storey window nearby and started playing 'I Will Survive'. Then some Bob Marley, Marvin Gaye, Billy Bragg, Aretha Franklin and other classics. Some people were laughing and singing along. Some were crying. One woman was sobbing, singing, and sweeping all at the same time, a red bandana around her braids.

People were singing and shouting, not caring who they were next to or who would overhear. It didn't matter. You just bent over and started to sweep in a direction. Some people tried to organise others, but it really wasn't necessary. If you were near a bin, you'd set it upright and dump into it until it was full. If there was no bin in sight, you'd start sweeping the glass and rubbish in the same direction as the others. The glass glittered like a sinister river. But with all the brooms together, some of its potential danger was taken away.

If the bins became full, you'd collect things near it, hoping the Council would do something tomorrow or the next day to tackle it. But what the police did, what the rioters did, what the government needed to do – these were urgent questions but not for now, not for this moment. Today was about the people, the neighbours, coming together with whatever tools they could lay their hands on.

Gina stopped a minute and looked at the underside of her trainers. There was so much glass underfoot it looked like gemstones.

'Do you know the song "Diamonds on the Soles of her Shoes?" Mason sang a few lines for her. She knew it was an old Paul Simon song, but couldn't remember the words.

'Look at this,' Mason said. 'This is what we need. People coming together...' He couldn't say more, but she felt the same, looking at the mixed crowd of people: white ladies in their leisure suits and trainers; Caribbean auntie-types who took no nonsense from anyone; black barbers pulling a line together of brooms sweeping in time in front of their shops; the Italian deli owners offering cool drinks to people. Dads were there with toddlers mounted in backpacks, the kids' legs dangling and bouncing with the sweeping. A lady was there who looked like Alison, but she disappeared into the crowd before Gina could be sure. Pregnant ladies stayed with determined looks on their faces like no one could tell them to go home. Sikh men with their turbans, East Asian kids who looked a bit like Mason, uni kids from Goldsmiths who had dyed their hair unnatural shades of the rainbow – they were all there too.

The thought jumped into Gina's head, wondering if Amara would have been there, if she came back to London. Would she be here, on the streets for riot clean-up? Would they even recognise each other? She looked at the women in their fifties all around her. Some looked elegant and sophisticated, others worn out and angry. But they were there. They were giving a hand when it was needed. And they weren't alone. Everyone was there together, mixed up and sad and trying to make sense of it all. That had to mean something. It had to.

Chapter Thirty-Six

Bella missed her girl. She and her new young man had gone out, into these riots. When would she be back? Such a sweet child. Never hesitated before making a cup of tea, or looking after her grandmother.

She was nothing like her mother. What was it about Amara? It was always so difficult to know what she was thinking. She had confided in her father, not Bella. They were a team of two.

No, that's not fair. Amara had had a special connection with her father, unspoken between them. Aday would never have wanted something to come between her and Bella. But he couldn't help it, he had this instinct about the child. He read her moods, anticipated her words before she uttered them, knew when she was going to change her mind.

It all fell apart after he died. No one could read her, and she became that much more of a mystery. No one could reach her. And then the riots came to Lewisham, and they frightened her away, like a nightmare. Even once her ribs healed, there was no way to calm her back to how it was before.

Where was Drina? Why wasn't she back yet?

Bella rocked herself in her armchair to try to soothe her thoughts. She turned off the radio. Usually she needed the company but today it was only bad news and more bad news. All that terrible spreading of the riots. Like a wildfire ripping through the forest in a drought. She couldn't listen to it anymore, in French or in English. The stories about the fires, and the broken glass, and the looted stores, she couldn't bear it.

She was sweating, and her cotton dress was uncomfortable against the polyester fabric covering the armchair. Why didn't she have those linen covers made, like Aday had said? That was so long ago, but he had been right. He was right about so many things. She wanted to tell him so, but she had missed her chance.

The stories about the broken windows scared her. It took her back further, back before she met Aday. When she was a young nursing student, lying about her age, living in the dormitories with the other girls. She had no one she could tell about the horrors that happened in Vichy France. Even earlier, when she was a young girl still living with her parents and the radio announced the pogroms in Russia, and *Kristallnacht* in Poland, and the look on her parents' faces. She couldn't remember much about them seventy years ago, but she remembered their worried faces in those moments when they heard the reports about the streets in Poland filled with shattered glass, like broken crystal. Everything that came later came from those riots. Those bursts of anger, and the actors orchestrating and directing it.

Where was Drina? Shouldn't she be back by now?

But maybe she wasn't coming back? Amara and Drina started blurring together in her worried head. Maybe she had made up her mind that this wasn't the place for her. With her beautiful tanned skin, her lovely curly hair, such a nice collection of features and characteristics from everyone who came before her. Why could she not see that? You have to find your place in life. You can't expect anyone else to make your home for you. No one can make you belong. You do it yourself, by living, by engaging with people, by creating a community worth belonging to.

Somehow Bella had failed to teach that to her daughter. Or maybe she just lost her hold on Amara, in that year after Aday died, when she was pulling herself out of the depths and just trying to keep it all together. The house was a shell with no heart when he had gone. But Amara, she should have still felt the love, in any case. Family wasn't anywhere else. It was there, centred around where they lived, worked, and lay their heads down to sleep.

But Bella failed to reach her, back in 1977. And in the years since, there hadn't been any way to fix that. To explain what had already been overlooked. Amara didn't have that instinct, the pull to come home, to build a home near family and old friends. Once her father was gone, there was no way to bring her back in.

With Drina, Bella had a second chance. How many people get that? She wouldn't have chosen it that way, for the new mother to reject the child. But love grew out of that. Sustaining love.

Drina was a dear girl, always creative and head in the clouds. Not practical, never one for maths and certainly not going to business school this one. But does that matter? In the end, not at all. What matters is how you treat people. How you create a community around you, with kindness, that people want to be part of, those who treat you well. Together, with friendship, you can create a place that matters.

Somehow, the young girl knew that. From an early age, without having to be taught. Sure, she took some wrong turns at times, had that bad boyfriend and some friends who didn't prove to be loyal. But at the core, the girl had heart. And she stayed, which is more than you can say for a lot of people.

Bella started to laugh, thinking about Drina and her sugar sculptures. And chocolate, she was talking about chocolate lately! Chocolate boats! In this heat! They would all be swimming in it, at this rate. She needed to think things through, that girl. Sometimes things did end in a bit of a disaster.

But she wouldn't want her any other way, the dear girl.

She'll come home, and soon.

Acknowledgments

Inspiration for this story came from many places, but most importantly from my neighbours, dear friends and community in Lewisham and Greenwich in southeast London. There is nowhere else we would rather live, despite the challenges and unpredictability. I could not picture a more lively, diverse and creative place to be.

Thank you to Charlotte Ledger, Ajebowale Roberts, Arsalan Isa, and the whole team at One More Chapter for making this book about the kindness of strangers into a reality.

Thank you to David Renton, for sharing an early version of his book on fascism and racism of this era, *Never Again: Rock against Racism and the Anti-Nazi League 1976 – 1982*. I really appreciate him sharing his expertise and reading early drafts of the chapters about the Battle of Lewisham.

I am indebted to Rebecca Ronald and Mary Herbert, who each in their gentle and informative ways taught me elements about sculpture and painting, as well as finding your way in art school in the UK.

I am grateful to Katie Lumsden and Renee Miller for reading drafts of this book, and their painstaking and very helpful comments at the early stages. My gratitude extends to the entire Greenwich Writers group for reading chapters and offering candid and very helpful reflections along the way. Thank you also to the London Writers' Salon for establishing Writers' Hour, which helps me commit to a regular practice that keeps the words flowing.

No list would be complete without thanking my parents, Fred & Ede Bookstein, for the love, education and encouragement from my earliest days until now. Your unconditional support means so much.

And Kanatta, Kéo & Yvette – you three are my inspiration, my motivation, and my home. Thank you for all that you do, and all that you are.

ONE MORE CHAPTER

YOUR NUMBER ONE STOP FOR PAGETURNING BOOKS

The author and One More Chapter would like to thank everyone who contributed to the publication of this story...

Analytics
Abigail Fryer
Maria Osa

Audio
Fionnuala Barrett
Ciara Briggs

Contracts
Sasha Duszynska Lewis

Design
Lucy Bennett
Fiona Greenway
Liane Payne
Dean Russell

Digital Sales
Hannah Lismore
Emily Scorer

Editorial
Kate Elton
Arsalan Isa
Charlotte Ledger
Bonnie Macleod
Jennie Rothwell
Tony Russell
Caroline Scott-Bowden

Harper360
Emily Gerbner
Jean Marie Kelly
emma sullivan
Sophia Wilhelm

International Sales
Peter Borcsok
Bethan Moore

Marketing & Publicity
Chloe Cummings
Emma Petfield

Operations
Melissa Okusanya
Hannah Stamp

Production
Emily Chan
Denis Manson
Simon Moore
Francesca Tuzzeo

Rights
Rachel McCarron
Hany Sheikh Mohamed
Zoe Shine

The HarperCollins Distribution Team

The HarperCollins Finance & Royalties Team

The HarperCollins Legal Team

The HarperCollins Technology Team

Trade Marketing
Ben Hurd

UK Sales
Laura Carpenter
Isabel Coburn
Jay Cochrane
Sabina Lewis
Holly Martin
Erin White
Harriet Williams
Leah Woods

And every other essential link in the chain from delivery drivers to booksellers to librarians and beyond!

ONE MORE CHAPTER

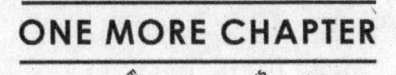

YOUR NUMBER ONE STOP FOR PAGETURNING BOOKS

One More Chapter is an award-winning global division of HarperCollins.

Sign up to our newsletter to get our latest eBook deals and stay up to date with our weekly Book Club!
<u>Subscribe here.</u>

Meet the team at
www.onemorechapter.com

Follow us!
@OneMoreChapter_
@OneMoreChapter
@onemorechapterhc

Do you write unputdownable fiction? We love to hear from new voices. Find out how to submit your novel at
<u>www.onemorechapter.com/submissions</u>